A PERTURBING PROPOSAL

Lovely young Clemency Barsford had dreamed since girlhood of wedding her childhood sweetheart, Damian Prior. Then the handsome baronet was declared missing in battle in far-off America, and Clemency's life and future were suddenly empty.

Now one man proposed to fill that gap.

A man whose face was scarred by war. A man whose heart chilled with pain at the very mention of love. A man who bore the title Lord Rodger Colbourne, but who was known to those he filled with pity by another name: Lord Caliban.

It was he who asked Clemency to be his bride. . . .

LORD CALIBAN

Be sure to read this other Signet Regency Romance by Ellen Fitzgerald:

A NOVEL ALLIANCE

SIGNET Regency Romances You'll Enjoy

(0451)
- [ ] **FALSE COLOURS** by Georgette Heyer. (131975—$2.50)†
- [ ] **AN INFAMOUS ARMY** by Georgette Heyer. (131630—$2.95)†
- [ ] **POOR RELATION** by Marion Chesney. (128184—$2.25)*
- [ ] **THE VISCOUNT'S REVENGE** by Marion Chesney. (125630—$2.25)*
- [ ] **THE MARRIAGE MART** by Norma Lee Clark. (128168—$2.25)*
- [ ] **THE PERFECT MATCH** by Norma Lee Clark. (124839—$2.25)*
- [ ] **A MIND OF HER OWN** by Anne MacNeill. (124820—$2.25)*
- [ ] **THE LUCKLESS ELOPEMENT** by Dorothy Mack. (129695—$2.25)*
- [ ] **THE BLACKMAILED BRIDEGROOM** by Dorothy Mack. (127684—$2.25)*
- [ ] **THE RELUCTANT ABIGAIL** by Miranda Cameron. (131622—$2.50)*
- [ ] **THE MEDDLESOME HEIRESS** by Miranda Cameron. (126165—$2.25)*
- [ ] **A SCANDALOUS BARGAIN** by Miranda Cameron. (124499—$2.25)*
- [ ] **THE FORTUNE HUNTER** by Elizabeth Hewitt. (125614—$2.25)*
- [ ] **A SPORTING PROPOSITION** by Elizabeth Hewitt. (123840—$2.25)*
- [ ] **BORROWED PLUMES** by Roseleen Milne. (098114—$1.75)†

*Prices slightly higher in Canada
†Not available in Canada

Buy them at your local bookstore or use this convenient coupon for ordering.

NEW AMERICAN LIBRARY,
P.O. Box 999, Bergenfield, New Jersey 07621

Please send me the books I have checked above. I am enclosing $_____ (please add $1.00 to this order to cover postage and handling). Send check or money order—no cash or C.O.D.'s. Prices and numbers are subject to change without notice.

Name_____

Address_____

City_____ State_____ Zip Code_____

Allow 4-6 weeks for delivery.
This offer is subject to withdrawal without notice.

Lord Caliban

Ellen Fitzgerald

A SIGNET BOOK
NEW AMERICAN LIBRARY

NAL BOOKS ARE AVAILABLE AT QUANTITY DISCOUNTS WHEN USED
TO PROMOTE PRODUCTS OR SERVICES. FOR INFORMATION PLEASE
WRITE TO PREMIUM MARKETING DIVISION, NEW AMERICAN LIBRARY,
1633 BROADWAY, NEW YORK, NEW YORK 10019.

Copyright © 1985 by Ellen Fitzgerald

All rights reserved

SIGNET TRADEMARK REG. U.S. PAT. OFF. AND FOREIGN COUNTRIES
REGISTERED TRADEMARK—MARCA REGISTRADA
HECHO EN CHICAGO, U.S.A.

SIGNET, SIGNET CLASSIC, MENTOR, PLUME, MERIDIAN AND NAL BOOKS
are published by New American Library,
1633 Broadway, New York, New York 10019

First Printing, March, 1985

1 2 3 4 5 6 7 8 9

PRINTED IN THE UNITED STATES OF AMERICA

1

Beatrix!

Clemency Barsford frowned. That name was frequently on the lips of her mother and her married sister Justine whenever Clemency happened to enter the parlor or the second drawing room or her mother's sitting room. Their conversation ceased abruptly as she entered and they always looked as if they wished she would leave. In her presence, they had very little to say about Beatrix save that she was Clemency's cousin and that she would be living at Sayles indefinitely. They did not say why this had happened or from whence she had come or—and this was the most important "or" of all—how she was related to Clemency.

She had picked up some provocative bits of conversation. At one point Justine had been saying, ". . . his brats on you. Mama—" ceasing with annoying abruptness directly Clemency appeared. At another time she had heard "disowned? He never should have been born!" She had the impression that the "his" of "his brats" and the "he" who had been so inconveniently brought into the world were one and the same. There were other similarly intriguing scraps and the resulting patchwork of information would soon be trotted out for the edification of Damian Prior, who would, she hoped, be able to provide the information she so ardently desired.

Clemency, seated atop Merlin, her roan gelding, was awaiting him in the woods stretching between their estates, more specifically near the half-ruined tower which had been part of a castle so ancient that no one remembered when it had been built or to whom it had belonged. She had no right to be there. The meeting had been arranged by an exchange of notes entrusted to Jim, one of the grooms in her father's stables.

"It is really too bad," Clemency muttered rebelliously, resenting anew the curtailment of her long enjoyable rides with Damian. In a regrettably short time he would be sent to join his Uncle Bruce, a colonel in the West Somerset Hussars, and train to be a soldier, while she would be in training, too—to be, as Miss Lewes, her governess, put it, a "proper young lady."

"I do not wish to be a proper young lady," she had told Miss Lewes with the frankness that had caused all the trouble. "I want to go soldiering with Damian."

The governess had looked shocked and, of course, she had repeated that impulsive remark to Lady Sayles. Summoned into her mother's presence, Clemency had listened to a long and boring lecture on the subject of propriety. Lady Sayles had looked at her youngest child sadly. Shaking her head several times, she had deplored the fact that she had allowed Clemency to run wild. "One forgets," she had sighed, adding with a trace of indignation: "Your brother and sisters are all so much older."

"As if it were my fault that I was born when Justine was eleven, Gerald sixteen, and Lydia nineteen," Clemency whispered.

Evidently her mother had forgotten that she herself had encouraged the friendship between Clemency and their near neighbors' son, Damian. Clemency had not been slow in reminding Lady Sayles of that fact.

" 'Twas all right when you were children, but you are now fourteen and cannot go tearing through the woods with Damian. I have been sadly remiss in my duties as your mother."

Following close upon this conversation, there had been a meeting with Miss Lewes and, in addition to teaching Clemency French, Italian, Latin, history, mathematics, and English grammar, there had been lessons in dancing, playing the pianoforte, sketching, and, above all, deportment. Her riding had been limited to short gallops with Jim in close attendance, and a note had been sent to Sir Anthony and Lady Prior, Damian's parents, concerning a friendship that could have dangerous ramifications if allowed to continue in the same way.

Learning about the note from Damian, Clemency had questioned him closely about those "ramifications" and found him no more enlightened than she herself. They had been similarly indignant over these parental strictures and defiantly ignored them as much as possible, continuing their rides in the woods. They had also continued to go swimming in their secret pool, which, ringed round with trees, was in the very middle of the woods. This activity, they agreed gleefully, must have sent their mothers and possibly their fathers, too, into the vapors. Certainly it was something no young lady of fashion would do!

"I shan't have to be a lady of fashion for four more years," Clemency addressed her other self, a habit that had grown upon her in what she termed the "empty years" before she was nine and met Damian in the old ruined tower. She had been roaming through it in hopes of finding an old spearhead such as her brother, Gerald, had picked up years before. She had already had some luck in that direction. She had discovered a small, cloudy glass bottle which her father had excitedly identified as a "tear vase," telling her that it was possibly over a thousand years old, dating back to the time when the Romans ruled Britain. Since then she had often invaded the lower reaches of the tower, keeping away from the steps which led to an upper room, mainly because they were narrow, cracked, and looked dangerous. However, one day she had seen Damian carefully coming down them. He had looked a little pale and shaken, but on seeing her, he had jumped down the rest of the way to say loudly and with a fierce look in his blue eyes, "Why do you trespass in mine castle, foul varlet?"

Upon being informed that he was the trespasser, he had offered to fight her for the right of tenancy. They had jousted back and forth with sticks picked up from the littered and broken floor, until Clemency had stumbled and fallen flat, bruising her chin and knocking the wind out of her stomach. More shocked than hurt, she had not cried, and Damian, helping her up, had complimented her on not being a "girl." That had been the beginning of a friendship their parents had originally encouraged, since Damian was an only child and just as lonely as Clemency.

She frowned. Of late, her mother and Justine had been

looking four years into a future when Clemency not only would have had her presentation ball and a Season in London but also would have been wed to some eligible gentleman.

"She does give promise of being a beauty," Justine had said. "Though I cannot imagine why she has grown so tall."

Lady Sayles had sighed. "Your papa had an aunt who was close on six feet. She died young, I understand."

That comment, suggesting a correlation between height and a youthful demise, had sent Clemency into a brief panic but, she recollected, she was nowhere near six feet tall. She was five-feet-seven and had not added a fraction of an inch since her twelfth birthday. Damian, on the other hand, had been small until last year, when he suddenly gained enough height to top her by at least two inches.

Damian.

She looked around her, wishing he would arrive. She had not seen him for a week and she missed him dreadfully. She would like to see him every day, all day. In fact, if she had to marry, she could not imagine joining her life with anyone except Damian!

She winced, imagining his reaction if he were ever informed of this desire. He would open his eyes wide and look disgusted. No one could appear more disgusted than Damian. He would sneer or perhaps he would only laugh and tell her that he wouldn't have a green-eyed, carrot-topped wench who was thin as a stick and who was always dirtying her hands digging about in old mounds. Her interest in the relics of the past was the one matter in which they diverged. His eyes were on the future, when he would be a soldier and fighting with his uncle in Spain against the little Coriscan corporal who had dared to make himself emperor of the French five years ago.

A lump swelled her throat. It would be hard to be without Damian. He was a wonderful companion, but more than that, she could not quite describe what she felt about him except that she experienced such a lift of spirits whenever he appeared. That had happened only recently and she was hard put to understand why he should seem so different to her than he had last year or the year before. She was positive that he had experienced no such feelings about her. He still called her "brat." The only time he was really polite to her was when he and his parents were bade to dinner at Sayles or she, with her family, was entertained at the Grange, where he lived. Then he was grave and cool. No one, to look at him, would ever guess how mischievous he could be or how much fun they had when they were together.

There was a wetness in her eyes. The time was drawing nearer when he would have to leave, and if the war did not end soon, he would have his coveted opportunity of fighting that horrid Napoleon and be exposed to dangers she did not like to contemplate. There were few families in the small community that had not sent a son to war. Even Lord Colbourne, whose hilltop castle had graced the countryside for five hundred years, had espoused the cause and gone, much to the distress of his widowed mother whose only child he was.

Clemency's parents disapproved of the young earl's decision, thinking it wrong to leave his lands in the care of a steward. "If he dies, his estates will go to a cousin, who is not at all the thing!"

Clemency's eyes lighted. Lord Colbourne had not died. According to Damian, he had not even been wounded, and he had been twice decorated for bravery beyond the call of duty!

She forgot about Lord Colbourne in thinking about Damian. Maybe he, too, would be similarly fortunate. That he was brave went without saying . . . But where was he? He should have arrived by now, unless, of course, he had had trouble getting away, as occasionally happened now that his parents had been alerted to her mother's cavils. She hoped that this was not one of the occasions, because she longed to hear what he might have to say about Beatrix. He had an ear to the ground when it came to local gossip, and even though this Beatrix was her cousin, it was possible that he knew more about the girl than her mama had been willing to tell her.

"There you are!" Damian exclaimed, leading Cora, his brown mare.

Clemency looked down quickly and produced the smile of which her mother and governess did not approve. It started with her lips curving up, spread to her eyes, and seemed to have the cooperation of all her features. It was glowing, beatific, and transforming. It radiated such happiness that there was no doubting her sentiments.

Miss Lewes was wont to say, "A young lady should never reveal what she is thinking."

Lady Sayles agreed. "A smile should be a mere twitch of the lips. There is something vulgar in the way that you smile, Clemency."

Damian smiled back at her, bringing two dimples into play. He said from the lofty eminence of the five months that divided them in age, "Good afternoon, infant."

"I am not an infant." Clemency leaned forward and extracted a twig that had been caught among his blond curls. Tossing it down, she added, "*She* will be here tonight and everyone's in such a pother. Mama and Justine are forever whispering secrets."

"Ah, hah!" Damian had the bad grace to look knowing. "I expect that's because of *him*."

"Him?" Clemency repeated with pardonable anger. "I do not understand you." A sense of being ill-used by everyone caused her to cry out, "I do think that's too bad of you, Damian. If I knew something *you* needed to know, I would tell you."

"What do you not know?" Looping the mare's reins around one hand, he came nearer, smiling up at her with his dimples more prominent than ever and a teasing look in his eyes. "Come down," he ordered. "It gives me a double crick in the neck to look up at you."

"Very well." Clemency slid off Merlin's back and confronted Damian. "Now, tell me!" she commanded.

"In a minute." Taking Merlin's reins from her, he tied the gelding and his mare to the low-hanging branches of separate trees. "Let us sit by the pool," he suggested.

"Very well, but I cannot go swimming. Justine would notice that my hair was wet. And besides, this . . . Beatrix will be here soon."

"I don't want to go swimming either. But it's pleasant by the pool."

"It is that," she agreed.

A few minutes later, sitting on the grassy bank of the pool, its still, mirror-bright surface reflecting the surrounding trees, the top of the tower, and the cloud-streaked sky as well, Damian, lying back, said, "This Beatrix is the daughter of your Uncle Nigel."

"My Uncle Nigel?" she repeated. "I do not have an Uncle Nigel!"

"True enough," he agreed solemnly. "He is recently dead."

"Recently? You must be funning me," Clemency accused crossly. "I've not heard of it."

"Nor of him, I know. If they did not care to acknowledge him while he was living, 'tis not surprising they'd not prate of his passing. He . . ." He paused at a snuffle from Cora. "She's thirsty," he commented. Rising, he moved through the trees, returning a few minutes later with the needful mare. Typically and perversely, he waited silently until the horse had drunk her fill and he had led her back to her tree, before providing any further enlightenment to his increasingly impatient companion.

Finally, settling down beside Clemency, he said, "Your Uncle Nigel was your father's youngest brother. He was a rum sort who was . . . compelled to marry the daughter of a cit. He was subsequently disinherited, not for that but . . . for other things. Does that satisfy your curiosity?"

"Who was the cit?"

"A lawyer's clerk in London."

"Why was he compelled to marry the girl?" Clemency demanded. Before Damian could answer, she continued, "I know . . . I expect she was with child."

Damian turned a bright pink and visited a disapproving look on her. "Where did you get such a notion, brat?"

"I see she was." Clemency nodded sagely. "Much the same thing happened to our Jim with Maria, the miller's youngest daughter. I passed the linen cabinet one morning and heard Jane and Rose talking about it. Jane was very angry because she'd been walking out with Jim. She called Maria a sly minx who knew what she was doing and—"

"That is enough," he interrupted sternly. "You should not have eavesdropped, brat."

"Oh, I know, but it was interesting." Clemency grinned. "And Papa's brother did the same thing?"

"Yes, but you must never say that I told you about it," Damian warned.

"You did not. I figured it out for myself!" Clemency said triumphantly.

"You should not have done so." He frowned.

"No matter. I expect that this Beatrix is the daughter of the daughter of the lawyer's clerk?"

"That's true."

"I wonder what happened to her mother?"

"She died when Beatrix was born."

"Oh, how sad. Poor Beatrix, never to have known her mother. I trust this uncle of mine did not marry again?"

Damian's eyes widened in surprise. "He did not, but why should you think he would not?"

"Because Mama and Justine did not speak of siblings. There is only Beatrix. I hope she will like me. It will be lovely to have a companion my age. I heard Mama say that she was fourteen and a little over. She'll be like a sister. Justine has never seemed like my sister, and Lydia acts as if she were my aunt. Just think, she's already thirty-four!"

Damian had a commiserating look for her. "I know it's been hard for you, Clemency, with both your parents so elderly."

Clemency nodded solemnly and then nearly blinded him with her beguiling smile. "But I have you, Damian."

Another flush mounted his cheeks. "Er . . . yes, but I expect I'm not like a female."

"Not in the least," she agreed happily. "I am glad you are not." She added frankly, "Even though I am *sure* I shall cherish Beatrix, she could never replace you in my esteem."

"Nor you in mine, brat," he agreed, moved by an emotion he could not quite understand.

They stared at each other wordlessly, and then, breaking a silence that was beginning to be too long, Clemency said, "I wonder when she will arrive."

"I heard she will be here by this evening," Damian told her.

Though matters, on this particular occasion, were out of her hands, Beatrix Barsford's penchant for doing the unexpected was involuntarily aided by the fact that Lady Sayles discovered that the family coach needed repairs. Consequently, that vehicle would not be fixed until the following morning and Lord Sayles forbade his wife's pressing the post chaise into service, saying he needed it to drive into Porlock to inspect a mare that was being offered at auction.

"I do not know how long 'twill take, and though Minehead's not many leagues from here, you'd best send for the chit tomorrow."

"She's expecting to come this afternoon," Lady Sayles protested.

"With Nigel for a father, I am sure she's used to sudden shifts of plan."

"I wonder how he happened to live at Minehead," Lady Sayles said. "Such a mean little place, though I suppose he thought the sea air to be beneficial."

"My brother did not know the meaning of the word 'beneficial.' It was money drove him there—or the lack of it. He didn't have two groats to rub together, I am sure."

"That poor child," Lady Sayles murmured. "I'll send for her first thing in the morning."

Mrs. Tilton, the housekeeper, had tartly warned Beatrix that her "fine relations" had probably changed their minds about taking her to live with them. " 'Twouldn't surprise me," she had commented with a toss of her head. "Some addition to an earl's household you'd be."

Beatrix, however, was used to disregarding everything the woman said and, accordingly, she was ready and waiting when the coachman rapped on the door with the butt end of his whip at eight the next morning.

Coming out in her neat black garments, her hat firmly on her head, her hands encased in black kid gloves, a reticule over one wrist and the handle of her bandbox over the other, Miss Barsford met the coachman's surprised stare with a small smile. Lifting huge blue eyes framed by improbably long lashes several shades darker than her blond locks, she said softly, "I expect you've come for me. I shall be pleased to accompany you."

"Very good, Miss Barsford." He looked at her narrowly. Primed on tales from his fellow servants as well as his own memories of Nigel Barsford, whom he remembered as handsome, feckless, and not above cadging a coin or two from him or anyone else who'd lend it to him, or rather give it to him, for promises to return it were never fulfilled, he thought he saw something of her father in her wide blue eyes and her straight little nose. However, she was tiny and the wildness that had been easily discernible in Lord Nigel was completely lacking in her. Everything about Miss Barsford suggested a composure amazing in one so young. He liked her voice. It fell very pleasantly upon the ears. He also appreciated the fact that she was not weeping. He could not abide blubbering females, even though the loss of a father might have provided a proper excuse for such a display. In fact, it was surprising that the girl was able to maintain her poise, especially in view of being summarily bidden to new and strange surroundings. Of course, Sayles would certainly be more to her liking than the small mean cottage she was leaving. His late lordship had fulfilled all the dire predictions mouthed by those servants who had known him as a child. He had fallen from grace early and never risen again.

"I must say farewell to Mrs. Tilton," the girl informed him, and moved back toward the door.

"Do not be long about it," he said gruffly. Had he spoken that way to Lady Clemency, he would have been dubbed impertinent and must have received a strong set-down from Briggs, the butler, but Lady Clemency's origins were impeccable. There was no baseborn mother lurking in her background.

"I shall not be long, sir," the girl answered meekly.

She knew her place, he decided, and that was all to the good. Probably she would have the position of companion to Lady Clemency. Judging from what the maids said, Lord and Lady Sayles were of two minds concerning Nigel Barsford's dying request that they provide a home for his orphaned daughter. Briggs, whose memories of his late lordship were particularly grim, would be pleasantly surprised by Miss Barsford, he decided. In common with himself, the butler would undoubtedly consider her quite unexceptional.

The housekeeper saved the girl the trouble of seeking her inside. She emerged from the cottage just as Miss Barsford was about to enter. The coachman eyed the new arrival appreciatively. She was an unexpectedly pretty piece, not more than twenty-five or twenty-six unless he missed his guess. She had a neat figure and a heart-shaped face brightened by large hazel eyes. Her hair was a ruddy gold and to look at her was to be visited by memories of his youth. He had a sigh for the forty years that had come and gone since he had had a reason for such fancies. He noted that there was little warmth in the farewells exchanged by the pair. He was not surprised, nor shocked either. Having known Lord Nigel, he could well imagine that he had employed many such housekeepers. And women of Mrs. Tilton's ilk were rarely pleased at a love nest built for three.

He helped the girl into the coach, and if he had been able to see inside, he would not have been surprised to discover that little Miss Beatrix Barsford had not cast so much as a backward glance at the housekeeper or the cottage where she had lived for the last four years.

Clinging to a strap, Miss Beatrix Barsford was half-triumphant and half-daunted by her journey or, more specifically, her destination. Recalling her father's stories, told her when he was drunk, despairing, and homesick, she could not remember a time when she had not longed to see the great house, longed to live there, and now she would, but not as she had planned. In her daydreams, she had envisioned a family party.

It would consist of Lord and Lady Sayles, their children and grandchildren. Two coaches would be bearing them to the sea for a picnic and then either a storm or a tidal wave or an earthquake or, better yet, all three would combine to destroy them. And after they were drowned or crushed by falling stones, her father would be restored to his rightful position as Earl of Sayles, while she would be lady of the manor. Unfortunately, in spite of her many prayers directed at God or the Devil, the Sayles family, untouched by these cataclysms, remained in excellent health, and she, Beatrix Barsford, was going there as a poor relation, taken out of charity!

"Do not look so dour, Beatrix. You could have been in the workhouse, you know."

That had been Mrs. Marjorie Tilton's comment, followed by one of her annoying little titters. Beatrix made a fearful face at this memory. She knew full well that Mrs. Tilton would have been pleased if there had been no uncle to rescue her from so horrid a fate. She herself hoped that Mrs. Tilton would have a difficult time securing another protector. Unfortunately, there was little likelihood of that.

Among the few mourners at her father's funeral had been a Mr. Ephraim Graves, merchant, and one of Lord Nigel's many creditors. Marjorie Tilton knew him well. Her soft persuasions had kept him from pressing his bills. Now that her lover was dead, Beatrix, seeing them glancing at each other over Lord Nigel's coffin, had no illusions as to where the wench would go. She wished the trull would go even further, and wondered whether hell was as hot as it was reputed to be. However, as she had already learned, it was futile to harbor such wishes. Beatrix drew a long hissing breath, hating Mrs. Tilton, who had not been above striking her when she felt she deserved it and who had kept her valuables under lock and key so there was no possible retaliation in the form of purloining a favorite ornament as she had done during the tenure of the previous "housekeeper."

The maid had been blamed for the theft and turned off without a character. The silly little wretch had cried as if her heart would break and whined about her wages going to support her sick mother and a consumptive brother. Tears, Beatrix could have told her, were utterly useless. She had cried, too, when her father had not had a winning streak at the tables or when he had cheated and been caught and expelled from one club or another, events which resulted in their having to tighten their belts and pawn their clothing.

She had been no more than eight when she had stopped crying and resorted to methods that kept food in her stomach. Her fingers were deft. It was easy to snatch pies and buns from counters or carts. No one had ever suspected her. No one ever would, but, she reminded herself, she would never need to steal again or, when there was no mistress present, fend off her father's creditors or crawl with him out of windows in the middle of the night to escape an importunate landlord. If she could not be lady of the manor, at least she would be comfortable, and perhaps . . . But it was foolish to dwell on possibilities so soon. She leaned back against the comfortable squabs of the coach and dreamily pretended that she was Lady Clemency Barsford being borne home from a visit to the seaside.

2

Clemency, sitting in the wide stone window of the tower, was glad it was so deep-set into the wall. There was plenty of room on the sill. She would not need to stand on the floor, much of which was crumbling beneath her feet. She trembled as she remembered the shower of stones that had clattered down in the moment before she had thrown herself at the window and, fortunately, been able to ease herself into the aperture. Trying not to look as terrified as she felt, she stared down at an equally shaken Beatrix. Her cousin looked even smaller than usual—mainly because she was on the ground, many feet below.

"Oh, my dearest Clemency," Beatrix cried. "Are you sure that the sill will continue to bear your weight?"

"It is hard stone and cannot possibly give," Clemency assured her, hoping that she was right.

"But the floor is also stone," Beatrix wailed.

"The floor is . . . is different, 'tis not built into the wall like the window. But do go and fetch help, Beatrix, dearest. I do not wish to . . . to remain here any longer than necessary." She moved, and a shower of small stones dislodged from the window fell, causing Beatrix to back away swiftly.

"You see . . . it's not safe. Oh, Clemency, if only I'd not been so curious about that room! I never, never should have suggested that we go—"

"I was just as curious," Clemency interrupted. "You must not blame yourself."

"I do wish I'd been the one to go first," Beatrix moaned.

" 'Tis as well you did not," Clemency comforted her. "You're not used to clambering among these old stones. I am. And we could not know that the floor would give way."

"You . . . you might have been k-killed," Beatrix sobbed.

"But I was not," Clemency reminded her through stiff lips. "Please, I beg you'll go back to the stables. Tell Jim or Rob. They can fetch ropes and a ladder or something."

"Will any ladder stretch that high?" Beatrix asked timorously.

"I expect they must, else how would anyone ever finish the top floor of a house," Clemency said bracingly, wishing that Beatrix, in her terror, were not filling her with new fears. "Please do go and fetch help," she repeated urgently.

"I will . . . I shall ride like the wind. Only I . . . I hope I know the way back to the stables."

"Molly will know. Just let her have her head," Clemency advised, and in another second had loosed a sigh of relief as her cousin dashed away.

In spite of her fears and in spite of the fact that it had been at Beatrix's urging that they had gone up the steps to the tower room, Clemency had an affectionate smile for her. Beatrix was everything she had hoped she might be, a real friend and a loving companion—and she was beginning to be less shy and self-effacing.

"She is like a little black shadow," had been Justine's comment when Beatrix arrived. "She moves so softly and she seems afraid to open her mouth."

"Poor child," Lady Sayles had been moved to comment. "What a life she must have led. My heart goes out to her."

Lord Sayles was of the same opinion, and from being suspicious and wary of his brother's child, her parents had been won over by Beatrix's eagerness to please them and her almost miraculous anticipation of their every need. She seemed to know when Lady Sayles wanted a fan or a shawl. When the *Morning Post* was mislaid, Beatrix found it and gave it to Lord Sayles. Clemency, missing a book she had been reading, was delighted when Beatrix retrieved it for her. In a matter of a fortnight, all three of them were determined to make poor Beatrix happy. Miss Rathbone, the seamstress from Porlock, was summoned and set to work fashioning several gowns for Beatrix, who had been coaxed into half-mourning rather than the rusty black she had worn upon arrival. The violets, the whites, and the grays had proved most becoming to her fragile beauty. As she modeled the new creations for her benefactors, her gratitude had been lovely to witness. It had also surprised Lord Sayles, who had actually said that she must take after her mother's side of the family, for her father did not have a grain of thankfulness in his whole body.

Damian, wary at first, had also been won over. Clemency frowned. Though she knew it to be unworthy of her, she could wish that Damian had not become quite so fond of Beatrix. In the last six weeks they had achieved a friendship that seemed far closer than the one she shared with him. When the three of them were together, Clemency could not help noticing the series of special little looks they were wont to exchange, hinting at a secret understanding that both were reluctant to share with her. Yet, when asked if she liked Damian, Beatrix, surprisingly enough, did not appear over-enthusiastic.

"He's a pleasant-enough boy, but young," she had replied.

"He is our age. In fact, he's five months older than I am and three months your senior."

"That," Beatrix had said thoughtfully, "is the trouble."

"I do not understand you," Clemency had begun. She had been unable to pursue the matter. Their conversation had taken place in the third-floor schoolroom, and Miss Lewes, arriving, had turned their attention to Latin declensions.

Clemency moved restlessly and gasped in fright as she seemed to feel a corresponding movement beneath her. She looked down. It was so very far to the ground. If she were to fall, every bone in her body would be broken! She cast a fearful glance toward the trees. How long had Beatrix been gone? It seemed a long time. Had she become lost? No, Molly would certainly gallop back to the stables once she had been given her head. Clemency looked down at the trees and wished heartily that she might see Damian come walking or riding through them, but now that she thought about it, she had seen very little of him in the past fortnight. She wondered if he had been purposely avoiding them. Perhaps it embarrassed him to spend time with the two of them when he so obviously preferred to be alone with Beatrix.

She groaned. Six weeks ago, the idea of anything or anyone interfering with their friendship would have been unthinkable. Yet, she could not blame him for turning to

Beatrix. She was as beautiful as a fairy princess and she was so little her head barely came to Damian's shoulder. Clemency could see that that pleased him. Oddly enough, he also seemed to be pleased that Beatrix was not as athletic as they were. On their walks through the woods, Beatrix could not leap over a stream. She had to be carried across, which Damian had done more than once. Though Beatrix continually protested that she was far too heavy a burden for him, he had laughed and told her fondly that she weighed no more than a feather! And one day when Molly had managed to pull away from the branch where she was tied and had galloped back to the stables, Damian had borne Beatrix before him on his horse, depositing her at the edge of the woods. Beatrix had teasingly called him her knight-at-arms. If she, Clemency, had ever said such a thing, he would have dubbed her a great silly, but he had appeared unexpectedly gratified by Beatrix's remark.

Clemency's hand stole to her breast. It seemed to be actually paining her, but of course it wasn't a real pain. It arose out of her sense of loss. Coupled with it was shame because she had for a moment thought that her friendship with Beatrix was not nearly so satisfying as the one she had been wont to enjoy with Damian. It seemed very mean of her to begrudge Beatrix her closeness with Damian, she whose life had undoubtedly been so hard and so empty.

In the eyes of Lord and Lady Sayles, one of Beatrix's most admirable qualities was her reticence regarding the hardships of her existence with her rackety father. She spoke of him only in the most glowing terms. Her only regret seemed to be that because of his kindness and generosity to his housekeepers, they were often strapped for funds. "But," she had finished loyally, "I would not have wanted him any other way."

And where was Beatrix now? Clemency wondered. Surely she should have reached the stables already. She stared into the forest, seeing only the tree shadows on the sunlit ground. She strained her ears in the hopes of hearing horses' hooves or perhaps the rustle of leaves disturbed by someone trudging along a path. She also had an anxious glance at the sky. The sun seemed definitely lower than it had been when Beatrix had started for the stables. It must be close on four in the afternoon. What if Molly had shied and tossed her off? She might have struck her head. Then she would not be able to summon help. Clemency shuddered and then was immediately aghast at how mean-spirited that supposition had been. She had been thinking solely of her own plight rather than that of poor little Beatrix, possibly lying unconscious in the woods, her golden curls red with blood from the wound in her head. Clemency could almost see the horrid sight.

"No," she whispered, realizing at that moment how lonely she would feel without Beatrix. She had never really had so close a female friend. And—Her thoughts were interrupted by a sound. Horses' hooves. Someone was riding toward the tower. She leaned forward eagerly and then cried out with fear as more stones went tumbling to the ground. As they did, she heard a snuffle, as if the approaching horse, also hearing them, had been startled by their clatter as they bounced down the sloping sides of the keep. In another second a horse and rider had come into the clearing. The horseman was casually clad in an open-necked shirt and breeches which seemed to be part of a uniform, for they were dark blue with a red stripe running down them. She could not see his face, for his head was bent and he seemed to be soothing his mount, a spirited chestnut, who was doing a regular dance.

Though she was much relieved to see possible help in the offing, Clemency was reluctant to call down to the man for fear of further startling his mettlesome horse. However, if she did not call to him, he might ride away.

"S-sir, oh, s-sir," she cried, and was annoyed at the quaver she heard in her voice. Also, as she had feared, the chestnut reared and shook its small beautiful head nervously from side to side. Fortunately, its antics failed to unseat its rider.

"Softly, softly, Valerian," the man said. He raised his head and turned angry brown eyes on Clemency. "Are you the chit who has been throwing stones at us?"

Stung, Clemency said indignantly, "I was not throwing stones at you, sir. And I am not a chit. My name is Clemency Barsford, and I . . ." Inadvertently she leaned forward again and her hauteur vanished as more stones fell. "Oh!" she gasped, and then added, "I . . . I am sorry that I am f-frightening your horse, s-sir, but there is no help for it. Each time I move, more s-stones f-fall and there . . . there does not s-seem to be a way back through the room behind me. My c-cousin has gone to f-fetch the g-grooms, but—"

"Good Lord," the man interrupted. "You mean you cannot get down?"

"No. C-could *you* f-fetch help, do . . . do you think?"

"You are . . . marooned on that sill?"

"Yes, I am, sir. I do wish you . . . might find a ladder or a r-rope."

"Wait," he said abruptly. Dismounting, he led his horse to a nearby tree and tied her to a low-hanging branch. In another moment he had stridden around the side of the tower, and in a few moments she heard his footsteps coming across the lower floor.

Alarmed, Clemency cried, "I beg you'll not try to get up here, sir. A ladder's needed, or a rope."

"So you said, but I'll be careful," he called from below.

"But the stairs are broken."

Laughter actually threaded through the tone in which he answered, "I've seen worse."

"But 'twill do you no good to come up here," she insisted. "Most of the floor's fallen."

"I see it has, but I also note that some remains." He was silent, but she heard the clink of his spurs as they hit the stone risers. She expelled a short annoyed breath, longing to tell him that he could not help her—but obviously he was not a man who heeded warnings or, she feared, listened to reason.

"You poor child!" he exclaimed, his voice nearer now. "It has given way."

She turned her head cautiously. Her eyes widened as she looked into a sun-browned face that was almost too beautiful for a man. Even in her peril, she could only marvel at features so regular that they could have been carved by a fine sculptor. But her discerning gaze also noted lines on his tanned forehead and deep circles under his eyes, which were not as dark as they had seemed before. Rather they were hazel and gold-flecked. He did not give her time to make any other assessments. He took an experimental step into the room.

"Oh, sir," she cried. "Please, on your life, do not come any further."

He gave her a reassuring smile of great sweetness. " 'Tis

your life we must consider, my dear. And believe me, I know where I may step and still remain aloft. I have trespassed here before . . . this tower, I believe, lies on the property of your father, Lord Sayles."

Clemency nodded. She was unable to answer because he was treading on the rim of the floor, which was all that remained. As he neared her, she closed her eyes, and if she had not been clutching the side of the window, she would have put both hands to her ears so that she would not hear the crash that must surely follow his foolish, foolish maneuvering.

"It is as I thought, my dear child. . . ." His voice was miraculously nearer. "What is left of the flooring is strong enough to bear me and, ergo . . . you, if you're not afraid. And I cannot believe you are—else you'd never have ascended those crumbling steps or made your way to that window."

Clemency opened astonished eyes and found him no more than a foot away from her. "Oh," she remarked amazedly. "The floor must be much stronger than I imagined."

"It is, most assuredly. Now . . . will you give me your hands and let me lead you back to the doorway?" He spoke soothingly and calmly, as if he had no notion of his own peril. "Can you forsake your aerie?"

Looking up into his face, Clemency was suddenly much less frightened. "I . . . I believe I can," she discovered.

He reached out his hand. "Keep very close to the wall. Let your back know it."

She found she could actually laugh. "What an odd way of putting it," she commented. "As if my back had eyes, too."

"It has sensation, which is equally useful. Be careful. I know you must be extremely surefooted."

"I am," she replied staunchly.

"And I beg you'll not look down. Look only at me."

She slipped carefully down from the window. However, as she stood on the foot or so of flooring that remained, she felt herself caught and knew it was her gown. Carefully she eased it off a projecting piece of mortar, and with her back against the rough stone, edged toward him. "I will have to go slowly," she explained.

"I'd not have it otherwise." He held out a slender brown hand. Another step and she was able to reach out toward him.

His fingers, long and slender, were warm against her hand. His smile was equally warm as he said, "You *are* very brave, child."

She gave him a fleeting smile but did not reply. If she were to reply, she knew that her voice would be trembling even more violently than before.

"Now, come . . . a step at a time, and step where I step. If any stones are dislodged, do not be afraid. You will not follow them. Trust me."

"I do," she managed to whisper, edging forward, resolutely keeping her eyes only on her feet.

He moved very slowly, though at one moment he came to an abrupt stop as a fall of stones crashed to the lower floor. "Do not look," he warned.

"I will not," she assured him as they started forward once again.

"There," he said. "Now I will go ahead of you on the steps, and you follow me as before. Try not to put your feet on any broken edges."

"Oh, we're on the steps!" she discovered, a thrill of pure happiness running through her. Looking down, she suddenly remembered Damian coming down those same steps, his face pale. She forgot him as quickly. The peril was not quite at an end. Some of the treads were badly cracked. She followed her rescuer, and finally they were standing on the rock-strewn surface of the ground floor.

"Oh," Clemency said weakly, and began to tremble. To her great embarrassment, tears ran down her cheeks as she stared up at the man who had led her out of terror and threatening death. "Oh, I . . . I . . ." To her further confusion, she could quell neither her tears nor her trembling.

"My poor child." He caught her in his warm embrace and held her tightly against him, the while he murmured gentle, comforting words to her and ran his hand through her tangled hair. " 'Tis all right . . . my dear. 'Tis all right," he murmured. "You are safe now, poor little bird."

A few moments later, all too conscious that she was no longer a child to be petted and coaxed out of a fear that should have left her immediately she felt solid ground beneath her feet, Clemency said, "I do thank you, sir. I am feeling much better now." She stepped back, and so did he.

"I did not mean to make such a cake of myself," she added regretfully. "I am past fourteen and should—"

"And should be proud of the way you were able to follow my instructions," he assured her. "I wish to hear no excuses. None are necessary. Are you aware of how many people twice or three times your age would have become completely frozen with fear, unable to take so much as a step? You are an uncommonly brave child—brave and, I fear, a little foolhardy, else you never would have traversed that floor in the first place."

"There was more of it," she explained. "And I wanted to show Beatrix . . ." She broke off. "Oh, dear, I do wonder what happened to her. I fear she must have met with a mishap, else she would have returned by now."

"She went to find help?"

"Yes. She's new here and I . . . we ought to look for her." Clemency moved forward impulsively and then stumbled and fell.

With a startled exclamation, her rescuer bent to help her up. "I pray you did not hurt yourself," he said concernedly.

"No, but I . . . I feel so weak." She lifted her startled eyes to his face. "I cannot think why."

" 'Twas an ordeal, your sojourn there"—he pointed upward. "I think I must take you back to Sayles, and it will mean confessing that I am a trespasser."

"A trespasser!" she exclaimed.

"Was I not, Lady Clemency?"

"I will say 'thank God' for that, sir," she added rather shyly. "I have told you my name. May I not know yours?"

"Have I not given it to you?" He looked at her quizzically. "I feel as if I have known you a long time. But of course I have not. I'm Colbourne. Rodger Colbourne."

"Lord Colbourne! And you live in the castle. And are home on leave, then? From Spain."

"Well, my child, you seem to know a great deal about me."

She blushed. " 'Tis not I . . . though I am sure our fathers are acquainted. 'Tis Damian who told me how you had been twice decorated for bravery."

His face darkened. " 'Twas more luck than bravery," he

said almost harshly. "There were others who deserved it more, and . . ." He paused. "But I'll not burden you with my plaints. Damian, is it? Damian Prior. I do remember the lad. He is about fourteen?"

Something in his words and in his face had hurt her. She did not know why, but she did have enough sensitivity not to question him about it. She said only, "Yes, he is, and soon will begin training with his uncle. He is in hopes that the war will not be at an end by the time he is ready to fight. I am sure that it must be over in four years' time—do you not agree?" She gazed at him anxiously.

"I wish I could agree." His smile was rueful.

"Oh, dear," Clemency sighed.

He gave her a long look. "Am I to understand that young Damian is your good friend?"

"My best friend," she said, thinking that she could hardly wait to tell Damian about her most fortuitous meeting with his hero. "We have known each other forever," she said.

"Forever," he mused. "I cannot think that is very long."

"Since we were nine," she amended. "Five years."

"I expect that is a long time at your age," he agreed.

She nodded. "I will miss him when he goes."

"Well, you have a few more years to wait before that happens," he comforted her. "And perhaps the war will be over." He glanced through the shattered wall of the tower. "The sun is on its homeward path and I am thinking we must join him. Come." He took her hand again. "Watch where you step."

"My horse is tethered over there," she said as they came outside. "In that little glade."

"We'll attach his reins to my saddle. I cannot think that you are in any condition to ride."

"I . . . expect I am not," she admitted reluctantly.

"I beg you'll not pull so long a face over that, my dear. 'Tis only natural . . ."

"Mama will be so angry. She does not like me going to the tower—but Beatrix wanted to see it." She clapped a hand to her forehead. "Oh, dear, I hope nothing's happened to her, but I fear it has—else she must surely have returned by now!" She twisted her hands together. "I have been remiss.

Oh, do let us hurry back . . . we must send people out to look for her."

"Very well. Your horse is in that glade?"

"Yes, tethered to a tree. I'll fetch him."

"No, I will," he said firmly. "You stay where you are, young lady." He strode off and was back more quickly than she had anticipated. "Are you sure you left him there?"

"You couldn't find him?"

"No."

"Gracious, I expect I did not tie him securely enough. Oh . . ." She gave him a distressed look. "They will be worried at home."

"Come," he said, and moved to the tree branch where he had tied his chestnut. "I'll put you up on Valerian, and please hold tightly to the saddlebow. I shan't be long in mounting, but meanwhile he'll want to show you that he's a horse of spirit. However, I assure you that there's no harm in him."

"I know that," Clemency laughed. "He's only young."

"Young and daring." He smiled down at her, and lifting her to the saddle, he sprang up behind her before his steed could lift so much as a hoof. "Come, then, we'll go. Onward, Valerian!"

Beatrix had lain in the grass after dismounting and giving Molly her head.

Had Clemency fallen to her death yet?

Beatrix loosed a long hissing breath. She had never expected her cousin would survive her walk across that crumbling floor. An earlier visit to the tower and a close examination of that upper room had shown her that the flooring was badly cracked and must give way. It had been even easier than she had imagined to get Clemency to venture out upon it. The silly thing had wanted to queen it over her—show how much braver she was than poor shrinking little Beatrix. The cracking of the floor beneath Clemency's feet had been wonderfully pleasant to hear. She had expected that any moment she would be watching her plunge thirty feet to her death, but instead, Clemency had leapt for the window and saved herself, at least for the nonce. It had been most unfortunate, but that windowsill could not hold her for long. Beatrix was reasonably sure of that.

Staring up at the sun, Beatrix wondered how long she had been hidden in this copse. It did not matter. She was sure she had been there close on two hours, and it was time and past that she returned to Sayles. She looked down at her wrist. It pained where she had struck it against the rock to make it bleed, but she would have to appear as if she had been hurt. She had used a sharp-pointed rock to add a long scratch to her arm, one that had cut through her sleeve. It had been no easy task to tear the material, and she had hated to spoil her new riding habit—but there would be other habits, other gowns, many others, if she reigned alone at Sayles.

Of course, there would be wild grief over Clemency, but gradually that would die down. Lady Sayles had other children, after all. She had complained that Clemency had so much energy it made her tired. She had also praised Beatrix's restful manner, and she was especially grateful because Beatrix did not mind reading to her by the hour. Lord Sayles liked her, too. They would eventually come to regard her as their daughter.

Damian might be disturbed. He was uncommonly fond of the wench and had actually talked of betrayal when Beatrix had met him that night—two weeks since—and swum with him in the pool. He seemed to have forgotten that it was he who suggested it. Naturally, swimming was not the only reason he had wanted her to come. She giggled. He had been a very clumsy lover, and though he denied it hotly, she knew he had never been with a woman. He had been half-excited, half-ashamed when they parted. She smiled contemptuously. He had not showed his face for two weeks now, or was it more?

She could get him back, she was sure of it—now that Clemency was out of the way. She would be lady of the manor in truth. She knelt and began to rub dirt into her face. Then she tore her stockings, and taking off one boot, tossed it among the bushes and set off for Sayles.

She waited until she was in sight of the manor before coaxing tears into her eyes, but as she was about to start for the road, a horse passed her. On it were a man and a woman—Clemency! Crouching down beside an adjacent bush,

Beatrix watched in shocked amazement and then moved back among the trees. It would never do to arrive at the exact same time. She must wait and let them worry. She lay down amid the deep grass, and now there was no need to try to coax tears into her eyes. Unbidden, they came, leaving white streaks on her dirty face, and if her wounds were false, her dirt artful rather than actual, her tears were real.

3

The ballroom at the Grange was bright with the light from candles in a center chandelier and in wall sconces set between floor-to-ceiling mirrors. A huge round moon framed in the long windows added its radiance to the occasion. Clemency, clad in a pale green muslin gown crisscrossed at the waist with matching ribbons in a satin that also edged the hem, was going through the patterns of a country dance with Damian, extremely handsome in his Brummell-inspired black evening clothes. She was enjoying herself more than she had anticipated, considering that this event would not be enlivened by an announcement of their engagement.

Though she had pleaded and Damian had argued, neither her parents nor his would consent to so binding a tie. "You are but seventeen and five months," her mother had said with a coldness emphasized by the frosty look in her faded hazel-green eyes. "And Damian himself is not yet eighteen. He is far too young and too heedless, if not actually wild, to be saddled with a wife, especially when he is about to be posted to Canada."

"Mama, I cannot imagine why you believe that Damian is wild or heedless," Clemency had retorted crossly. "He is not. He is extremely levelheaded and his friend Lieutenant Palmer tells me that Damian is already in line for a promotion."

"How would Lieutenant Palmer know that? He is not even in the same corps."

"They are friends and Lieutenant Palmer has visited him at his barracks."

"Young men always stick together," her mother had retorted.

Clemency blinked back tears. She knew she should not be

anticipating a time when Damian would not be present, but she could not help it. Moving reluctantly into the arms of another young man, she caught sight of Beatrix dancing with Lieutenant Palmer. She was in good spirits tonight and her partner was looking at her most ardently.

In the last three years, Beatrix had become even more beautiful and she was surpassingly graceful as she twirled around. Many of the gentlemen present tonight had wanted to claim Beatrix as their partner for the cotillions and country dances, but she favored Lieutenant Palmer above them all.

"You are very pensive tonight, Clemency," Damian remarked a few minutes later as he reclaimed her for the final pattern of the dance. He muttered, "I am passing warm. Will you join me in the garden?"

"Wait for me by the fountain," she muttered back.

"Good girl," he approved, and very properly escorted her to the edge of the floor before bowing and disappearing through the draperies that masked the garden doors.

Fearful that she would be immediately surrounded by partners demanding dances, Clemency moved as close to those same draperies as she might, the while keeping a weather eye turned on the thin elongated figure of Miss Lewes. She was glad that the governess was chaperoning them rather than Lady Sayles, who at the last moment had come down with a quinsy and taken to her bed. Lord Sayles had joined his host in the cardroom. A wary glance across the room showed her the thin, elongated figure of the governess seated on one of the spindly chairs reserved for dowagers and companions. She swallowed a giggle as she remembered Beatrix's christening Miss Lewes "the grasshopper." She did bear a faint resemblance to that insect as she engaged in animated conversation with another lady. Fortunately, she was not looking in her direction and Clemency was able to follow Damian into the garden.

Once outside, she made her way down a path bordered by a high yew hedge, and a second later she was by the fountain which stood in the middle of the rose garden. As she looked for Damian, he came from behind to sweep her into his arms. "My dearest love," he breathed.

"Oh, Damian, I—" Whatever else she might have said was silenced by his lips. She returned his kisses with fervor.

"Oh, Damian, my very dearest," she murmured when finally he released her, I wish—"

"Do not say it," he told her huskily. "It cannot be helped."

"But, Canada," she mourned. " 'Twill be such a very long time between leaves."

"No matter. On my first, we'll be wed. You'll be of age then."

"Of age!" she repeated. "Oh, no, we cannot be separated for so very long a time!"

"Silly gudgeon." He grinned. "I expect I will be home before six months are up, and in six months you'll be near enough to eighteen that your parents will not dare withhold their consent, nor mine neither."

"Oh, that is true," she said happily. "I'd not thought of that!" She sobered quickly. "But six months, and fighting the Americans . . . Oh, I do wish I were Beatrix!"

"Beatrix!" he repeated. "Why would you want that?"

He had spoken with his usual disdain, and Clemency was momentarily diverted. "Why do you not like her? You did once . . . and very much."

"No reason," he said evasively. "Tell me, my dear love, why should you, blessed with beauty and the world's goods, wish to change places with a wench taken out of charity?"

"Do not put it that way," Clemency protested. "You make her sound as if she came from some orphanage. She is my uncle's daughter, after all."

"And he was a loose screw, right enough," Damian retorted. "You haven't answered my question."

"Well, Mama allows her so much more freedom than she does me. Beatrix went driving with Lieutenant Palmer yesterday. And even though we have known each other all our lives, she'll not let me go out with you—alone. She says we must consider what people will say. It is all so ridiculous. She seems actually to distrust you. I cannot think why."

He put his arms around her and placed his lips against her ear. "No more can I, my dearest. Unless she has been listening to a little bird."

"A . . . little bird?" Clemency pursued, even though she wished she had not brought the subject up. She hardly liked to be discussing such matters with Damian so close to her she could hear his heart beating.

"You know the saying," he responded.

"Mama'd not stoop to have any of the servants spy on us."

"Perhaps she does not need to employ a *servant*," he said meaningfully.

"Beatrix?" Clemency moved away from him and turned to face him, her eyes large with indignation. "Truly, my love, you are wrong. She is my good friend."

"She is not mine," he said meaningfully.

"She always speaks very well of you to me."

"She's very clever," he said dryly.

"Oh, dear, I wish you'd tell me what passed between you."

"Nothing. I only wonder if Beatrix is really a friend to anyone."

"I have just told you—" she began.

"Oh, Clemency," he cut in. "You are so good and so trusting. And we have wasted enough of our precious moments discussing your cousin."

"I cannot think why you've formed such a dislike for her," she persisted. "There must be a reason."

"Damn her," he said roughly. "I have no reasons . . . only intuition. Enough of Beatrix, my beloved, enough, enough, enough!" Pulling her back into his arms he kissed her until she was breathless. "God," he murmured brokenly, "I love you so much, Clemency. You are my heart's treasure."

"And you are mine, my own darling." Tears began to roll down her cheeks. "Oh, what shall I do when you are away? It was bad enough when you were in training and I saw you so seldom . . . but I did see you. Now . . . oh, Damian, I shall be only half-alive. God, when will these ridiculous wars end?"

"They will have to end, you know," he said.

"But not soon enough," she said woefully.

"Clemency, dear . . ." Beatrix, with Lieutenant Palmer behind her, came hurrying toward them. "Miss Lewes is searching for you. You'd best go inside. I said you must have come out for a breath of air."

"You could not invent a better excuse than that?" Damian demanded coldly.

"Dear Damian," Beatrix sighed. "She caught me quite unawares."

" 'Tis true," Lieutenant Palmer said. "Lord, what a dragon!"

"You didn't tell her that I . . . that we were together," Clemency said nervously.

"No, of course I did not, my dear. But she has noticed that Damian is absent."

"How observant of Miss Lewes, particularly when there is such a crush inside," Damian commented.

"I say, Prior, you mustn't take it out on us," Lieutenant Palmer said. "As I told you, the woman's a regular dragon."

"And, unfortunately, a very observant one," Beatrix remarked ruefully. "However"—she turned to Clemency—"I will go back with you and say I found you in the cloakroom, whence you'd gone to repair a tear in your gown or some such thing."

"Now, that should suffice." Lieutenant Palmer's darkly handsome face was wreathed in smiles. "But, Miss Barsford, I must say I am loath to let you return so soon."

"Oh, but I must," Beatrix murmured. "You'd not want to toss my cousin, here, to your dragon."

" 'Tis an old dragon, and most of her teeth are drawn, I think." He was evidently attempting to speak lightly, but he did not quite achieve the tone he was seeking.

"But there is still fire in her nostrils." Beatrix put her little hand on his arm. "I pray you'll not be cross, Ralph."

"Not if you promise to join me here again. . . ."

"I will try," she assured him. "But now, Clemency, we'd best go."

"Yes, I know." Clemency reached for Damian's hand, and pressing it, said, "I will bid you good night."

"Good night, love," he said feelingly.

As luck would have it, Beatrix's clever excuse failed miserably, for as they approached the cloakroom, they met Miss Lewes coming out. Even so, the resourceful Beatrix might have evolved another equally effective explanation had not Miss Lewes spied a leaf in Clemency's hair, the sight of which moved that lady to scold them furiously in one breath and order the coach in another.

"If only she could be persuaded not to tell Mama." Clad

in her peignoir, Clemency sat on the end of Beatrix's bed.

" 'Tis a pity she's above bribery," Beatrix agreed.

Clemency gazed at her in shocked surprise and then she laughed. "Oh, you are such a tease. Anyhow, were I even to breathe bribery, she would go rushing off to Mama with that tale and add another sin to my calendar, if so it might be called." Her bosom swelled with righteous indignation. "A mere matter of seven months keeps us apart. I do not feel seventeen. I love Damian. I want to marry him and be with him, and now, due to Miss Lewes, I will be watched so closely that . . . Oh, it is outside of enough!"

Beatrix said gently, "You will see him in church tomorrow."

"Under Mama's eye. What *can* she have against Damian, whom I have known all my life."

"I expect she does not want you to have your heart broken," Beatrix said reasonably. "It's a very chancy thing to be a soldier. Look at Lord Colbourne."

Summarily deflected from her melancholy musings, Clemency actually glared at Beatrix. "I wonder that you dare mention his name," she said coldly, "after what you said last Sunday in church of all places—and in full hearing of several other people. Lord, I do hope he did not hear you—he was not far away."

Beatrix looked down. "I was not aware anyone heard me until afterward," she said ruefully.

"I do not believe that," Clemency retorted, her voice swelling with indignation. "You did not trouble to lower your voice. It goes beyond anything to . . . to make sport of him in that cruel way, calling him 'Lord Caliban' after all he's suffered in defense of this country, in defense of you, if you'd stopped to think of it."

"I pray you'll not tax me about that again," Beatrix said angrily. "It just slipped out, seeing him so dark-browed and limping and his face so swollen and scarred. He does look horridly ugly—even you must admit that, Clemency."

"I admit nothing of the kind!" Clemency glared at her. "He is not ugly. He is . . . changed." She swallowed a lump in her throat as she remembered how he had looked when she had first seen him. "Mama has a passing acquaintance with his physician and he has said that the swelling will go down . . . and his scar will look less noticeable in time.

Furthermore, his leg will grow stronger. "But if he really looked as badly as you implied . . . I would never describe him in such terms. And other people, people who have always envied him, have taken to calling him that too. Damian told me so."

"One more black mark against me in Damian's book, I see," Beatrix commented. "I vow, I thought he was going to hit me, and right in front of the vicar, too."

"It was ill done of you, especially in view of all he's suffered, with his poor little wife dying in childbed and the infant with her."

"I have said I was sorry." Beatrix hung her head. "As I have explained, the name just slipped out . . . on the spur of the moment. I had forgotten just how much I owe him for helping you down from the tower that day." She shivered. "Just imagine if he'd not arrived when he did."

Clemency also shivered. "I will never cease to be grateful to him."

"Nor I. You cannot imagine how terrified I felt when Molly threw me and I lay unconscious so long, waking just at sundown. I was so sure something terrible had happened to you." Beatrix threw her arms around Clemency, holding her tightly. "If anything *had* happened, I should have wanted to die too."

"Shhh, dearest." Clemency kissed Beatrix's cheek. "Neither of us died and nor are we the worse for the experience." Her eyes grew somber. "But poor Lord Colbourne. That is why I wish . . . But no matter, 'tis done. You cannot call back your words."

"I would apologize to him, but I fear that would only make matters worse. Still, I pray you'll not think ill of me when I tell you that it is for the best that your mother will not allow you and Damian to wed before he goes to America. Supposing he . . . well, you know what can happen in a war."

"I pray you'll not even think of such a thing!" Clemency cried.

"Oh, my love, my dear love." Beatrix's arms tightened about Clemency once more. "I want only for you to be happy. But one must think of the future. Supposing you were to have his child and—"

"I want his child," Clemency interrupted. "If anything were to . . . to happen, at least there would be an heir. As it is . . . Oh, God, why am I talking this way?" She slipped off the bed, adding reproachfully, "I wish you'd not filled my mind with these terrors, cousin. 'Tis bad enough to think on Damian's leaving in less than a fortnight without the added fear of his never returning!"

"I meant only to be practical, my love," Beatrix assured her. "I am sure Damian will return, and so must you be."

"I am," Clemency answered with a touch of defiance. "I will bid you good night, Beatrix." she hurried out of the room, closing the door with a slight slam.

Beatrix regarded the door thoughtfully. She had made an error, something that both annoyed and alarmed her. Seeing Lord Colbourne limping up the aisle, she had remembered his untimely appearance and rescue of her cousin, thus ruining all her plans. But by inventing that nickname, she had come close to alienating Clemency, and her suggestion that Damian might not return had driven a further wedge between them.

"I wish he would die," she muttered bitterly. Ever since that time three years ago when they had lain together, he had treated her as if she were some abandoned wretch from the streets! In retaliation, she had dropped little hints into the ear of Lady Sayles suggesting that Damian was wild and reckless and not above dallying with the village girls, the while he paid court to Clemency. She had managed to turn that lady against him, forestalling the possibility of any marriage between him and Clemency, at least while they were yet so young. However, it would be deadly dull when he was gone—he and Lieutenant Palmer.

Ralph Palmer was mad for her. He had actually asked her to run away with him, and while he had not mentioned marriage, she had half a mind to oblige him. He was handsome, and if he was not Damian, she could make do. Anything would be preferable to staying here with Clemency and pretending to an affection she was very, very far from feeling. If, as had been promised long ago, she and Clemency were to be presented at court and have a Season in London, there would be an incentive to remain. However, Clemency, damn her eyes, was not yet eighteen and nothing Lady Sayles could say or do could dissuade her from her love for Damian.

"I can only hope that the child will outgrow him once he is away," Lady Sayles had told Beatrix. "But if she does not, I fear I will have to let them marry. Her father's fond of Damian, and though I have told him about his peccadilloes, he says they are common to young men of his years. So . . ." Lady Sayles had shrugged. "I have no choice."

She did have a choice. She could insist on Clemency's going to London—but Lady Sayles was past middle age and Beatrix was sure she dreaded the idea of bringing out two debutantes. She might have exerted herself were Clemency willing, but she was just as happy to be free of the responsibility. That she did not waste a thought on herself was also obvious. Beatrix's position had not altered in three years. She was still a poor relation, and if the Sayles family settled a dowry on her, it would be adequate but not lavish, nothing to attract a wealthy suitor. She turned her mind back to Ralph Palmer. He had kissed her and she had felt a response deep within herself. In that moment, she had desperately longed for more than a mere embrace. With the exception of Damian, she had not been loved by a man since she was thirteen, a long time for a female as passionate as herself to go wanting. Of course, Ralph was off to America, but wives could follow their husbands across the seas—and she was pretty sure that with a little urging, he would marry her. And even with the war raging, it would be exciting to see a new country. Lieutenant Palmer did not have a title, but Damian was only a baronet. And what was there for her here? She could not spend the rest of her days as Clemency's companion and reading to Lady Sayles—and in Clemency's present mood, she might be closeted with her mother more and more. Anything was preferable to that. Ralph Palmer was not "anything." He was a very personable young man and he loved her. She wondered how long he had waited in the garden. She hoped that he was still there. It would not hurt him to cool his heels or his blood. He would be the more ardent when they met again.

Clemency, head down and staring unseeingly at the new spring grass, was walking through the fields that lay between the Grange and the woods bordering the stretch of land where Colbourne Castle stood. Her mother and Miss Lewes, now more companion to Lady Sayles than mentor to Clemency, would have been shocked if they had known she had come so far unescorted and on foot. They did not know. She had told them only that she was going to walk in the garden.

The Grange was misnamed, she thought, lifting her head to stare at its uneven sprawl of roofs. It was not a farmhouse or, at least, it had not been a farmhouse for some two hundred years. Damian's ancestor had been a wealthy yeoman who had performed some service for James I and had been rewarded with a baronetcy. Since that time, the family's wealth had increased, and numerous additions to the Grange had turned it into a large manor house with a vista designed by Capability Brown. A manmade lake reflected both the house and Colbourne Castle rising on its high hill. Looking from lake to house, she felt her old resentment stir. If her parents had been as reasonable as they were now prepared to be, she would not have had to wait until Damian came home on his postponed leave next month. They could have been wed and she dwelling here with his recently widowed mother, possibly awaiting the birth of her first child.

She loosed a quavering sigh. It had been a month since Damian's last letter, seven months since she had last seen him. He could not have returned, not even for his father's funeral, because he was in a place called Buffalo, which was in New York, and the British forces had captured it. It had been a bloody battle but Damian had emerged unscathed. In the letter describing the event, he had also mentioned Beatrix, there with her husband, Lieutenant Ralph Palmer. Clemency had not shared this information with her parents. Since her scandalous elopement—"gone like a thief in the night" was the way her father had scornfully described it—Lord and Lady Sayles had forbidden Clemency to so much as mention her name.

She had had considerable difficulty convincing them that she had not been a party to her cousin's plans. In fact, she was ruefully positive that they still suspected her of helping Beatrix get away.

"How else was she able to remove all her garments from her armoire? She would have needed a trunk as well as a bandbox, and surely she could not have carried them herself."

Lady Sayles had impaled her daughter with a suspicious stare. "You must have aided her."

"Our daughter has long had a passion for the romantic exaggerations of Mrs. Radcliffe," Lord Sayles had mused.

"She writes mainly about secret passages and ghostly mansions," Clemency had retorted, "not elopements. I did not help her, Papa. She did not give me one inkling of what she had in mind, not one."

"You were very close," Lady Sayles had insisted.

"I thought we were," Clemency had said, said out of a depth of bewilderment and grief. "Now I . . . I do not know what to think." She had burst into tears and fled to her chamber.

Tears came to her eyes now. For the thousandth time she wondered why Beatrix had not taken her into her confidence. Had she feared that Clemency might betray her? Did she not know her better than that? Once more she recalled their discussion on the night of the Priors' ball. She had been angry with Beatrix because of poor Lord Colbourne. Had her cousin taken her strictures ill? There was no guessing her state of mind. By evening of the following day, she had fled with Lieutenant Palmer, and nothing more had been heard of her until Damian's letter.

She blinked because the sunlit roof of the Grange was turned iridescent by her tears. She wished she had not gone walking. She was being racked by too many memories, but she was in no mood to go back to the inevitable questions and the scolding she would undoubtedly receive. By now her mother must have guessed that she had not restricted her walk to the gardens. Bitterness engulfed her. It was very, very hard to be treated like a child when she was eighteen and could have been married! Lucky Beatrix, to be with her husband in America. If she could have been with Damian . . . For her own peace of mind, she had to stop agonizing over those frustrated hopes. She would go home soon. However, at present the backs of her legs were aching. She had walked much farther than usual. She had passed the Grange and was nearly to the top of a small rise of ground. She could see the castle particularly well from here. It was really in a remarkable state of preservation. She had always loved its tall keep, and there was the pennant flying from the top of that tower. It signified that Lord Colbourne was in residence. She frowned, remembering Beatrix's cruel jest. It was amazing how it had caught on. Rose had told her that the village children spoke of the ogre's castle and of Caliban's Keep.

"Cruel," she muttered. "And on many counts." To make sport of his honorable wounds, to leave Sayles without so much as a word of gratitude to her parents for all they had done for her. And surely she might have left one whom she had extolled as her "dearest friend" a note. At first Clemency had been unable to believe that Beatrix had not left her a message. She had taxed the servants, waited for the post for weeks after Beatrix's departure, expecting that surely she must hear from her, but she had not. It was strange, very strange. Sometimes she felt as if she had never really known her cousin.

She turned away from the sight of the castle and started back the way she had come. Reaching the fields, she veered off from a clump of trees hard by a stream. Not far from that stream were two narrow, upstanding stones on which odd symbols had been cut. The people from their tiny village gave them a wide berth, saying that they were set there by witches, but Clemency had once found a flint arrowhead at the base of one. She had tendered it to a frankly envious Damian. She remembered him asking how she could always find objects that no one had ever seen before. " 'Tis simple. I look for them," she had answered.

She had been lucky, she thought as she went in the direction of the two stones which, when she was little, she had called "the enchanted maidens." Beatrix had laughed at her for that. Since the coming of Beatrix, she had stopped visiting the "maidens." Coming upon them now, she had the odd fancy that they were welcoming her back. If her cousin had been party to her thoughts, she would have teased her and called her "childish."

Though only two months older than herself, Beatrix, she realized, had never been childish. Games bored her. Britain's historic past also bored her. She looked ahead to balls and drives in fast curricles and, above all, London. She knew the city. She described its fine palaces and huge mansions. She had also talked of the Prince Regent and his mistresses. Not long ago, she had told Clemency that she would not mind serving him in that capacity. Clemency flushed, remembering that she had asked her cousin if a mistress were some sort of elevated housekeeper. A memory of her cousin's derisive laughter echoed in her ears.

"A mistress sleeps with the master," she had giggled. "And in return he dresses her in silks and hangs diamonds round her neck, but I beg you, child, do not tell your mama that I have poured such information into your innocent little ears."

Though Clemency was not much wiser concerning the occupation of mistress, she had not sought any further explanations from her mother. Beatrix was always ordering her to remain silent in regards to the bits of gossip she imparted to her. Some of it, she picked up from listening to the servants' chatter. She was never above eavesdropping, Clemency recalled. She also seemed to know what was going on in the village. She had even glimpsed the late Lady Colbourne, whom she described as small, dark, and all eyes.

"Her name's Inez," she had said. "She does not speak a word of English. He jabbers to her in Spanish. I am told he met her in Portugal, but she's actually from Madrid. There's a tale that he rescued her from some French officers who were about to ravish her. Judging from the way he looks now, I would say 'twas out of the frying pan into the fire."

Beatrix had laughed at Clemency's shocked and indignant protests. She had added, "I wish I might go to Spain. They say that the men are ever so handsome. Dark flashing eyes . . . dark hair, long lithe bodies. They must be wonderful lovers."

Thinking about her cousin's constant references to far-off places and handsome men, Clemency found herself less surprised at her actions. Lieutenant Palmer was dark, handsome, and given Beatrix's love of romantic adventure and— The pounding of hooves put an end to her reflections. Looking around, Clemency saw a huge black horse galloping in her direction. The animal bore a saddle but its reins and stirrups swung loose over its heaving, foam-streaked flanks. She leapt from its path but actually felt its hot breath as with a neigh that was close to a shriek it tossed its head and rushed through the trees.

"Marcus . . . Marcus . . ." a man called hoarsely. "Damn you, Marcus . . ."

Clemency stared about her. Someone had been tossed from the stallion's back, and from the sound of his voice, he was not very far away. She looked around but did not see anyone.

"Where are you?" she called. "Have you been hurt?"

"Where . . . are you . . .?" came the strained response. Evidently the rider had been hurt.

"Here by the maidens!"

"The . . . maidens?"

Clemency bit her lip. She had not meant to blurt out that childish name, especially at a time like this. "I am by the standing stones."

"I am upstream . . . by a large oak . . . with long branches . . ."

"That span the stream? I know it!" She hurried in that direction, and reaching the oak, she saw a booted foot. She quickened her steps and in another moment had come upon the fallen horseman. He lay on his side, one hand outstretched, grasping a small thorny bush, as if he had been trying to pull himself up. She did not see his face immediately, only his tousled black hair, which fell in waves over forehead and cheek. She did see his mouth and found his lips compressed as if he were in considerable pain.

She knelt beside him. "Are you much hurt, sir?" she asked gently.

He half-raised his head. "I do not know," he muttered. "My horse shied at something . . . I was not attending. My leg . . ."

"Have you hurt it?" she demanded anxiously.

"I am not sure. It does not feel well, but then, it seldom does."

His voice sounded familiar to her. She had heard it before somewhere. At the ball? Had he been one of the young men who had tried to pry her away from Damian? No. It was an older memory. She was sure of that, and into her mind flew images, images connected with the voice she was hearing now. The cadences had been different then—soothing, soothing the fears of the frightened young girl he had subsequently drawn across a shattered floor to safety!

"Lord Colbourne!" she exclaimed.

He tried to lift his head, but his position was still too awkward. "Do I . . . know you?" he asked.

"We have met, but you may not remember. No matter." Gently she pushed the tangled hair away from his eyes. "Oh, your cheek is scratched and bleeding. Does it hurt much?"

"I do not feel it."

"Even so, I'd best clean it. Then I'll go for help to the castle."

"It's a great distance away and the hill is high, hard to climb," he protested.

"Then perhaps I'd better seek help someplace nearer, but first your cheek. I'll ease your head onto my lap if you do not mind."

"If *you* do not mind." There was an edge of bitterness to his tone. "You'll not like what you see. I must warn you that of late some people in the village have taken to calling me Lord Caliban."

"Oh!" Clemency cried. "Oh, dear, I did pray that you'd not heard that cruel joke."

"Ah, good, you are forewarned and know what to expect when you look upon the ogre of Caliban's Keep." His laughter was harsh.

"My lord, I beg you'll not take those ill-conditioned remarks to heart," she said unhappily.

"They are not far from the truth, I expect."

"Oh, please, I cannot bear to hear you talk so. It hurts me."

"Does it? Why?"

"Because it is so far from the truth."

"Look closer and you will disagree."

"I do not disagree," she protested, actually hating Beatrix at this moment. But she could not think of her—she must tend his wound. She had been wearing a white fichu. Taking it off, she dipped it in the stream, and gently easing his head onto her lap, began to wipe the blood away. "I hope I am not hurting you," she said anxiously.

"Not at all. Is the scratch deep? If so, 'twill add a needed symmetry to my contenance."

She glanced at the scar that seamed the left side of his face, running from hairline to jaw and, she realized with a relief tinged by horror, narrowly missing his left eye. She also noted that it was no longer the vivid red it had been that day in church. It was much paler, and she guessed that in time it would differ little from his normal complexion. His features had the same beauty she remembered, save that in repose there was a bitter twist to his mouth that had not been in evidence four years ago. She said reprovingly, "I pray you'll not talk such nonsense, my lord. I see very little change in you."

"Very little change?" he echoed incredulously. His golden gaze was fixed on her face. "From when? We do not know each other, do we? I could not have forgotten one so lovely as you . . . with eyes green as any water nymph's and hair the color of flame."

His compliments brought a deep flush to her cheeks. Damian had occasionally praised her coloring—but always teasingly. He had said she had cat's eyes and hair the shade of a fox's brush. She swallowed a lump in her throat. She did not want to dwell on Damian at this moment. To think of him was to see him lying as helpless as poor Lord Colbourne, but with wounds unhealed by time. She said, "I am Clemency Barsford, my lord."

"Clemency . . . Barsford," he repeated uncertainly. "Of course, I know the name . . . your father's Lord Sayles . . . but where . . . ?"

"I pray you'll not think on it now, my lord. Will you be all right if I leave you? I think it would be best if I did not go to the castle—since my fiancé's house is so much nearer . . . the Grange, you know."

"The Grange . . . Damian Prior's gone to America, so I have been told."

"His mother remains in residence. I will pile grasses under your head and mark the place where I left you." She began to pull up handfuls of grass.

"You are, in truth, an angel of mercy," he said softly.

"One good turn deserves another, my lord." She smiled.

He eyed her in silence for a moment, his forehead creased as he evidently searched his mind trying to place her. "You do look familiar, Clemency Barsford," he said as she eased his head onto the grass. "How do I know you?"

"Do you remember the tower . . . with its broken floor and the—"

"Ah," he interrupted. "Of course I do! But you are never that child?"

"I am, my lord."

"Clemency . . . Barsford. Yes!" He half sat up, wincing with the effort.

"I pray you will lie down, my lord," she admonished. "And do not stir, for you will only hurt yourself. I will be back very soon, I promise you."

"I do thank you," he said, relaxing.

"Are you comfortable?" she asked anxiously. "Do you need more grass beneath your head?"

"I am very well, my dear."

"I shall be back as quickly as I may," she repeated.

The butler, who answered Clemency's frenzied knocking, was well-known to her and admitted her immediately. Fortunately, Lady Prior was downstairs. She had been half an invalid since the sudden and unanticipated death of her husband, but Clemency's description of Lord Colbourne's accident served to bring her out of her apathy. She summoned servants and ordered that the head groom, who, she explained to Clemency, had almost as much knowledge of medicine as the local physician, accompany them. "I will have a room readied for him," she told Clemency briskly.

"I do thank you, Lady Prior," she said as she hurried out to lead the men to where Lord Colbourne lay.

He was lying with his eyes closed as Clemency and the men returned. From the expression on his face, she guessed that he was in considerable pain, but as she bent over him, he opened his eyes, and glancing at the men behind her, actually managed to smile as he said almost gaily, "I vow, my dear, this is more than a mere good turn. I am much in your debt, Miss Barsford."

"Never," she said softly. "I owe you my life."

"You do refine upon it too much," he chided. "May I have leave to call upon you when I am more myself?"

"Oh, you must," she exclaimed. "I will look forward to it, and I pray it will be soon."

"And so do I," he said, a smile flickering briefly in his somber pain-filled eyes.

4

"Such magnificence, my dear." Miss Lewes sat on the edge of a Louis XV chair covered with a green-and-gold Aubusson tapestry all delicate scrolls and stylized flowers. She gazed wide-eyed at a ceiling painted with a pastoral landscape depicting nymphs, shepherds, and the sun chariot piloted by a golden Apollo. It was centered by a huge crystal chandelier. The walls were paneled in ivory and ornamented with gold. The rest of the furniture was also French. There were delicate painted cabinets, a long couch to match the chairs, and console tables covered with fine marble. A huge fireplace was surmounted by a carved marble mantelpiece decorated with artfully sculptured leaves through which peeped mischievous little faces.

Clemency nodded absently. This was her second visit to the castle. Her first had taken place a week earlier, when she, with her parents, had been bidden to dinner.

The invitation had been issued shortly after Lord Colbourne, recovered from a fall that had fortunately resulted only in a twisted ankle, had come to pay a courtesy call on Clemency and her parents.

He had proved a most gracious host. The dinner had been delicious, and afterward he had showed them through some of the state rooms, giving them interesting and amusing anecdotes concerning the several reigning monarchs who had stayed in them.

There had been Anthony Colbourne, who, upon entertaining Queen Elizabeth on one of her numerous progresses, found himself not only poorer in purse but bereft of a magnificent Cellini cup which had taken her majesty's avaricious eye. The Lord Colbourne who had welcomed Charles II had possessed a beautiful wife whose charms had strongly appealed to his majesty. However, her lord had proved less generous than his ancestor, which meant that he had to content himself with his hereditary earldom rather than the dukedom that the king had dangled before his eyes.

Lord Colbourne had recounted these tales with great charm, and her parents had been delighted. However, Clemency, following them from room to room, had been distressed by the emptiness of the place and by the unhappiness she saw reflected in their host's eyes when his face was in repose. Equally distressing to her had been the painful limp that had replaced his once graceful stride.

She had found it difficult to smile and jest with him, and, in fact, had been heartily pleased when the evening ended. However, before it had come to a close, she discovered that she and her host shared a passionate interest in antiquities, particularly those from Britain's past. As a boy he, too, had combed the grounds looking for spearheads and—he had laughed deprecatingly—perhaps a Roman shield or sword. He had been fascinated when she told him about her discovery of the tear vase and the flint arrowhead. He had expressed a wish to see the vase and had promised to show her some of the items he had found in the vicinity and during his travels through the country in the years before he had gone to war. That was why she had come this afternoon, and again she was painfully aware of the loneliness he must be experiencing amid all this luxury.

If only he had someone with whom he could share it. Certainly it was a great pity that his wife had died so young, and their child with her. It would be well were he to marry again. He had been a widower for some fourteen months. However, she doubted that he had any such intention. Probably he had been madly in love with the girl he had rescued and married. And in addition to that, he was oversensitive about his infirmities. She sighed as she remembered Beatrix's cruel remarks. These, repeated by those who were envious of his wealth and position, had served to increase his sensitivity. Thinking about that, she was glad her cousin had gone. In fact, she hoped never to see her again!

"I wonder what has happened to our host," Miss Lewes

murmured, effectively scattering Clemency's thoughts. "We've been here upwards of twenty minutes."

Clemency glanced at the beautiful Dresden china clock on the mantelshelf. It was nearly twenty-five minutes since they had been shown in here—and what was keeping him? Was he ill again? Judging from what he had said about his leg on the day of his fall, she guessed it must give him a great deal of pain. The thought of what he endured both physically and mentally distressed her anew. It was so manifestly unfair that Lord Colbourne, who was noble in the true sense of the word, must be visited by such anguish! She wished that there was something she could do to help alleviate his sorrow. Her gaze fell on her reticule. In it was the vase. Possibly she could coax him into searching out new antiquities. Though walking was difficult for him, he could ride, and there was a ruined castle in their immediate neighborhood. It overlooked the sea. The sea air was known to be beneficial to one's health. She wondered if he had ever thought of going to Bath or Brighton. Porlock was also on the sea, but it did not have the facilities of the other two towns. And Bath also had Roman remains.

In that moment, the door to the drawing room opened and Lord Colbourne, carrying a large teakwod box, limped in hastily. Clemency's anxiety fled as she found him smiling, albeit apologetically.

"Good afternoon." He looked interrogatively at the governess.

"My lord, this is Miss Lewes. Mama has the headache and could not accompany me."

"Miss Lewes, I am delighted to meet you." He bowed over her hand.

"And I, you, my lord," the governess said more timorously than usual. "Such a lovely room, so many rare treasures."

"I thank you." He smiled. "Or rather, my . . . er, buried ancestors would thank you, for it was they who accumulated most of what you find here."

"I can see that some of your furnishings are of considerable antiquity, my lord. And that box . . . Indian, is it not?"

"Quite correct, Miss Lewes. My uncle visited India some years ago and presented this box to me. I had some difficulty in locating it just now—which is why I was delayed. 'Tis a long time since I have looked at it—but it will explain what I was doing on Lord Sayles's lands that day we first encountered each other." His gaze shifted to Clemency.

"I remember that you called yourself a trespasser," she said.

"Fancy your recalling that," he marveled.

"I remember everything about that day," she replied, moved by several emotions. Gratitude and regret were uppermost, as once more she envisioned him guiding her across that shattered floor, risking his life to save her.

"As it happens, so do I," Lord Colbourne said. "You were so very brave, my dear."

"Brave," she scoffed. "I was terrified—and well you know it."

"Your terror traced no yellow streaks upon your back." He gave her an admiring glance. Turning to Miss Lewes again, he added, "I presume you remember what took place that day?"

"Oh, yes, my lord," she replied. "I was present when you brought dearest Clemency home." With a touch of her old sternness she added, "Lady Clemency was always far too adventurous for her own good—especially after her cousin arrived."

"Her cousin? Oh, yes, that tearful little girl who fell from her horse and failed to give the alarm. Whatever happened to her?"

"She eloped with an officer," Clemency said shortly, wishing that Miss Lewes had not broken the family rule and mentioned Beatrix. However, she recalled, he could not know that her cousin was the source of those cruel remarks that had caused him such misery.

"Eloped, did she? 'Tis not an unusual occurrence these days. I wish her happy and hope 'twas more than a uniform engaged her affections."

"Lieutenant Palmer seemed very pleasant," Clemency said. "He was Damian's guest."

"Ah, young Damian, who is due home soon, his mother has told me."

"Yes," Clemency corroborated, "in another month."

"And of course," he pursued, "you'll be wed at that time?"

"Yes," she said with a touch of resentment. "We should have been married before he'd left, but my parents would not hear of it!"

"You were but seventeen, my dear, and Sir Damian bound for America and danger," Miss Lewes reminded her.

"I would have gone with him, and gladly!" Clemency cried.

"You cannot know the hardships attendant upon traveling with an army, especially in such wild country," Lord Colbourne said gravely. "A soldier should be single-minded and alert at all times. He cannot be racked by concern over the loved ones he has brought with him."

"That is entirely true," Miss Lewes agreed.

Clemency noted that Lord Colbourne's eyes had turned very somber as he spoke. She wondered if he might not have been referring to himself. Had he been less cautious out of concern for his wife? She wished devoutly that the conversation had not taken this unfortunate turn. Forcing a smile, she turned her gaze on the teakwood box. "I must tell you, my lord, I am on fire to know what is in there." She put a finger on its carved top.

"Ah," His eyes brightened and an amused smile twitched at his lips. "I will show it to you in exchange for a look at your vase. But where is it?"

"Here, sir." She opened her reticule and drew out the small packet that contained the tear vase. Peeling away the paper and the cotton she had wrapped around it, she held it toward him.

He took it almost reverently. "Imagine . . . this object made of glass has survived all this time. And might have contained the tears of Claudius or even Julius Caesar."

"I have a feeling its owner was rather more humble," Clemency said.

"I have a feeling you are very probably correct," he agreed. "Ah, that these stones or, rather, glass could speak!"

"Imagine collecting tears," Miss Lewes commented.

"Tears were precious to the Romans," Lord Colbourne explained. "Perhaps in the act of bottling their grief, they were momentarily diverted from their sorrows."

"That is an intriguing idea, my lord," Clemency observed. "You might be right."

"I would prefer to be. Grief's a debilitating emotion and avails us little, since it cannot restore those whom we have lost. 'Tis better to leave them in the realms of memory and take up the reins of life again."

"That is not always easy." Miss Lewes spoke with uncommon bitterness and Clemency guessed that the governess was referring to the recent death of her mother.

"I agree, Miss Lewes," Lord Colbourne said sympathetically. "I was speaking of what one ought to do rather than what can be done."

They were veering toward dangerous shoals again, Clemency thought. She said, "I wish I might have shown you the arrowhead I found. 'Twas in very good condition. And my brother, Gerald, found an ancient spearhead near the tower."

"Near or in the tower?" Lord Colbourne asked interestedly.

"I am not sure," she said. " 'Twas in very good condition, though."

"Perhaps it came from the burial ground beneath the tower. They used to bury weapons with their dead, you know."

"The burial ground beneath the tower?" Clemency repeated.

He flashed a smile at her. "I am not entirely sure there is . . . but I think it might explain this." He lifted the lid of the teakwood box and took out an object wrapped in flannel. Unwrapping it, he revealed a goblet of a greenish metal chased with stylized figures of animals.

"Oh!" Miss Lewes exclaimed. "You *found* that?"

"You might almost say it found me . . . I literally stumbled on it. It was projecting up out of the earth that lay beneath a break in the stones of the dungeon floor—in that tower."

"The dungeon floor?" Clemency stared at him in consternation. "What dungeon?"

There was a teasing quality to the smile he turned on her. "Did you not know that there was a dungeon beneath the tower floor?" he asked blandly.

Clemency gazed at him in amazement. "I never did. Damian, neither—nor Gerald, at least he never said so."

"You might say I stumbled on that, too. 'Tumbled' would be closer to the truth. There is a fall of masonry inside, part of an older wing. I was a curious lad and I was poking about that and accidentally knocked down some of the stones. I saw a gaping aperture, and in coming closer, I tripped over another stone and fell upon a rocky flight of steps."

"Oh, were you hurt?" gasped Miss Lewes.

"The wind was knocked out of me, but other than that, I took only a few bruises. Not enough to deter me from going down those steps into darkness. I had a tinderbox in my pocket and I struck a flint to light my way. I was hoping . . . I do not know exactly what I hoped I'd find." He grimaced.

"Did you find something horrid?" Clemency asked.

"Horrid and . . . also sad. I discovered a rude cell with the remnants of a rusty chain on the wall and a heap of bones beneath."

"Not human bones!" Miss Lewes said in shocked accents.

"I am afraid they were. Some poor prisoner chained and forgotten," he said ruefully. "They gave me quite a fright, and I dropped my tinderbox."

"Oh, dear," Miss Lewes said. "You might have lost your way."

"I did for a bit, and stumbling on the stones, I fell and found this half-embedded in the broken earth, and sticking into my stomach as well."

"Did you have any idea what it was?" Clemency asked.

"I felt the smoothness of the metal. I dug around it with both hands and finally pulled it out. Then I crawled back toward what I hoped was the stairs."

"And was it?" Miss Lewes demanded.

He smiled at her and shook his head. "It was another cell, half-filled with bricks where most the wall had fallen. Mine might have lain with those other bones had it not been for a gust of air coming from the opening. After a few more false starts, I finally gained the stairs and came out with this goblet."

"Gracious." Clemency released a caught breath. "That was an adventure." Half-enviously she added, "It's a wonder that I never found that opening myself."

He winked at her. "Mainly because I closed it with more stones, having claimed it for my own. In those days, I fear I recognized no territorial rights. And there's worse to tell." He had another teasing smile for Clemency. "On that day we met, I confess that I was in hopes of a similar find. Time was lying heavy on my hands and I wanted something to do that might turn my mind from . . . other matters." A somber look flickered briefly in his eyes and vanished as he added, "Consequently, I was not only trespassing, I was contemplating thievery, though with little hope of success. Such discoveries are not made every day. I found this goblet over sixteen years ago."

"Sixteen years ago, Lord Colbourne?" Clemency questioned. "You must have been very young."

"I expect I was, though I did not think so—since I was recently turned thirteen."

"Really." Clemency's rapid mental calculations gave him an age of twenty-nine, which, since she was approaching her nineteenth birthday, made him little more than ten years her senior. She had not thought him so young. Pain had etched too many lines upon his face, she thought regretfully. He had had more than his share of sorrow—since his father had died when he was seven, and his mother a year after he joined Wellington's forces. She remembered someone telling her that his maternal uncle had helped raise him, but that man was dead too. There had been too many deaths in his life.

"You did make a marvelous find, my lord." Miss Lewes had been reverently handling the goblet. "I would say that this is bronze."

"I agree—bronze and probably dating from a time before the tower was built. Beowulf himself might have drunk his mead from it."

"As long as it was not Grendel." Clemency laughed. "I would hate to have him or his mother lurking beneath our tower." She examined the goblet. "These animal pictures etched into its surface—they are so well done. And so painstaking. I would not have thought the ancients so accomplished. I do thank you for showing it to me."

"I wish to give it to you, Lady Clemency or, rather"—his hazel eyes gleamed gold with laughter—"or should I say that I am returning it to you."

"Oh, no, you must not," she protested. "I could not take it."

"Come, by rights it belongs to you. 'Twas taken from

beneath your tower—or rather purloined. You must have it. I insist."

"You are very kind, but I will not take it unless we make an exchange."

"An exchange?" He looked at her quizzically. "What manner of an exchange?"

She touched the tear vase. "You must have this."

"No . . ." He shook his head. "I was the trespasser, not you."

"Had you not trespassed when you did, my lord, I'd not be here to argue with you at this moment." She held out the tear vase. "Please," she said softly. "I do want you to have this."

Looking into her face, he ceased to protest. "I think you do." He reached for her hand and pressed a kiss upon it. "I will cherish it, my dear."

At his touch, a most unexpected and surprising sensation went through Clemency. She had never experienced anything like it, not even when Damian had kissed her lingeringly upon the lips. She could define it only as an odd excitement that turned her hot and cold at the same time. It also confused her so much that she was extrememly glad when Miss Lewes insisted that they had remained far too long.

"We must go," she agreed.

"May I hope that you will come again soon?" he asked.

"We shall . . . and you must come to see us," she said. "And I do thank you for this treasure."

"And I, for mine," he returned.

She was still thinking about her odd reaction to his kiss as she and Miss Lewes were being driven back to Sayles. She did not understand it and she did wish that the governess was not chattering so much. Generally, Miss Lewes was considerably more self-contained, but she had been most impressed by their host. "So charming a man, and so handsome, too. That scar has not marred his features, not at all. In fact, I think it has only given him character. 'Tis a pity about his leg, but one hardly notices it. His eyes are really beautiful—do you not agree? In some lights, they are the color of amber. He does seem extremely taken with you, my dear."

"Only because I helped him," Clemency said quickly. "For no other reason, I am sure."

"I am not so sure," Miss Lewes returned. "From my observation . . ."

Clemency was spared the governess's observations by reason of their arrival at Sayles. Coming into the hall, she saw a letter on the silver tray that stood on the table just inside the door. Her eyes widened as she recognized Damian's black scrawl upon the envelope. Lord Colbourne faded from her mind as she picked it up. She had not heard from Damian in over a fortnight.

"Clemency!" Lady Sayles came hurrying down the stairs. "You have been an age. Oh, dear, I do not mean to sound as if I were scolding you, only . . ."

Clemency regarded her mother in surprise and concern. Lady Sayles's eyes were red. She looked as if she had been weeping—which was unusual for her. "Mama, is your headache worse?" she asked solicitously.

"No . . . I mean . . . Clemency, my dearest, a message came for you . . ." Lady Sayles's lip quivered. "I must tell you . . ."

Clemency was aware of a great throbbing in her throat. She held up Damian's letter. "Yes, I have only just found it . . . on the table. This is what you meant, is it not, Mama? Damian is . . . is not a very good correspondent." She would have gone on talking, saying anything because she wanted to forestall her mother's divulging of the message she saw written in her reddened eyes and on her trembling mouth.

"Clemency," Lady Sayles said insistently, "Damian is . . . is missing in action. He is presumed dead."

And so it was said.

Clemency stood quite still, staring at her mother. "Presumed?" she questioned in a low voice. "*Presumed* does not mean . . . dead. They only *think* he is dead. They are . . . they are not sure." Looking into Lady Sayles's doubtful, distressed, and pitying eyes, she repeated firmly, "They are not *sure*, Mama."

Her mother put an arm around Clemency's shoulders. "They are very nearly sure, my dearest love. A comrade saw him fall bleeding, and as he lay on the ground, another soldier ran his bayonet into him. His friend could not go to his assistance . . . because he was in the midst of the fighting himself. After the battle ended, he and others went to look for the wounded and the dying. They could not find the . . . the body, but 'tis believed that those human scavengers that haunt the battlefields dragged it away to rob it."

Clemency gently disengaged herself from her mother's embrace. Her voice was also gentle as she said, "You must not call Damian an 'it,' Mama. Not until you are quite, quite sure that he is dead."

"Oh, my dear, I am sorry." Lady Sayles's voice broke. "But there is very little hope, you know."

"I do not know." Clemency shook her head. "I do not. I am sure I would feel it if he were dead. I do not feel it, Mama. I do not feel it, and they, whoever they are, they do not know it." She looked at her mother defiantly now. "They do not know it." She added, "I think I shall go up to my room now." A random thought struck her. "I should not have given it away so quickly, I fear. But of . . . of course I did not dream I should be needing it quite so soon."

Her mother regarded her apprehensively. "I am not sure I understand you, my dearest."

"I am talking about a vase, Mama . . . a vase for tears." Clemency hurried up the stairs.

5

"London," Clemency said numbly. She was standing in the back parlor, whence she had been summoned just as she was about to go riding, something she usually did in the mornings. However, it had been blustery when she awakened. Autumn had come early this year, she thought, and then remembered that it was within three days of October. What had happened to the summer? she wondered. It did not matter. She fixed her eyes on a point equidistant from her mother and her sister Justine.

Pregnant, placid, and adamant, Justine looked uncommonly like Lady Sayles. They could easily have been sisters, and certainly they were in agreement, presenting a solid bulwark of decision. It was a decision, she reasoned bitterly, that was calculated to change her life.

" 'Tis a pity your papa sold the town house," Lady Sayles said. "But we will stay with Justine, and together she and I will arrange your presentation at court. Justine will procure you a voucher to Almack's, no small favor, I can tell you. Fortunately, she is a friend of Mrs. Drummond Burrell, who, as you know, is one of the patronesses."

"I do not want to be presented at court." Clemency's green eyes were stony. "I do not want a voucher to Almack's. I . . . I want to remain here."

Justine, who was knitting a garment for her expected infant, looked up from her work to say, "You will change your mind once you see London. It is an exciting city. You cannot stay here and rusticate forever."

"No," Lady Sayles agreed. " 'Tis time and past that you had your London Season. "And—"

"And married?" Clemency interrupted angrily. "I shall never marry. Do you not understand, Mama? Damian—"

"Damian is dead, poor lad," Justine said firmly. "But you are alive and young. You'll not be young forever. You've passed your nineteenth birthday. You should have been in town a year ago. But no matter, you will be just as welcome now. You are a mite too thin, but you are still beautiful. You have a large dowry and impeccable ancestry. I see no reason why you should not have as great a success as I did."

"But—" Clemency began, only to be silenced as Lady Sayles said, "Justine was voted an Incomparable by the Dandies who sit in the Bow Window at White's." She added complacently, "Not that I approve of such a distinction, but still, it was a mark of approbation."

"And," Justine said, "I was married within five months of my arrival."

"Damian—" Clemency began.

"Damian," Justine interrupted a second time, "was a charming young man. However, he was only a baronet. You could do considerably better on the marriage mart, my dear. I am told that the Marquis of Stralem is in town for the Season. Also the Earl—"

"I beg you'll not talk to me of them," Clemency flashed, and had a sudden vivid recollection of a time when she was going on seven and Justine had turned eighteen. Justine had been as slender as herself in those days, and her eyes, now so calm and cool, had been filled with fire. She had stood in this very parlor, alternately sobbing and screaming her defiance at their mother because she and Papa had given their permission to Lord Farnsworth to press his suit.

"But I do not love him, Mama," Justine had cried, her eyes flashing.

"He is of impeccable lineage and your papa and I approve," Lady Sayles had said with a calm that further infuriated her daughter.

"I do *not* approve," Justine had cried tempestuously. "I love Charlie Edgecombe. I will marry no one but him. We . . . we are plighted!"

"You are not plighted," Lady Sayles had returned. "That decision is not for you to make. Sir Charles is a feckless young man who has no means to support a wife. He is known to be a gambler who will bet on anything. I will not stand by and see him squander your dowry on which turkey will walk across the road first or whether Lady Such-and-Such will be delivered of twins! I have it on very good authority that he is already heavily in debt—and not a year out of Oxford. Your dowry would not suffice to keep him from his inevitable retreat—debtors' prison. You will marry Lord Farnsworth, and that is final."

Justine had gone sobbing from the room. She had tried to run off with Charlie Edgecombe, but her plan had been discovered and she locked in her room. Now, twelve years later, she was Lady Farnsworth, happily anticipating her fourth child and calmly outlining a similar destiny for her younger sister, quite as if Damian had never existed.

"I cannot go to London," Clemency said positively. "I do not want a Season. I will never marry. I am quite content to remain at home with you and Papa." She glared at her mother.

"Nonsense," Lady Sayles retorted briskly. "You will go to London, Clemency. You are to leave at the end of the week. It is all arranged."

"I will not!" she cried, and stamped her foot.

"What is all this pother?" Lord Sayles appeared in the doorway. He had a stern look for Clemency. "I could hear you all the way down the hall. A lady never raises her voice."

Clemency whirled on him. He had spoken as if she were still in leading strings. "Papa, I cannot go to to London. I cannot have a S-Season. Not when Damian . . ." Her voice broke.

"Damian is no more, child," Lord Sayles said. "A sad ending for a promising young man. However, life must go on."

"We do not know that he is . . . is dead. He . . . was only presumed dead," Clemency moaned.

"If he were not dead, we should have had some word of him by now," Lady Sayles said reasonably. "It has been five months, my love. You cannot immure yourself in the country. You are not his widow."

"I wish I were!" Clemency exclaimed. "I feel like his widow."

"Once you are in London, you will meet other young men," her mother said inexorably. "You will go about to routs and dances and—"

"I do not want to meet other young men! How can I dance and enjoy myself knowing that Damian is . . . is gone? I love him. I will never cease to love him. My heart is in the grave with him."

"Nonsense," said her father unsympathetically. "Such talk belongs to bad plays and silly novels. Your mother and I are most anxious to see you creditably settled."

"Yes, my dear, once you are married and have a home of your own and children, you'll see how quickly you'll forget Damian," Justine assured her. "I once thought myself madly in love with someone who was entirely wrong for me. And—"

"Charlie Edgecombe," Clemency interrupted. "And have you quite forgotten him, Justine?"

"Lud, yes," Justine said comfortably. "I would be hard put to tell you what he looks like now."

"I will never forget Damian. His image is inscribed upon my heart forever and ever! I will not go to London, I tell you. I will not have a Season. And I will never marry anyone!"

Her father's eyes blazed with anger. "You will do as your mother and I tell you to do, Clemency!" Striding to her side, he took her by the shoulders and actually shook her. "Let me have no more arguments. You will be leaving for London in three days, and that is final. Meanwhile, I want you to go to your room and stay there—until I say you may come down!"

"I am not a child!" Clemency pulled away from his restraining grasp. "How dare you treat me as . . . as if I were some infant." Turning on her heel, she fled from the room. It gave her some small satisfaction to open the front door and then slam it behind her as hard as she could. Moments later, she had reached the stables and was waiting impatiently while Rob, one of the younger grooms, saddled Elvira, her mare. She noted his curious look and guessed that her distress was easily discernible, something else that must have angered her father—since a lady was not supposed to reveal her emotions to the servants.

"Oh, God," Clemency whispered as she guided Elvira out of the stables. "Why do I have to be a lady?" Touching the mare's flank with the tip of her whip, she urged her into a gallop and headed for the woods.

She had ridden along the well-known paths, threading through trees turned gold and orange. Showers of leaves floated down from the high branches, and again she wondered what had happened to the summer. She had hardly marked its passing. She did recall being surprised at the masses of flowers in the garden and wondering how they happened to be there—and then they had drooped and died almost before she knew it. Days had ceased to mean anything to her. Time itself meant nothing. She was no longer anticipating a moment when she would look through one or another window and see Damian riding up their circling driveway.

She had not intended to go to the pool, but habit intervened. Almost without being aware of it, she reached the small glade that hid it from view. Dismounting, she tied Elvira to her usual branch, and passing between the trees, settled down on a bank covered with dry and yellowed grass, brittle to the touch. Red and gold leaves floated on the water, but she did not see them. She was envisioning herself and Damian reflected in those pellucid waters where they had so often swum. A slight smile curved her mouth as she thought how shocked her mother and Justine would be had they access to her thoughts.

Justine.

"Oh, God," Clemency murmured plaintively, "do not ever let me be like her, forgetting poor Charlie so easily! But I could not forget Damian, I could not." Unbidden, other visions came to her—the battlefield strewn with the bodies of scarlet-coated soldiers, their dark blood staining their bright uniforms. She moaned as she saw, in her mind's eye, the coward with the bayonet thrusting it down, down into the heart of Damian—Damian of the golden hair and the mischievous blue eyes, who had teased her so unmercifully when they were younger . . . only to turn ardent and so loving. She would never forget the amazed look in his eyes when he came home on leave the first time—she had turned sixteen, and he had looked at her as if he had never seen her before. And, of a sudden, he was no longer her old playmate—he was someone new and different, delightfully different. Beatrix had teased her about her change of heart. She had been angry with her cousin, who had made her feel silly and gauche. She would not think of Beatrix—she would think of Damian . . . how passionately he had kissed her before he left her all those months ago. Months? It had been a year.

"I will come back, my darling. I promise you that. Wait for me."

He had promised, but promises counted for nothing upon a battlefield, where soldiers with bayonets . . . "Oh, Damian . . ." She raised her eyes to the sky. "Oh, what shall I do? I cannot marry and forget you. I am not Justine!"

She did not know how long she had lain there when she heard the sound of a horse. She sat up immediately, looking warily about her. Whoever was riding through these woods had no right to be here. She tensed as Elvira lifted her head and whinnied. Clemency's tension increased. Had the mare alerted the horseman to her presence? She rose quickly, her heart pounding heavily. There were vagrants and poachers in the woods. However, there were keepers, too, vigilant men on the alert for trespassers. Unfortunately, none of these were mounted. They walked, and the poachers crept. Who could it be? She stood very still, listening, at the same time hoping that Elvira would remain silent.

Then suddenly a voice she knew murmured, "Well . . . and whose horse might you be, madam?"

Clemency released a long quavering breath and came out of the glade, a few feet away from the man on horseback. "She is mine, Lord Colbourne," she said, forcing a smile. She had not seen him for nearly two months, she remembered. He had called twice—once just after she received the news about Damian, and then he had come a second time. He had not stayed long, and she had been glad of that, being too depressed to see callers, even Lord Colbourne.

"My dear . . ." He wheeled his horse around. "You should not be out in the woods alone. You cannot know who is lurking in them."

"I know," she acknowledged. "I thought you might be a poacher when first I heard your horse. I am very glad you are not."

"And I am indeed glad to find you. I passed by your house and found your parents much concerned about you. They did not know where you had gone."

"And you agreed to find me for them?" she inquired edgily.

"No." He swung down from his saddle as easily as he had all those years ago and limped toward her. "I have come because I hoped I might see you. Rob, at the stables, told me you were headed for the woods. What's amiss, my dear?"

"Did not my parents tell you what they had in mind for me?" she demanded bitterly.

He shook his head. "No, they did not. But perhaps you will tell me."

"They want to send me to London for a Season. In fact, they have made all the arrangements—and without one word to me! I cannot go. I cannot dance and go to routs and picnics and ride in the park with the gentlemen they will compel me to meet." Tears came into her eyes. "But they will make me go. They . . . they do not care that . . . that Damian is dead. They t-tell me I . . . I will forget him. I am not Justine. I will never forget him, not while I breathe! But they do not understand . . . they will not understand . . ." She broke off, vainly trying to swallow her sobs. She had not meant to weep.

"My dear . . ." He put a comforting arm about her shoulders. "I know well what you must be suffering. I know well what it means to lose someone you love with all your heart and have your friends and family tell you that it is time and past that you put away your mourning clothes, but at least my people waited until a year was up."

"Oh, my lord . . ." She looked at him remorsefully. "Your poor wife . . . 'twas a bitter blow. I am so sorry to lay my grief on you."

His arm tightened about her shoulders. "Who better, my dear Lady Clemency? Are we not friends?"

"Oh, yes, we are . . . we are." Something else occurred to her. "My parents respect you, my lord. Can you not persuade them to let me remain here?"

"I cannot take that liberty, my dear. They'd not listen. I am sure they believe they have your best interests at heart."

"But they do not! Oh," she cried passionately, "I do not want to become like Justine, so complaisant. She was not always so. They forced her to give up the man she loved. She even tried to run away with him, and now . . . she says she doesn't even *remember* him! Oh, I am *not* like her. I will not marry at their command—but what can I do? They will be at me and at me . . . they will never give me any peace." She turned a stricken face toward him. "I . . . I am sorry. Again, I am thinking only of myself."

He was silent a long moment, staring at her intently. Finally he said, "I know all that you are feeling, having suffered it myself. I . . ." He paused, and a slight flush spread over his face. "I have an alternative for you which I hesitate to broach, save that it might be a solution to your problem and relieve the pressure under which you are suffering at this moment."

Clemency regarded him perplexedly, not understanding his words or the deepening flush that lent an even darker tint to his scar, turning it blood red. It looked almost as if the slash were newly cut. Had it been a bayonet that had left that cruel mark? Even in the depths of her anguish, she longed to comfort him for all that he had endured in body and in mind. But he had spoken about a solution to her problem. "What alternative could there be?" she asked dubiously.

He cleared his throat, and for the nonce, his gaze, usually so direct, was fixed upon a spot above her head. "I have said that we have both suffered the loss of those we loved. When Inez died, she took a large part of my heart with her. For a long time, I cursed the fate that had taken her from me. I was sure that I would never recover from that cruelest of blows. I was doubly unhappy—for you see, Inez was not happy here. The climate was too harsh and she was very delicate. She missed the warmth of Spain and she also grieved for her family. They were all killed by the French soldiers." His face darkened. "They would have done for her, too, but I saved her from them. We fell in love at first sight. She traveled with me—lived with me near the battlefields, and nursed me so devotedly when I was wounded—but she wanted me to remain in Spain. There were places where we might have been safe, but I, I fear, was selfish—I wanted to come home, and she came with me. I blame myself for her death."

"Oh, no, I . . . am sure she would have been miserable had you left her behind."

"But I should have stayed with her," he sighed.

"You had your duties, too," she said softly. "Your lands."

"That is what I told myself. But you can imagine how I

felt when she died . . . and the child with her. I was sunk in misery."

"Oh, I know . . . I understand."

"I know you do, my dear. And I do want to tell you that as time went on, I began to feel a little better. I found that life was not so cruel as I had believed. I began to read and study. And then you mentioned your tear vase and I recalled the goblet—as well as my old interest in antiquities, but . . . I am getting away from my point." He cleared his throat a second time. "My dear Lady Clemency, we have met but seldom, but each time I have seen you, I have found myself longing to see you again. I have missed you these last months, but I have been deeply sympathetic. I sympathize with you now. We are in similar circumstances, you and I. My family consists only of a childless uncle, a geat-aunt, also without issue, and a second cousin whose wildness has resulted in his being transported to Australia—something I could not prevent. Naturally my aunt and uncle are concerned and tell me I must marry again for the sake of a line they do not wish to die out. Your family is determined to push you into marriage with some bridegroom as yet unknown. Might we not join forces and . . . and hands in friendship if not in the love I gave to Inez or you to Damian? I promise that if you consent to be my wife, I'll expect nothing more than your friendship, nor need you think of heirs at present. I . . . do believe we might deal well together."

She regarded him in stunned amazement. She tried to speak, but the words piled upon her tongue and she had perforce to swallow them. It was a moment before she could say, "I . . . I do respect you, my lord, and . . ." Tears filled her eyes. "I must . . . must . . ."

"Think," he supplied. "Yes, you must think or, rather, ponder deeply upon my proposal. I know it must come as a shock to you, and I am prepared to wait for your decision. When did you say your parents intend to leave for London?"

"In three days."

"Then I'd best have your answer by the day after tomorrow. Thursday." Apologetically he added, "That's scarce time for a life-changing decision."

"Thursday," she whispered. "I . . . do not know what to say."

He had a commiserating look for her. "I am sure I have shocked you. Perhaps I have also frightened you. If you feel you'd rather not entertain so unusual an offer, I must tell you, I can easily understand your position. And I will abide by your decision and not presume . . ."

He was speaking so quickly, and her head was whirling. She held up a protesting hand. "Please . . . I do not know what I feel, as yet, my lord."

"I hope you will know by Thursday." He moved away from her. "May I have your permission to tell you what I also hope?"

She regarded him in surprise. He had spoken hesitantly, almost shyly, and suddenly he seemed much younger. "Yes," she said softly, "you have that permission, my lord."

"I am very fond of you." He fixed his eyes on her face now. "I would miss you if we were not to see each other again, so whatever you decide, please do not let it make a difference in our friendship."

"I will not. I would miss you also, my lord," she said frankly. "And may I also say that I . . . I am greatly honored."

"It is I who am honored by your agreeing to consider my offer." Taking her hand, he kissed it.

A sensation she had experienced once before returned, and was even more intense and more inexplicable. It left her full of confusion, and oddly enough, a heaviness around her heart seemed to vanish.

He released her hand. "I will ride with you until the edge of the woods."

"I would like that."

They rode in silence. Then, as they reached the driveway leading to Sayles, he stopped his horse and said, "Though I loathe anything that borders on the clandestine, I would not like to meet you under your mother's eyes. Would it be possible for you to join me at the tower on Thursday? I will be there well before any time we decide upon, for I'd not have you linger there alone."

"Yes, I will come," she agreed. "But it might not be easy, so do wait."

"I will. I promise. Shall we say three?"

"Three it is, my lord," she said shyly.

He gave her a long look. "Three on Thursday, and until then, farewell."

"Farewell," she murmured, watching as he started down the long driveway toward their gates. He did not look back. However, as distance diminished horse and rider, she felt a sudden throb of fear in her throat. She had disobeyed her father, had not gone to her room, had defiantly ridden into the woods, causing both parents to be alarmed. Her homecoming would not be pleasant. She would be locked in her room tonight and perhaps they, scenting rebellion, would keep her there or watch her closely every minute until it was time to leave for London. Meanwhile, he would wait beside the tower in vain, for she could not tell them about this unorthodox proposal. They would be shocked or disbelieving—and she could not bear for Lord Colbourne to be hurt . . . and meanwhile, he was at the end of the driveway. Clemency spurred her mare forward, urging her into a canter. She caught up with Lord Colbourne just as he turned out of the gate. "My lord . . . I cannot wait until Thursday," she cried.

He pulled his horse to a halt, staring at her in an astonishment mingled with apprehension. "Do you mean that . . . that you cannot consider my proposal?"

"No, I will marry you as . . . as soon as you wish."

"Oh, my dear"—his eyes brightened—"I should like it to be very soon. Shall we tell your parents . . . now?"

"Please," Clemency said.

The date of Clemency's wedding was set at the end of October, which would allow the banns to be proclaimed three times in St. James's Church in the village. However, the ceremony itself would be performed in the chapel at the castle, and the newly wedded pair would remain in residence for the fortnight it would take to make Lord Colbourne's London house ready to receive them, the mansion having been unused since 1809, and before that, only intermittently, it being the custom of the earls of Colbourne to live in the country.

Though a flustered Lady Sayles had said she wished his lordship had fixed his wedding date for that same period, because three weeks would hardly give her enough time to ready her daughter's bridal clothes, there was no doubting her joy over a match that united her daughter to a man who was rich, handsome, and a matrimonial prize. Justine professed herself to be totally in agreement with her mother, even though she admitted somewhat grudgingly that Clemency's triumph was greater than her own, since her husband was a mere viscount of rather recent vintage. The Farnsworths had been ennobled during the reign of George II, while the Colbournes had been barons initially and earls since 1336, a date that preceded the Sayleses' title by a hundred years. Clemency's father was also elated. Not only was his daughter marrying a man of wealth and impeccable ancestry, there was a practical side to the arrangement. He would be spared the expense of launching a daughter in society.

The ceremony would take place on a Thursday, which surprised Lord and Lady Sayles but caused the bride to laugh when her intended suggested it. Her parents were quite annoyed because she refused to explain the reason for her laughter.

On the morning of her wedding, Clemency woke early. A glance out of the window showed her that autumn reigned in all its glory. The trees were red and gold and yellow and even pink. Asters and chrysanthemums bloomed in the garden.

Propped against several pillows in the bed in which she had slept for most of her nineteen years, she let her gaze wander around her room, at the white paneled walls, the small fireplace under a mantel which bore a clock and a tattered rag doll named Lucy, which had been her most cherished toy when she was little. There was also the china dog which Damian had won for her by tossing hoops at a fair camped on the meadows not far from their estates. There were chintz curtains at her windows, and her two chairs were covered with petit point worked by her sister Lydia, whom she barely knew, since Lydia had married a member of the Douglas clan and lived near Inverness in Scotland.

She had already sent a silver fruit bowl and her apologies for not gracing Clemency's wedding with her presence, it being too short notice for her to make the proper arrangements. Clemency had received similar excuses from Gerald, who lived at another family holding in Yorkshire. She had not expected he would come. He had not even attended Justine's wedding. Gerald rarely visited Sayles. He and his father differed greatly in their feelings concerning the house. Gerald wanted to add a new wing and Lord Sayles refused his permission, saying that when he was gone would be time enough to make changes. He had often accused his son of wanting to put on his shoes while his feet were still in them.

Little as she knew about her brother, Clemency feared that her father's accusations were not far from the truth. She smiled. It would be a relief not to hear them quite so often. Lord Sayles's diatribes concerning Gerald were often delivered over the dinner table, notwithstanding her mother's complaint that they gave her indigestion.

A smile curved Clemency's lips. It would be pleasant to be away from the family. She would not have to listen to her mother's endless criticism of herself and her siblings, either. Of course, life at Sayles was not all scolding or forcing one into propitious marriages. She had had some good times under this roof, too. And her room was comfortable. It was certainly more cozy, she was sure, than the immense chamber she would soon occupy in the castle. She had not seen the bedrooms yet, but she had seen the two drawing rooms, the music room, the library, and, just the day before yesterday, Lord Colbourne had taken her to the long gallery.

Clemency had been amazed at the number of paintings that lined the paneled walls. They dated back to the time of Edward IV. Those portraits of the Lord and Lady Colbourne of the period were not too well-executed. They began to improve in Tudor times, and she had been intrigued by that group with their narrow suspicious gaze which, she guessed, owed as much to the character of the times as to the style of painting. Her ancestors, too, were narrow of eye and wary of countenance, as if, almost, they expected a stab in the back from some enemy or from an enemy of the capricious Henry VIII. The Lord Colbourne of the Elizabethan period, however, had had some of the look of his descendent, and the artist had actually captured a twinkle in his eye as well as a mocking twist to his mouth. He had been holding a small model of a ship.

"He looks almost piratical," she had observed.

"He sailed with Drake," Rodger had replied laconically.

Rodger. That was her bridegroom's given name—one of them. He had been christened Rodger John Anthony Charles

David Colbourne. She preferred Rodger but it still seemed strange on her lips, who had always called him Lord Colbourne. However, she must become accustomed to using it, accustomed to him, not as her savior, not as her friend, but as her *husband*. It required an adjustment in her thinking that she had some little difficulty in achieving, particularly since, much as she revered him, he seemed remote, and rather than her bridegroom, the husband of the late Lady Inez Colbourne of the black eyes and the blue-black hair, whose enigmatic smile and somber gaze were to be seen in the portrait painted by Sir James Carmody just after her arrival in England.

It had been impossible not to note the pain and regret in his eyes when he had paused before this latest addition to the gallery, hung close beside his own portrait in scarlet regimentals, looking supremely handsome. He had looked, in fact, like the man who had rescued her five years ago. Had it been only five years? It seemed much longer. Mentally she veered away from those recollections and fixed her thoughts once more upon Inez.

Sir James had caught a trace of melancholy in her glance. She had been smiling, and so the contrast of eyes and lips was marked. She had also been garbed in black.

"Sir James had wanted her in glowing colors," Rodger had explained, "but when I met her she was in mourning for her family. The Spanish ladies take their mourning seriously. I did coax her into colors finally. There was a yellow gown . . ." He bit his lip and turned away, saying a second later, "Some flowers bloom best in their native soil. They should not be transplanted here where the winds blow cold from the sea." They had left the gallery after that and he had shown her other rooms and other treasures.

Clemency sat up in bed, hugging her knees and thinking of the woman or, rather, girl whose place she would be taking, but she could not really take Inez's place, any more than Rodger would be taking Damian's special niche in her heart. She thought of Justine, whose portly husband had arrived for the wedding, contrasting him with her vague memories of Charlie Edgecombe. Charlie had been slender and dashing, a golden stallion of a man. Lord Farnsworth was stolid and heavyset. He must have added at least two stone since last she had seen him. At least there was not so much contrast between Damian and Rodger—and what about the contrast between herself and the Spanish woman? She found herself unwilling to dwell on that. She thought of Damian again.

"I will not forget him," she vowed, clasping her hands and feeling beneath the fingers of her right hand the blazing diamond circlet which was part of the Colbourne family jewels and her betrothal ring. "No matter," she promised. "I will *not* forget you, my Damian." It was some comfort to remember that her bridegroom did not expect her to forget the boy she had loved for the better part of her life, any more than she would expect him to forget Inez. Besides their relatives, there would be two ghosts at their wedding, and because of herself and the man she was about to marry, both would be welcome.

Castle Colbourne stood on a high hill. It was a square building with a round keep, which had once sheltered the family as well as a goodly number of servants and men-at-arms. During the ensuing centuries, when sieges became less frequent, various generations of Colbournes had added to the newer building. Their tastes had not been similar and so the house had several wings, the most comfortable of which overlooked the drawbridge and a moat overgrown with water lilies and stocked with carp. It was a pretty sight and the windows of the bedchamber and sitting room she would occupy gave her a pleasant view of it. Rodger's apartments were next to it—and a connecting door led into his dressing room and thence to his bedchamber. There was much the same arrangement in Clemency's house, but it had been many years since her father had used his suite of rooms. She wondered if the same situation would prevail once she took up residence at the castle. She was rather daunted by the idea and preferred not to dwell on it at this precise moment.

She sent another look around the chamber she had occupied for so long a time and which, in a matter of three hours, would become yet another guestroom, its furnishings shrouded in dust covers and its bed stripped of sheets. It was an odd feeling, one she had not experienced when she thought of living at the Grange. She knew the Grange. Colbourne Castle was still strange to her, and remained, though she was trying hard to abolish that thought, the residence of the little Spanish girl whose rooms she would be occupying this night.

The chapel was located in another wing of the huge structure. It had been built in 1663, shortly after the Lord Colbourne of that period had reclaimed his lands and castle from the Roundheads. Though he was not a religious man, the fact that the Puritans had quartered their horses in the chapel of the old wing, built by his remote ancestors, had infuriated him. Fortunately, his mother, anticipating such an event, had removed the stained-glass windows from the former chapel and buried them in a safe place.

These, in all their Italianate glory, were fitted into the new walls, and though the young man was not a papist, he hired stone workers, sculptors, muralists, and woodcarvers to fashion as splendid a place of worship as they could conceive—given the considerable amount of money he furnished for the enterprise. The result ran to heavily carved pews, made from the finest mahogany, to a high altar fashioned from marble under a magnificent sculpture of Christ on the Cross, to patterned marble floors and traceries of metal on the doors. There was a crystal chandelier and there was also considerable use of gold leaf on murals depicting scenes from the Bible and the New Testament. The result dazzled the eye and embarrassed succeeding generations of Colbournes, who considered it overdone—especially for a family whose religious observance ran to occasional appearances in the local church, generally on Christmas, Easter, and at funerals. However, it was fine for a private wedding—and much to the relief of those servants who stood ready to light all the tapers in the chandelier and wall sconces, the sun, which had been in hiding for several days, emerged to shine brightly through the windows, casting red, green, and yellow sunbeams on the newly scrubbed floors, causing the small assemblage of wedding guests to exclaim in delight.

Clemency, wearing the lace veil that had belonged to her great-grandmother and which had been worn in turn by her grandmother, mother, three aunts, and her own two sisters, was garbed in a white silk gown hastily sewn by Miss Sprague, the village seamstress. Standing beside her father, she gazed in the direction of the altar, where her bridegroom stood next to Lord Farnsworth, pressed into service as best man. Rodger was garbed in a brown coat, gold silk waistcoat, buff breeches, white silk stockings, and shoes with silver buckles. His hair, worn in a Brutus crop, was beautifully arranged and his cravat was marvelously complicated. He looked so handsome that it took her breath away. Indeed, it seemed to her that she had never really seen him before. Yet, at the same time, she was distressed by the way he was holding himself, so stiffly, one hand resting on an ebony cane he seldom used. He was not looking at her, not looking at anyone, she thought, and could actually feel his tension.

As she moved toward the altar and saw Mr. Humphrey, the old vicar who presided in church every Sunday, her own tension increased and she had a craven impulse to run from the chapel, but, inexorably, her feet, suiting their steps to those of her father, were bringing her toward the altar. Rodger moved forward to stand beside her, as words she barely heard for the pounding in her head were being said.

"Do you, Rodger . . ." The old man enunciated Rodger's long string of names, and after a few more words he asked the question that would unite them. Rodger answered in the affirmative, and now the old man, who had baptized and confirmed her, was facing her.

"And do you, Clemency Elizabeth Virginia Grace . . ."

Did she possess so many names herself? She had forgotten them. The vicar was regarding her interrogatively. He must have asked *the* question, and she had not meant to hesitate. "I do," she said quickly and clearly.

More words were being said, and Rodger was pressing a ring on her finger. The metal was cool against her skin. A moment later, he bent his dark head and brushed her lips with his own. He had a fleeting smile for her before he stepped aside to allow her parents, her sister, Lord Farnsworth, and a tearful Miss Lewes to congratulate her. Other felicitations were given her by Rodger's Uncle Arthur, a tall and heavyset man who bore no resemblance at all to his nephew, and by Lady Valerie, Rodger's great-aunt, who was immensely old and leaning on an ebony cane much like his own. Then someone shyly called her Lady Colbourne, and she turned to find Rose, her abigail, in her best gown, smiling at her with tears in her eyes, while Clemency for one wild moment wondered whom she was addressing since Inez was dead.

6

The wedding feast was at an end and finally the guests left. Clemency's parents were the last to go, with Lady Sayles drawing her daughter aside and saying something about not being too surprised at her introduction to married life.

"I fear—and Justine has chided me for being remiss—I have not been explicit enough upon this subject. So much has happened so hastily and 'tis so long since I myself was wed, I did not think to warn you about what you might expect." There was a faint color in Lady Sayles's faded cheeks. She continued nervously, "I . . . I must assure you that it is all perfectly respectable, and once you are accustomed to your change in status, I am sure you will find it quite to your taste. I . . . did." So saying, Lady Sayles flushed even more deeply. She patted Clemency's hand, kissed her on the cheek, and bade her good night, leaving her daughter perplexed and unwillingly thinking of Beatrix.

" 'Tis ever so pleasant being with a gentleman, so I have been told." Unbidden, her cousin had gleefully provided a description of practices she had not understood—save that it had shocked her to learn that kisses were not restricted to cheek or mouth and that parts of her body, never on view save when her abigail was dressing or undressing her, were seen by a husband and fondled as well. She had found the idea rather horrid, but now she remembered it, and sitting in the chamber, which was even larger than she had anticipated, she tried to imagine what would happen in the course of an evening that was not over yet.

Rose's attitude added to her perplexity. The abigail was smiling broadly as she brought out Clemency's nightshift and peignoir. These garments were new and far finer than the gowns she usually wore. Her peignoir was lacy and her shift was lawn and lavishly trimmed with lace. There were blue ribbons threaded through it at the neckline. Sitting at the mirror while Rose brushed out her hair, she stared into the glass and was surprised. Save that her eyes seemed wider than usual, she looked much the same.

"There." Rose stepped back. "Such pretty 'air as your ladyship 'as."

"Thank you, Rose," Clemency said in a subdued tone of voice. It occurred to her that Lord Colbourne had never seen her without the Psyche knot she generally wore, but now her hair hung loose about her shoulders—flowing to the middle of her back. She had never been quite happy about its color, and to her mind it seemed particularly red on this night. Lord Colbourne, she recalled, had once compared it to flames, and Damian had called it foxy. She ought not to be thinking of Damian at this moment. Strange that he did not seem *dead*.

Death and Damian—it was a peculiarly incompatible notion. Yet he was dead—there could be no doubt of that—and she had become Lady Colbourne, married to the man who had once saved her life . . . and now that life belonged to him. Belonged to him? Did one *belong* to one's husband? *Husband?* He *was* her husband, this man who had once seemed so remote, this man whom Beatrix had called Lord Caliban. How horrible to fasten so cruel a sobriquet on so handsome a man. Caliban was not only ugly of form but also ugly of spirit. Lord Colbourne—Rodger . . . he was Rodger to her now—was . . .

"Should your ladyship care to retire?" Rose asked.

"Retire . . ." Clemency repeated, looking at an immense four-poster hung with green chintz curtains matching those at the window and the spread, now turned back, exposing snowy linen sheets. She said, "I expect so."

The mattress proved to be soft, and the pillows also. She sat against them while Rose smilingly bade her good night.

Once alone, Clemency gazed at the fire. Its flames were reflected on the walls of a room which could have swallowed her own bedroom at home. Now that Rose had blown out the candles on the dressing table and mantelshelf, leaving only one candle on the table near her bed, the place seemed cavernous. She stiffened as the flame of her candle suddenly wavered as if caught in a breeze—the window? No, the door, opening, had caused that draft, the door that led to his dressing room and to his bedchamber.

Clemency glanced at the door in question and found Lord Colbourne—Rodger—standing on the threshold. He was wearing a long red-and-gold brocade dressing gown and at his throat was the white frill of his nightshirt. Her heart was beating fast. It did seem strange that he should come to her room dressed in this manner. She forced a smile. "Good evening, my . . . Rodger."

"Good evening, my dear." He stepped to the foot of the bed and gazed at her . . . How? She was hard put to define his expression. Could she call it concerned, worried, regretful? She was not sure, and while she was searching for a comparison, he said, "I hope you are comfortable, my dear."

"Very. 'Tis a lovely room," she said brightly.

"I had hoped to make more alterations . . . but these last three weeks have been rather hectic. The furniture is, I think, too heavy, but it will be changed. I thought a golden wood might be more to your taste."

"It does sound pleasant, R-Rodger." She was annoyed at herself for the nervousness she could not quite quell. She thought regretfully that he must have noticed it also.

He said, "I could wish it were still summer. The gardens look bleak at this time of year."

"I do not think so. I thought the chrysanthemums quite beautiful, and the dahlias. I have no preferences as to seasons—each has its own beauties."

"I must agree with that." He nodded. "But 'tis lovely in the spring. You are comfortable?"

"Quite." She repressed a smile. He had already asked her that and received an affirmative answer. It occurred to her that he might be quite as nervous as she. Though the light in the room was dim, she knew he must be flushed because his scar was flaming. As she searched for some word to put him at his ease, he said, "Then I will bid you good night."

"You . . . you are leaving?" she asked.

He nodded. "You do not need to be afraid of me, child. I have said that our marriage is based on our mutual need for protection against our overeager relatives. I do not want you to be intimidated by the fact that we have been pronounced man and wife. The words may be binding but they are not constricting. We have had but scant opportunity to really know each other. However, in the days that follow, I hope we will rectify that matter." He moved to the side of the bed, and bending, kissed her lightly on the forehead. "Good night, my dear. Sleep well and in peace." Before she could answer, he opened the connecting door and closed it softly behind him.

Clemency looked after him. She was surprised and touched. She had expected . . . She did not know what she had expected. Beatrix's giggles were in her ears, a ghost from the past that seemed to be mocking her. Was there another ghost flitting around here or had Inez left the room with the man she, too, had called husband?

She slid down among the pillows and closed her eyes. Sleep did not come as quickly as she had hoped. Opening her eyes again, she watched the fire die down and was still watching as the embers turned gray.

In the days following her marriage, Clemency spent considerable time going through the castle. Sometimes Rodger accompanied her, but more often it was Mrs. Ames, the housekeeper, a pleasant-faced woman in her middle fifties who had also worked for his lordship's mother. She was very quiet and self-effacing but, Rodger had confided, immensely efficient. When going through the house, Mrs. Ames carried a formidable array of keys. These, Clemency found, unlocked cabinets, closets, and rooms heavy with dust and closed for years. She wondered why. They were large, airy, and some had an admirable view of the distant sea. They would be excellent for guests, she thought, and she would like to get new furniture for some of the suites. Though there was no faulting the main part of the castle and the wing in which her bedroom was located, these others had been badly neglected, something she did not scruple to tell the housekeeper.

Mrs. Ames took her comments in good part and, in fact, appeared extremely pleased at her interest. "I was in 'opes that 'er late ladyship'd want to do somethin' wi' 'em. But, poor little creature, she was so ill most of the time, an' 'sides, she was used to livin' different. All this wood 'n' stone seemed to scare her."

"I can understand that," Clemency had replied. "Spanish houses are, I believe, made of stucco and much airier than those we occupy."

Later, discussing her ideas for changes in the west wing, Clemency was careful not to stress the bad condition of the rooms for fear Rodger might believe her critical of his late wife. He was in immediate agreement with her. "I suppose as time goes on, we will want to entertain, and certainly you have my leave to deal with those rooms as you please."

There had been a certain relief in his tone, as if he were glad she had found something to occupy her time and would, in consequence, not require his constant attendance on her. He had, she guessed, become accustomed to living alone, and the adjustments he was now making were not easy for him. There were times during the next few days when he disappeared into the library and did not emerge for hours, and always after their midday meal he rested. However, he did not neglect her. On the morning after their wedding, they had gone riding and he had taken her over an estate which was larger than she had first imagined. At the foot of the castle-crowned hill, there were a number of tenant cottages adjacent to fields of grain and barley. She had been introduced to some of the occupants and found they all seemed to welcome his lordship with pleasure and an obvious affection. He was a concerned landlord and deeply interested in their welfare.

She also met Mr. Frazier, his estate manager, who, again, had been in his mother's employ. He was very cordial to her but she noted that his attitude was wary, as if he were reserving his judgment until she had been there long enough for him to decide whether she was the proper bride for Rodger. She appreciated his concern. It was clear that everyone connected with the estate had a great affection for the earl, something he had won rather than inherited.

As for herself, each day she spent with him proved enriching. In addition to riding with her, he sat with her in the library and read aloud from his favorite books. His interests were eclectic. One night she might hear poems by Blake and thrill to his rendition of "Tyger, Tyger," or he would tease her by choosing some of the more eerie passages from Mrs. Radcliffe's novels. They had friendly arguments over the merits of Sir Walter Raleigh, whom she revered and he derided as hotheaded and thoughtless. He had also promised that when spring came they would journey to Devon, where they would see the hut-circles she had once mentioned. He seemed excited by the idea of showing her London. He had been shocked to learn she had never visited the city. He spoke at great length about its museums, its palaces and churches, its parks, and its theaters, which he himself had not seen for a long time. "We will discover it together," he had told her with one of his warming smiles.

By her second week at the castle, she was much more at ease in the enormous establishment, and with the pressure of her parents' plans ended, she reasoned that she should feel perfectly happy. She *was* happy. She was having new clothes made for her forthcoming wedding journey. Her husband had surprised her with the present of a beautiful young chestnut gelding which she immediately named Apollo. Rodger was unfailingly kind and courteous to her, but still she sensed that rather than becoming closer to her, he seemed to be withdrawing from her—if not physically, mentally. He had a habit of falling into long silences and staring at the floor. On the last two nights, he had failed to come to her room. Instead, he had bade her good evening in the hall outside her sitting room. She feared he could not bear to see her in the chamber he had once prepared for his first bride, until she learned from the housekeeper that Inez had never had a separate suite of her own. She had slept in his lordship's room. Clemency had been surprised and depressed by that knowledge. Had she married a man whose spirit was still inextricably entangled with that of his late wife?

She was gloomily sure of it on a day when he had retired early to bed with only the briefest of good-nights, and no more than a peck on her cheek. The following morning, she learned he had gone out riding. She did not see him all that day. Despite a midday meal, excellently prepared by Mrs. Phipps, his wonderfully accomplished cook, Clemency had scarcely tasted a morsel. In the afternoon, she had gone to the library in hopes that he might return and join her—but he did not. Later, upon questioning his butler, she learned that his lordship was seeing tenants. She took a nap in the afternoon, and awakening after six in the evening, declined supper and went to the music room, where she played a few pieces on the pianoforte—an instrument that she had been meaning to try. It was beautiful. Its case was painted with scenes of ladies and gentlemen engaged in exchanging the time of a Renaissance day and its tones were particularly resonant. She hoped he might hear them and join her—but he did not. Finally, at an early hour she went to bed, and helped to undress by a sober-faced Rose, she cried herself to sleep.

She awakened to a hand on her shoulder. "Oh, milady," Rose said anxiously. " 'Is lordship . . ."

"Wha . . ." Clemency muttered.

" 'Is Lordship, 'e be in a rare takin'."

Clemency sat up immediately. "What's the matter?" she demanded anxiously.

" 'E's groanin' . . . sounds as if 'e's in 'orrible pain."

Clemency reached for the peignoir flung over the end of her bed, pulling it around her in the same moment she reached the floor. She flung open the connecting door between their rooms, hurried through the dressing room, and came into Rodger's bedchamber, nearly bumping into Jenkins, his valet.

"What's the matter with his lordship?" she demanded, and gasped as she heard Rodger moaning.

Jenkins, a tall, thin man with mouse-colored hair, gray eyes, and a pallid complexion, eyed her coldly. " 'E's been out riding, an' 'e walked in the fields wi' Mr. Frazier, much as I told 'im 'e should favor 'is leg." He added with a frown, "Best come out of 'ere before 'e spots you, milady. 'E wouldn't want you 'ere."

Ignoring the valet's protest, she stepped toward the bed. A candelabrum on the table showed her that the sheets were much disarranged. Rodger, his leg lying outside the covers, looked deathly pale. Beads of perspiration were on his forehead and his mouth was compressed as if he were endeavoring to stifle the groans that issued from him every so often. Hurrying to his side, she sat on the edge of the bed. By the light of the candles she could see the flesh was badly scarred. Deep grooves ran up it on either side. The limb, however, was not crooked. It had been set very well—considering the conditions under which the surgeon had labored. However, the muscles were tight and knotted. That condition was not new to her. Damian had once suffered it while they were swimming. She had been forced to pull him to the bank, else he must have gone under. Afterward, at his instruction, she had massaged the tense muscles until they relaxed and the cramp he had suffered had gone. She moved back against the foot of the bed and began to massage his leg gently. Tears stood in her eyes as she felt the deep welts. He must have suffered agonies.

"Clemency," Rodger muttered, "you should not . . ."

She gave him a startled glance and found him staring—or rather glaring—at her. "Shhhhh," she cautioned. "Just lie back and try to relax."

He made an effort to pull his leg away. "Mustn't look . . . 'tis so ugly. . . . Fetch Jenkins, I beg you. Mustn't look at Caliban's limb."

She drew a long hissing breath. "I beg you'll not be so foolish," she scolded, continuing her massaging. "Does this not feel a little better?"

"It does . . . but it is so ugly," he rasped.

"It is not ugly," she disputed. "It is only hurt, poor leg. I have it on very good authority that it will improve in time, so close your eyes and relax, my dearest."

"Dearest . . . your dearest," he muttered. "Am I?"

His question produced a reaction that startled her with its intensity. It seemed as if something that had been taut and strained had been released, and she experienced such a rush of love and affection for this man that it left her weak and shaken. "You are my very dearest," she whispered, wanting to kiss and caress him. She dared not yield to that temptation. She was not sure he would welcome such attentions from her. She continued to massage his leg, wishing that the muscles would respond more readily to her fingers. Damian had told her she had healing hands. She hoped devoutly that he was right. She moved forward, continuing to knead the scarred flesh. Finally, and much to her relief, she saw that the lines of pain were leaving his face as the muscles grew less tense. His eyes closed. His lashes were long and curling, she discovered, and his face was so beautiful in repose. She pushed the tangled hair from his forehead, noting with considerable satisfaction that he had fallen asleep. Then she heard a slight cough from the doorway. Looking up, she found the valet looking at her interrogatively, his expression half-apprehensive, half-hopeful.

"He's sleeping," she whispered. "I think I must stay with him in case he wakens in the night and needs me once again."

The man nodded, and moving out, closed the door softly behind him.

The bed was wide, and Clemency, smoothing the wrinkled sheets as best she might, blew out the candles and settled down far enough away from Rodger so that she would not move against him and perhaps hurt his leg again. She was glad that she had never been a restless sleeper. She was not sure she would even be able to sleep, listening to Rodger's quiet breathing so close beside her. The thought of his poor maimed leg brought tears to her eyes. However, she did find some consolation in the fact that his strange mood of the last few days was not based on his longing for his lost Inez but because of his own physical discomfort. She was pleased that she could help him and wished that she could help him more, wished, too, that she could also tell him how much she loved him . . . but perhaps he would not want to hear that. In the midst of all these complicated ruminations, Clemency fell asleep too.

"Clemency . . ."

She had been on the edge of wakefulness, and at the sound of her name, uttered softly and almost in her ear, she opened her eyes and blinked against the light that came flooding into the room from the window directly opposite the bed. A second later, she found herself looking into her husband's face, his cheeks and chin dark with a night's growth of beard, his eyes intent. He said, "I thought I must have dreamed that you were with me."

"You did not dream it," she said on a breath. "Your leg—how does it feel this morning?"

"Much better, thanks to you, my darling." Moving closer to her, he pressed a kiss on her cheek and then his lips moved down to cover her mouth.

Almost without volition she put her arms around him, responding joyfully to an embrace that was passionate as well as loving. When she could speak again, she whispered, "I was so afraid that . . . that . . ." She paused and flushed.

"That what?" he murmured, his fingers gently stroking her hair.

"That you did not . . . want me, that you still longed for Inez."

"You thought I did not want you?" he said incredulously. "To be with you is to want you—but I had attached conditions to your marrying me, and I feared you must still be missing Damian."

"No," she said quickly. "Oh, no, Rodger, my dearest love."

"You called me 'dearest' last night . . . and filled me with hope," he said. "You do care."

"Oh, so much, so very much." She put her arms around him once again.

"Oh, Clemency, my own . . ." he whispered, and then all speech ceased between them. There was a moment when she felt a surge of panic, but only for a moment. Soon all her fears were magically put to flight, and with a little murmur of pure joy she knew that nothing she had ever felt for Damian could equal the excitement and the rapture she experienced when she became Rodger's wife in fact as well as name.

There were times during the fortnight that passed before they went to London that Clemency wished strongly that she had already visited the city. Then Rodger would not have been so anxious to show her its delights. In fact, she looked back ruefully to the excitement with which she had greeted the disclosure of his plans for their wedding journey. He had said at the time, "I would like to show you Paris and Rome, but that is enemy territory still, though I think Napoleon will soon be bested. One day I will take you on the Grand Tour, but meanwhile I hope you'll find London as beguiling as I do."

The idea of seeing the city without the exigencies attendant upon being a debutante proved extremely beguiling. "I am sure I will," she had responded excitedly, going as far as to clap her hands.

Why had she clapped her hands? she wondered crossly. Why had she been so enthusiastic?

As the time for their journey drew nearer, Rose busied

herself with mending such garments as needed it and conferred with her mistress as to the wardrobe she would take to London. Clemency's response to these questions bordered on the distracted. She was more than ever visited with worry over Rodger.

Too much walking on the city streets would be hard on his leg, and he was very reluctant to use his cane. Furthermore, a confidential discussion with Jenkins had served to enlarge her fears on that point and had added new ones as well, as the valet explained that his lordship's health had suffered in Spain. " 'E caught this fever, an' that weakened 'im. 'E's also very prone to the quinsy—seems like hardly a winter don't come but 'e's bedded down wi' it. Runs an 'igh fever, 'e does. Only you mustn't say as I told you, milady. 'E don't like to be reminded of 'is 'ealth."

"I never would," she had assured the man, but their conversation had led her to devise a strategy that would let him rest without his being aware of it. She would, she decided, train herself to recognize the little signs that pointed to his fatigue, not an easy thing to do since he was generally determined to conceal all weariness and pain. However, she was beginning to know him very well, and once she was sure that he was overtired, she would pretend that she was exhausted and insist that they must go home. It might disappoint Rodger. He wanted her to see as much of the city as possible, but at least he, who was convinced of her honesty, would suspect nothing.

She would have to be careful. It would be disastrous if he ever guessed that she was coddling him. Knowing him as well as she now did, she was only too aware of how much he regretted the loss of the splendid physical prowess he had possessed before being so grievously wounded. He loathed his infirmities and tended to be abnormally sensitive about them. In consequence, her cousin's cruel jest had found a particularly vulnerable target. His reference to Caliban on the night she had come to him showed that it still rankled. His distress hurt her almost physically. Anything that touched him wounded her. Indeed, she wished that there were some way she might transfer his ills to herself. She would have borne them gladly, loving him as much as she did. She had never dreamed that that much-touted but extremely elusive emotion could be so fulfilling, diminishing everything that had occurred in her past life. Indeed, she had not known what living meant until she was truly joined with her husband.

Rodger seemed to love her equally. On the night before their departure for London, they retired early, but he showed no disposition to sleep. Instead, his lovemaking was incredibly exciting yet at the same time wonderfully tender. Later, cradling her in his arms, he confessed that he must have loved her a very long time without realizing it.

"When did you realize it?" she asked.

"I think realization began to come on the day you told me your mother was forcing you to go to London. The thought that I might not be able to see you every day hit me almost like a physical blow."

"That's when you knew you loved me?"

"I was not aware of it at that precise moment, but I did know I would miss you terribly. You were already a part of my life."

"And you," she whispered, "are my whole life."

"Am I, my own darling?"

"Have I not proved it?"

"You have," he agreed, and kissed her lingeringly.

"Then," she murmured a few moments later, "why do you need to ask for assurances?"

"Because I want to hear you say them."

"And I want the same from you. You did make me so dreadfully unhappy."

"When?" he demanded in surprise.

"I expect you were in pain. It must have been your poor leg, but you were so cold and cross with me, hardly speaking to me . . ."

A low laugh broke from him. "It was not my leg that was troubling me. It was you."

"Me," she demanded amazedly. "Had I done something to displease you? Why did you not tell me?"

"You'd done nothing, my angel. You were there and I wanted you so desperately, but I feared to frighten you, and—"

"And I wanted you to be with me. Oh, dearest, did you ever see two people more at cross-purposes?"

"No"—he kissed her—"never." He kissed her again, and

she, feeling his need, responded joyfully. Much later, they fell asleep in each other's arms.

Determined on her strategy, Clemency did not want to like London. However, once she arrived in that most beguiling and exciting city, she found she would have to make a few alterations in her plans. She would like London while they were driving in her husband's curricle or post chaise or riding in Hyde Park. She would dislike it when they were on foot and when they were bidden to balls and routs—as had happened almost before they set foot in the Palladian mansion on Arlington Street that William Kent had designed for Rodger's grandfather a little more than half a century ago.

Fortunately, Lord Colbourne showed no more disposition to accept the invitations than she to receive them. "If we are ever asked why we did not put in an appearance, we will pretend that the invitations were mislaid by a careless servant, whom we dismissed," he said with a whimsical smile. "I do not want to be half-crushed at a rout and nor do I want to make conversation over a dish of tea. I will see that you are well-partnered at balls. I have a large acquaintance in London, but first I want to show you my special city. I hope you'll find it to your liking."

She thought it safe to reply, "If you do, I am sure I will."

His London proved to have a much wider circumference than she had anticipated, and Clemency soon found him to be as excited as a boy as he pointed out places that had awed or thrilled him when he had last stayed in the city—which had been on the occasion of his second visit in 1808—just before going off to fight in Spain. She also found that her strategy needed alterations, for when she had pretended tiredness in the middle of a walk through St. Paul's Cathedral, his face had worn an expression of such deep disappointment that she had hastily revived and told him that a seat in a pew would suffice. However, her protest did produce some beneficial results. He was more concerned over her possible fatigue and less eager to show her all London in a week's time.

Unfortunately, when they came to the British Museum, she was so fascinated by the wonders on view—the Egyptian collection with its great painted sarcophagi and its partially unwrapped mummies, the Roman group with busts and jars, the barbaric masks and weaponry that Captain Cook brought back from his expedition to the South Pacific, as well as the biological specimens in the basement of the museum building. It was while she stood gazing in wonder at a jar containing a giant octopus that a side glance at her husband showed her that he was leaning heavily on his cane, a grim expression on his face.

"Oh!" She came to his side. "I have not meant to tire you, my dearest."

His chin went up, his eyes blazed with a resentment she had never seen before. "I am not in the least tired," he said coolly. "Whatever gave you the idea that I was, Clemency? I am not quite an invalid, you know."

She could have wept. Inadvertently she had done what she promised herself she would never do. She had wounded him in his vulnerable pride. She made a quick and, she prayed, convincing recovery. "I was actually speaking of myself, my love. The backs of my legs are aching fiercely and I do think I have seen enough of these unfortunate creatures." She looked pleadingly at him and was pleased to see the tenseness receding from his face.

He gave her a quizzical glance. "I am inclined not to believe you, but if, as you say, you are tired, do let us go."

Much relieved by his capitulation, Clemency, reiterating assurances concerning her own fatigue, came out of the museum. It had been a narrow escape, she thought as they finally reached their house. She must remember his pride at all times. He had been close to being angry with her, and she could not bear that. Consequently, it was with a deep sigh that she sat down on a chair in the hall and removed her slippers.

"I have never walked so much," she complained. "That building is a regular rabbit warren."

To her greater relief, he said, "I must apologize, my dear. The museum always fascinates me and I forget that it can be a tiring experience as well."

"But certainly interesting, I do agree."

Much to her surprise, he came over to her, and drawing her out of her chair, he held her closely in his arms, rubbing his chin against her curls. "You are an angel from heaven. Your good qualities are manifold, but you are a most inexpert liar.

I *was* becoming very tired in the museum. I wish I had not been, and please, I beg you will not restrict your pleasures on my account."

"I do not . . . I spoke only because I—" She came to a stop as he put a gentle hand over her mouth.

" 'Methinks the lady doth protest too much.' " He gave her a tender smile. "But I do need to rest. May I hope that you, being so very weary, will share my couch?"

"Oh, I most certainly will," she agreed delightedly.

Rodger dropped into an exhausted sleep the minute he put his head on the pillow, and Clemency, lying wakeful beside him, was doubly regretful. He had seen through her stratagems and now it would be very difficult for her to curtail his activities with the excuse of her weariness. She would have to think of something else—but what? She racked her brains but nothing occurred to her until, her eyes ranging around a room she usually saw only at night, she noted that the walls were very dingy. They needed a new coat of paint, and some of the furnishings in the mansion depressed her. Rodger's late mother had developed a most unfortunate passion for the Egyptian style, so popular at the turn of the century. Chairs with their arms finished in sphinx heads were to be found all through the house. There was also a sofa with the head of a crocodile at one end and its tail at the other. She repressed a shudder. It occurred to her that she would very much like to make some purchases herself, and the walls needed repainting. Redecorating would take a great deal of time and she would be less free to go sightseeing. That might disappoint him, but by the same token, she doubted he would suspect her motives. He himself had complained that the dining room was too dark and gloomy, and she thought the drawing rooms could be much improved. She would speak to him on that subject immediately after he awakened. No, perhaps she had better wait until later—so that he would not become suspicious or . . . Unexpectedly, she too fell asleep.

Clemency had expected some manner of argument from Rodger, but she was agreeably surprised to find that he was in complete agreement with her.

"The house does need some renovation. It could be made much lighter and airier—a fit setting for you, my love, who have the sun in your hair. All I ask is that you leave the library untouched. We'll need some retreat."

"I would not think of redecorating the library," she assured him. "Particularly since you tell me a great many of the books were amassed by your father. 'Tis a pity he died before you had a chance to know him better. It was even more of a pity that he never knew his son."

"I think it an even greater shame that he did not survive to know his most beautiful daughter-in-law," he replied.

The compliment had had the untoward effect of making her think of Inez, and it gave her a little chill. In the six weeks they had been wed, he had not referred to his late wife. He seemed totally concentrated on her. If something were to happen to her, would he find another to replace her in his affections, and would she, too, be forgotten? It was a daunting thought. A quotation from Byron's *Childe Harold* had arisen in her mind: "Man's love is of man's life a thing apart, 'Tis woman's whole existence."

She remembered disputing that theory when first she read it. Even loving Damian as much as she thought she had, he had not occupied her every waking thought. Rodger did. He *was* her whole existence and, she decided, if anything did happen to her, she would not want him to be lonely or grieving. His life had been disrupted enough already, and besides, nothing was going to happen to her. She had sailed into a safe harbor where no tempests could ever reach her.

7

Clemency's redecoration of the town house resulted in a parade of plasterers, painters, carpenters, and visits to drapery and furniture houses. It was a very busy time made busier by Rodger's insistence that she "upholster" herself, as he teasingly put it.

"My love, village seamstresses are very well, but London has some of the finest mantua makers in the world and it would please me to buy you a few gowns."

Rodger accompanied her and, rather than a few gowns, as he had specified, he insisted on a whole new wardrobe when Mrs. Bullitt, a dressmaker of impeccable taste, emphasized the fact that though they might bear a passing resemblance to each other, there was a great difference between the styles of 1813 and those of 1814 going into 1815. The waists were shorter, the colors more vivid, and because of a period of relative peace in France, French imports were swelling the English market.

Consequently, there were fittings and more fittings, until Clemency, her head in a whirl, was close to forgetting what she had purchased. It was with considerable surprise that on looking over her wardrobe she found a long wrapping coat of dark green, lined with silk and with two capes attached to the shoulders, a style she had always adored. This garment was a French import, as was the pelisse in white merino cloth. Merino being a popular material in England, too, she also had a gown of green merino. Another gown, also green, but made of kerseymere, boasted one of the new shorter waists, as did a green velvet dinner dress and a golden-brown silk evening gown so becoming, Rodger said, that she must have another ensemble of that same color for traveling. A silk plaid gown was trimmed with floss silk for afternoon wear, and there was an elegant frock of fine Indian muslin, embroidered with wreaths of white lace leaves and finished off with white satin ribbons, that was reserved for a ball at Carlton House.

Clemency had also become the possessor of several pairs of little kid slippers and some stouter boots for walking in a snow that was lasting for an unconscionably long time. In addition there were kid gloves, bonnets, her favorite among these being a high-crowned straw ornamented by bronze and green cock feathers. There was a set of cameos and a circlet of pearls which Clemency laughingly protested she did not need. Rodger had taken his family jewels from the vault and she had two sets each of diamonds and pearls, including a tiara that had been fashioned for his great-grandmother and made of diamonds—the most beautiful thing she had ever seen, she told him.

"And what am I to do with all these garments?" she demanded after having watched Rose reverently unpack them. She was with Rodger in the library, presently dubbed the "oasis from chaos." Fortunately, though, the work had been nearly completed, despite the fact that the workers were forced to trudge back and forth in snow that reached as far as the windows, having been falling for six weeks straight in a biting cold that left the Thames frozen solid.

"I would think my very beautiful bride, that the knell has sounded."

"The knell?"

"Those invitations keep pouring in and I feel that 'tis time and past that I satisfied the curiosity of certain of my good friends—among them the Prince Regent."

Any notion that Rodger had been teasing her when he mentioned that illustrious name fled on an evening in late February when their post chaise became numbered among the clutter of vehicles that lined the streets within walking distance of Carlton House.

Clad in her high-waisted, low-necked, clinging white gown beneath a white wool mantel lined with ermine and trimmed in white fox, her hands thrust into a muff of the same fur, Clemency, valiantly trying for an expression as blasé as those of the other guests, mounted the steps beside Rodger. Her husband, in evening attire, looked splendid. He had taken his cane and was making a great effort to conceal his limp. In spite of her excitement at seeing the other guests, among them some of the most illustrious names in the kingdom, Clemency wished that Rodger were not so abnormally sensitive about his infirmity. He had told her several times that she must not sit out any of the dances due to his inability to take part in them. "You will be besieged, I know, my dearest, and it will be my pleasure to watch you." He refused to accept her fervent assurances that she would not want to dance with anyone save himself.

"You must not be unfashionable, my angel. And I must tell you that to dance with one's husband is never *comme il faut* in this society."

He had spoken with an irony that seemed foreign to him. He had added, "I beg you'll dance, for 'tis a long time since I have been to Carlton House and I expect there'll be many wanting to speak to me, old friends from the guards, whose conversation must seem very tedious to you. I cannot think of anything duller to an outsider than tales of battle strategies."

His use of the term "outsider" had sent a little chill through her. Much as she assured herself she was being ridiculous, it seemed to her that she was seeing another Rodger, one who was almost a stranger and to whom she was an appendage he would as soon do without as he mingled with his old cronies. Was he wearying of her society? Or could he possibly imagine she *wanted* this glittering life into which he was thrusting her? A recent conversation came back to her, one that had given her much pain. It had concerned the Frost Fair, held on a Thames so deeply frozen that it supported what appeared to be most of the population of London—not excluding post chaises, coaches, and a carnival that seemed every bit as extensive as Bartholomew Fair. Rodger had wanted her to attend the festivities, had spoken of finding an escort for her, one Colonel Bixby, an old friend. He had not been pleased by her refusal.

"I'll not have you deny yourself these pleasures because of your old crock of a husband," he had said with an effortful smile.

"Old crock!" She had flung herself on him, pummeling him lightly with both fists. "How can I enjoy myself with you away from me? How can I make you believe that my only happiness lies in being with you?"

He had pronounced himself deeply gratified by her passionate assertions, but she feared he was not being entirely sincere. Loving him as much as she did, she still sensed that he was not entirely happy over her refusal to take part in activities in which he could not participate. Consequently, it behooved her to dance with those partners who presented themselves this night. She hoped there would not be too many.

"My love"—Rodger gave Clemency's elbow a tiny shake—"this is hardly the time to daydream. Look about you, please."

"But I am," she replied with a tardy glance around her at the sumptuous hall they had just entered. It was embellished by columns of Siena marble and decorated with bronze busts of ancient Romans fashioned by the Prince Regent's favorite sculptor, Nolekens. The floor, she noted, was black and white marble, suitable, she thought irreverently, for a gigantic game of chess. Glancing upward, she saw the stars glimmering through an oval skylight.

Thrust forward by the crowds behind them, Clemency and Rodger went up the marble staircase. Thanks to her height, she was able to glimpse the equestrian portrait of George II hanging on the side wall—or at least some of it. She was also able to see and admire the statues of Pallas Athena and Time in archways near the stairs.

By the time they reached the ballroom, hung in scarlet silk, with two orchestras playing for the vast assembly of nobles and notables, Clemency was quite dazzled by the array of paintings, mirrors, and sculpture she had viewed on the way. The ballroom itself was also magnificent, its walls graced by huge pier glasses rising from floor to ceiling and facing each other; they had the effect of enlarging the numbers of people present, making it appear as if half London were in that chamber. They also caught and threw back the lights from an immense crystal chandelier and from wall sconces all around the room.

Clemency had been rather daunted by the majordomo's stentorian announcement of the Earl and Countess of Colbourne, and on entering the ballroom, she found herself facing a battery of quizzing glasses held in the hands of interested gentlemen. Several very beautiful women smiled bewitchingly at her husband. He nodded in the direction of two or three of these, receiving welcoming and even flirtatious glances, bringing to her mind gossip repeated by Justine.

According to her sister, many of the great ladies of the *ton* could not tell which lover had fathered their children. She had also mentioned the beautiful Georgiana, Duchess of Devonshire, who, with her friend Lady Elizabeth Foster, lived at Devonshire House sharing the attentions of the duke. Lady Georgiana had also had many other amours as well. "As numerous as the stars in the sky"—Justine had spoken almost enviously. Had her sister wished to emulate the duchess? Clemency wondered. *She* did not. The thought of having a lover or sharing her husband with a mistress appalled her.

"Colbourne, as I live," drawled a tall, dark, heavyset gentleman, neatly but unostentatiously clad in a black coat similar to that worn by her husband. He strode up to them and cordially grasped the hand Rodger held out to him.

"Alvanley," he said. "Good to see you."

"It's very good to see you, Rodger, and looking so well. Where have you been this long time?"

"In the country," Rodger explained.

"In the country?" Alvanley made a face. "For your sins?"

"For my health, William, and, I might add, my happiness." Turning toward Clemency, he said, "May I present my wife?"

"Your wife!" Lord Alvanley's deep brown eyes widened. "This nymph whose beauty beckoned me from afar? You never found her in London!"

"No, in the country. My dear, this is Lord Alvanley, an old friend."

"I am delighted," she murmured.

"And I am overwhelmed." His lordship's gaze encompassed her form from head to toe. "Tell me, Rodger, which part of the country did you visit? Also tell me the shortest route there. I find traveling a dead bore, but journeys can end in lovers' meetings, I see."

Clemency swallowed a laugh. His compliments, uttered in a dry precise way, were almost a parody of the fulsome praise poured on ladies who had any pretensions to good looks. A glance at her husband showed her that he was similarly amused.

"I would never advise you to go to the country, Alvanley," he said solemnly. "The country must come to you."

"Ah, Colbourne, you've been away too long." Alvanley grinned. "And has Prinny seen you?"

"I glimpsed him in the crowd but I doubt that he has bent his gaze on me."

"He will . . . but I do not see how you could have merely glimpsed him. He does fill the eye tonight—with enough gold braid on his uniform to cover one of the sofas he is beginning to resemble."

"My dear William, that was quite in the Beau's vein. I have not seen him here tonight."

Alvanley's smile faded. "You've not heard of the incident in the Argyle Rooms, I take it. I can wish that I had not, save that I was there and could not avoid it, and 'twas not Brummell was to blame, though many will say 'twas so."

"Lord, man, you'll not be telling me that the Regent and the Beau are at odds?"

"Had either carried a dagger, we might have had an interesting murder. As it was, the fray was restricted to words. The Beau's been out of favor for quite a while and it all came to a head last July when Brummell, Henry Pierpoint, Henry Mildmay, and I all won at hazard. To celebrate this most unlikely event, we determined on giving a fancy-dress ball. The Beau insisted that the Regent be excluded. We agreed but, of course, someone dropped a word into the royal ear. He wrote to us and said he intended to come."

"How very like him." Rodger grinned.

"Entirely." Alvanley nodded.

"So of course you sent him an invitation?"

"Of course we sent him an invitation, Rodger. Poor Brummell was quite cheered. I think he had the idea that Prinny wanted to kiss and make up. Accordingly, on the night in question, we were all at the door waiting to make our bows like good little soldiers. The Regent arrived, gleaming with orders and done up in one of his fancy uniforms. He seemed in an excellent mood, bowed to Pierpoint, who was on one side of the door, then found Brummell on the other side. Without a word, he turned his back on him, a good-sized affront when you consider his increasing girth."

Clemency gasped, but Rodger continued to grin. "And then what happened?"

"The Prince Regent was looking at me." Alvanley rolled

his eyes. "I was so shocked I was momentarily struck dumb. Everybody at the door was in the same condition except for Brummell, who also turned to me and said in his coolest manner, and you know how cool that can be, 'Ah, Alvanley, who is your fat friend?' "

"How very like him!" Rodger exclaimed. "I expect he did not trouble to lower his voice?"

"On the contrary." Alvanley grimaced.

"And the Regent?" Rodger asked.

"I think he would have preferred a thrust from that aforementioned dagger. However, he sailed into the ballroom and then as an afterthought sent someone back to us, saying he'd like to converse with Mildmay. And of course, Henry, who was furious at the way he treated Brummell, would not go. He said it must be a mistake because his royal highness had had ample opportunity to see and speak with him and had taken no notice of his presence."

"Is Mildmay in his black books too?" Rodger inquired.

"No, just Brummell and, of course, Prinny's wife, the fair Princess Caroline, who is proving to have quite a little wit of her own, poor creature. 'Tis a pity she's not in her dotage, else they might have dealt reasonably well together."

Clemency, listening wide-eyed to this exchange, was once more indebted to her sister for some understanding of what his lordship meant. The Prince Regent, Justine had said, giggling, had a penchant for elderly mistresses. Even the beautiful Mrs. Fitzherbert, whom he had married, could give him six years. Lady Jersey, Justine said, was a *grandmother*!

"Well, Rodger, having given you some of the *on-dit* of the town and prevented you from making any *faux pas* when the Regent comes your way, I will leave you—though I hope we'll be seeing more of you soon." Alvanley turned an interested eye on Clemency. "I will understand the reason if we do not." He bowed over her hand. "Your servant, my lady."

"He seems very pleasant," Clemency said, watching his lordship stroll away.

"He is, though rather too full of gossip, in my opinion. He's considered one of the wittiest men in England. I am pleased to note, however, that he seemed most favorably impressed with you, my love."

"Do you think so?" she asked in surprise. "I thought his compliments rather fulsome."

"They were, but also he is sincere. How could he not be, with you outshining all the other ladies present?"

She flushed with pleasure but said, "Now I must think that you, too, grow fulsome, Rodger. From what my sister Justine has told me 'tis highly unfashionable to heap such praise upon your wife."

To her surprise, he frowned. "I pray you'll not listen overmuch to your sister. No doubt she also stressed the fact that it is equally unfashionable for a wife to love her husband?"

"She did . . . but reached a most inattentive ear." Clemency's adoring glance went unseen as Rodger bowed to an extremely rotund gentleman in a white uniform that had the effect of making his bulk seem enormous. A second later, she recognized the Prince Regent. Responding to Rodger's pressure on her arm, she was guided toward him, and falling into a deep curtsy, she looked up to meet a most appreciative glance from a pair of intensely vivid blue eyes.

"My Lord Colbourne," the Regent said warmly, "Alvanley has just filled my ears with praise for your most exquisite bride. I vow I did not believe half of what he said until this moment." Reaching out his hand, he assisted Clemency to her feet and retained a grip on her fingers.

"You are very kind, sire," Rodger replied.

"And you are very fortunate, my lord. 'Tis well to see you in London once again. And with such a welcome addition to our city." His gaze shifted back to Clemency's face.

"I do thank you, your highness," she murmured, and knew to her regret that she was blushing. Any hope that he would not notice what she feared to be gaucherie was flouted when he said, "Your color does you credit. I had begun to fear that modesty was out of fashion. I do hope, my dear Lady Colbourne, that you will do me the honor of dancing the next cotillion with me?"

She curtsied a second time. "I should be honored, sire."

"I shall come to claim you very soon," he said. The vivid eyes rested in Rodger. "I have always known you to be a man of excellent taste, Lord Colbourne. Again, I must applaud it."

Rodger inclined his head. "I thank you, sire," he murmured,

adding as the Regent moved away, "You are indeed favored, my love. The Prince Regent seldom dances."

She longed to tell him that she would have preferred to decline this favor, but managed to swallow her protests. To emphasize her feelings regarding dancing would only make him the more cognizant of his infirmity. She said softly, "I hope that I will be able to remember all the turns."

"If you do not, none will notice, given your lovely face and form," he said with a look that melted her resistance and made her doubly pleased that she had raised no objections to the honor conveyed upon her by the Regent.

There were times in the hectic month that followed Clemency's informal presentation to the Prince Regent that she wished sincerely that she had never agreed to their London journey.

The Regent's sanction expressed in the cotillion to which he had led her brought her to the notice of the *ton*. Invitations littered the table in the hall and filled the wastepaper basket after she answered them.

"In common with Byron, you awoke and found yourself famous," Rodger said teasingly.

"And with much less reason," she had responded ruefully. "I do wish we were back in the country."

Unfortunately, that remark angered rather than pleased him. "You must not make yourself a martyr to my disabilities," he had retorted sharply. "I myself am delighted to be in town again. 'Tis a long time since I have seen Alvanley and my other friends. I should not feel half so sanguine about leaving you were I not sure that you must also be enjoying yourself."

Castigating herself for inadvertently reminding him of his lameness, Clemency decided that once and for all she would try to ignore the fact that Rodger limped or was sometimes forced to rest because he had exercised his leg too much. She would be casual and seemingly unconcerned and she would become the popular young matron he obviously wished her to be. She dutifully designated a time when she would receive at home. Meanwhile, she accepted invitations to routs and made courtesy calls on various members of the *ton*. She was beginning to make friends among younger, newly married women like herself—but of these, she preferred the society of Lady Maria Kensington.

She, too, was married to a former officer. Gerald Kensington had been in the Yorkshire Hussars and wounded at Oporto. Sent home to recuperate, he found his father ailing and his estates badly managed. He had sold out and spent a great deal of his time in Yorkshire, a climate his lively wife decried as "insupportable."

Lady Maria was very good company and knowledgeable about shopping. An indefatigable bargain-hunter, she coaxed Clemency into going to tiny out-of-the-way *boîtes* where one could get "incredible bargains," at least according to her ladyship, who bought so many of these desirable items that the bargain aspect was soon dissipated. She also advised Clemency to stop perusing the pages of *La Belle Assemblé*. " 'Tis only an advertisement for Mrs. Bell, the wife of the editor, who has her own shop. She charges outrageous prices and is forever promoting that most uncomfortable Circassian corset, which you, being so divinely slim, certainly do not need," she had said frankly. Maria prided herself on her frankness and also on her knowledge. She kept Clemency half-shocked but definitely entertained by her confidences concerning various members of the *ton*. These generally centered on which titled lady was being indiscreet with what titled lord. Lady Caroline Lamb's scandalous behavior was much on her tongue, even though her affair with Byron was definitely at an end.

Not knowing much about the lady or the poet, Clemency had been inclined to pity the latter for his loss. She had felt deeply sympathetic over his club foot, which, she was sure, gave him much anguish. Maria had laughed over that. "You'll never need to pity Byron, who has all the ladies in London throwing themselves at him," she had said with her habitual naughtiness. "As for Lady Caroline, do not waste any sympathy on her. She is quite mad. One can only feel sorry for William Lamb, a charmer, my dear, and why not, since he is the illegitimate son of the entirely charming Lord Egremont."

"How can you know that?" Clemency had wondered.

"My dearest, only such innocents as you do not know it. Lady Melbourne had half London at her feet and the other half in less obvious places."

There was no disputing the fact that Lady Maria, gossip though she might be, was entertaining and a good friend. Clemency felt the richer for her company and she was making other friends as well. By the middle of March she was hard put to find a night when she might remain at home. There were invitations to the theater, the opera, and the newly organized Philharmonic Society, of which Rodger was a patron. There were also banquets and balls. Though her husband accompanied her to many of these, there were times when he was quite content that she attend them with one or another sprig of fashion. She finally met Mr. Brummell and he accompanied her to Covent Garden to view a play called *Isabella*, in which the great Sarah Siddons had made an earlier notable success. Mr. Brummell seemed to believe that Miss O'Neill, the actress currently attempting the role, might not duplicate her predecessor's expertise. He pronounced himself entirely in error after the first act and actually had tears in his eyes at the death scene—or so he said. Clemency did not notice them.

Though their box had been much besieged by aspiring young beaux and ladies longing for a closer look at her escort, Clemency had waited in vain for what Lady Maria described as one of his famous "set-downs." Beyond looking weary, he said nothing, and her comment to Rodger that she found him shy caused her husband to compliment her on her perspicacity.

"Brummell doesn't shine in public. His choicer witticisms are reserved for his special cronies, who repeat them and add more luster to his reputation."

"I like him," she had averred. She did not add that she particularly liked the Beau because he did not try to flirt with her as some of the other gentlemen did. She feared that Rodger, given these confidences, might find her gauche and unsophisticated. Judging from his attitude on the night they had gone to Carlton House, he was proud of her success and wanted her to be even more successful, something that Lady Maria was helping her to become. It was through her that she met Sir Clement Granby, a pleasant young man who aspired to be a dandy and had been much struck by the similarity in their given names.

"I bring good weather, and you forgiveness, a comfortable

blend, I'm thinking," he had said when Lady Maria introduced them.

Rodger, meeting him at White's, had approved him. He seemed delighted that on the days when he was unable to ride with her, Clemency could canter through the park with Sir Clement and also Lord Layard, another of Lady Maria's finds. Clemency feared that her lord's pleasure was double-edged, since her popularity left him free to visit the friends he had mentioned. He often met with members of his old regiment who were either home on leave or had sold out.

She did not ask what they discussed. The very air was heavy with words concerning Napoleon's coming debacle. Since his ignominious retreat from Moscow, the emperor had made one tactical error after another. These had culminated at Leipzig in October of 1814 with the Battle of Nations, which raged for three days, the sixteenth, eighteenth, and nineteenth of the month. He had met with a crushing defeat and his army of 350,000 men had been reduced to something less than 80,000. He had retreated to a France already mourning the loss of the 460,000 dead in the ruinous Russian campaign. In spite of the opposition to his schemes, evident even in his own legislature, Napoleon had been able to raise another army of 300,000 strong to drive the pursuing allies out of France. However, those who read the news coming across the channel each day were positive that by the end of March the emperor must be deposed.

It was near the end of that month when Clemency, seated at the large desk in the library, was writing an answer to Lady Pomeroy, who had desired the company of My Lord and Lady Colbourne at a dinner on Tuesday of the following week. Unfortunately, My Lord Colbourne, caught as he was leaving the house, had answered impatiently that he could not attend any functions that particular week. He had spoken brusquely and looked at Clemency as if she ought to understand that matters considerably more momentous than a mere dinner were in the offing.

It was not the first time he had addressed her in this manner, nor was it the first time that she had wished fervently that they might return to the country. She was certain that his ill humor was based in part on his physical condition. Nearly every day he was seeing one or many of his old comrades and discussing the conditions in France for hours at a time. Not only did this wear down his stamina, but it unfortunately brought back unwelcome memories of Spain. His sleep was restless, and once he had awakened her with a cry of, "Onward, men . . . charge."

"If only . . ." she muttered, thinking of home again. But she had learned her lesson. Rodger wanted her to enjoy herself and appeared to believe that her enjoyment must lie in becoming a glittering ornament to society. It had been weeks since he had mentioned their projected trip to Devonshire and, to all intents and purposes, their wedding trip to London gave every indication of changing into a permanent stay, something that despite her fondness for Lady Maria, she did not want. She wished she could bring up that trip to Devon again, but feared his reaction. He would probably suspect that she had an ulterior motive in mind, concerning his health, of course. She heaved a short impatient sigh, wondering if there would ever come a time when Rodger would cease to be so edgy on the subject. She was tired of walking on eggs, tired of being constantly on guard lest she wound his feelings. Yet, she told herself, she ought not to complain. She at least could be sure of her husband's love—which was something many young women in her circle could not say. Just the other day—

A tentative tap on the door roused her from these reflections. She looked up interrogatively. "Yes?" she called.

The butler opened the door. "If you please, milady, there's a person who wishes to speak to you."

"A person?" she repeated. "What manner of person. Travers?"

He regarded her apologetically. " 'Tis one o' them," he commented obscurely. "But she says as 'ow she knows your ladyship." Surprise and disbelief were mingled in his plump face.

"One of *them* . . . Travers? I am not sure I follow your meaning."

"Wot goes about 'andin' out tracts to the poor." The butler's countenance was further disturbed by a frown.

"A . . . Methodist?" Clemency asked tentatively.

"Some such, your ladyship. All in black she were, an' carryin' a Bible, which don't mean . . ." He cleared his throat and cast her an embarrassed look. "She . . . er, says as 'ow she 'opes 'er cousin'll see 'er."

"Cousin?" Clemency grew cold. "She calls herself my cousin?"

"Yes, your ladyship," sighed the butler. "Else I'd not be givin' 'er the time o' day."

Clemency's hand strayed to her heart, which seemed to be beating much faster than usual. "Where is she?"

"In the 'all, your ladyship."

"Please show her into the drawing room, Travers."

"Your ladyship'll see 'er then?" The butler actually sighed.

"Yes, I will see her. Tell her that I shall be with her directly. Did she give you her name?"

"Palmer, 'twas, your ladyship."

Palmer. Beatrix! But of course she had not needed that identification. The word "cousin" was enough. Clemency did not leave the library immediately. She remained at her desk both amazed and confused by the memories surging through her mind.

She had not thought of Beatrix in years. No, that was not true. She had most assuredly thought about her, and often enough in connection with Rodger, resenting her for her cruel references to his crippling injuries.

Lord Caliban!

She could not have wounded him more had she slipped a dagger between his ribs. And while wounds heal and leave scars, they generally do not carry with them the pain that she knew still afflicted her husband and, now that she thought about it, must be partially responsible for his extreme sensitivity on the subject. And she had just given orders to show this woman into his drawing room!

By rights, she should have had the butler turn her out into the street, but she could not do that to Beatrix! Even if her mother had, in effect, stricken her name from the family Bible, they were still first cousins, and once they had been very close.

Furthermore, from the few words dropped by the butler, a very great change must have taken place in the girl she had once known. One of *them*, the man had said disdainfully. In common with many servants, he had a distinct prejudice against proselytizers, particularly those who invariably exhorted the so-called "humble folk" to be content with their lot, quoting the difficulties sustained by the rich when attempting to enter heaven. Only Beatrix's claim of a close relationship had prevented Travers from turning her away.

Beatrix with a Bible? Beatrix turned Methodist? That did seem hard to believe, especially in view of her extreme boredom in church, her sighs, her groans, and her fidgeting. She had been far from religiously inclined in those days. Nor had she been overburdened with the strong conscience that popular belief attributed to Methodists, leaving as she had without a word to anyone. Once more Clemency was visited by her old confusion and hurt. She could have written from America—and what had happened to Lieutenant Palmer? And when had Beatrix turned Methodist—and why? These questions could be answered by only one person—the woman she had just instructed Travers to show into the drawing room.

Clemency frowned. Did she really want Beatrix under Rodger's roof? She had a strong impulse to summon the butler and tell him to usher the visitor out. The pulley hung on the opposite wall. Rising, she stepped toward it and stopped. She could not be so cruel, and besides, she *was* curious. Had Beatrix been in London long? The war was still raging in America. Had Lieutenant Palmer also been killed?

She smoothed down her gown, examining the skirt for ink stains and finding none. There was a convex mirror hanging on the wall near the door. She stared into it. Usually she smiled at the image it gave back to her—but she was not in the mood for smiling at her distorted countenance. She only wanted to see that her hair was smooth. No, she wanted to see if she looked as calm and composed as she wanted to be. Satisfied that she did, she turned away and hesitated at the door. Then, resolutely opening it, she went down the hall in the direction of the drawing room.

Opening the door, she paused on the threshold, staring at the small, thin, black-clad figure who sat on a straight-backed chair not far from the door, her hands folded in her lap, her eyes downcast and her Bible on the table next to the chair. Though her gown was neat, it was also old and patched. Clemency had a vision of the bedraggled sparrow she had seen on the window ledge sheltering from the chill March winds.

"Beatrix," she said tentatively.

Beatrix looked up quickly and rose hastily. She was even thinner than she had looked while sitting down. Her rusty garments hung on her wasted frame—her blue eyes seemed huge in her lean face and her cheekbones seemed much more prominent than Clemency remembered.

"Clemency!" Beatrix cried. "God be praised. He has shown me the way to you, cousin."

All of Clemency's burgeoning prejudices were replaced by pity. She hurried toward her cousin, her hands outstretched. "My poor Beatrix, what has happened to you?" she cried.

" 'Tis a long story, cousin, but before I begin . . . might I have a cup of tea? 'Tis a long walk here . . . from Chelsea, and I . . . I find myself much fatigued." Beatrix took a tentative step toward Clemency and then with a little moan fell into a dead faint.

8

Beatrix, lying in a bed the like of which she had not seen since she had left Sayles, was well satisfied with herself. She had fallen on the floor not far from the Bible that had dropped off the table, mainly because she managed to give it a surreptitious shove when she tumbled. She had not been sure whether or not she could manage that, but she had. It had lent an artistic touch, she thought with more pleasure than she had experienced for quite some time.

It had been no pleasure at all to find out that her dear Cousin Clemency was wed to Lord Colbourne and living at his imposing mansion on Arlington Street in the most fashionable part of the city. Whenever she had thought of Clemency, she had envisioned her in black, mourning the death of Damian Prior. Instead, here she was looking ravishingly beautiful, garbed in the very latest fashion, and why? Because she had the good luck to be the daughter of Lord Sayles, her father's oldest brother!

The old familiar fury pulsated through Beatrix's veins. She longed to throw something or jump up and down or pound the walls with both hands—but she could not.

She had not devoted much thought to how she would feel when she saw Clemency again. She had been mainly concentrated on the character she had created for herself some months back, one of several she had presented in the nearly two years since she had eloped with Ralph Palmer.

"Damn him," she muttered. "Double damn him, and may he fry in whatever hell he finds himself!"

Ralph, madly in love with her, had promised to marry her; he had spoken to the captain of the ship bearing them to

America, but because she had flirted with Major Culpepper the next night—and it had not been her fault the major had kissed her—Ralph had accused her of leading him on and canceled the wedding! Fortunately, Culpepper had been blown to bits along with Ralph, and he was the only other person who knew they had not been wed. However, for all they had been so friendly with her, none of Ralph's fellow officers had lifted a finger to help her after his death. They had been too involved in fighting the Americans.

She had sailed back to England with a common soldier, a blacksmith's apprentice before being recruited. She shuddered, recalling his rough caresses and his beatings, too, when half-sick from the motion of the ship she had refused to give him the pleasure he had demanded in payment. She had fled from him in Liverpool and gone on the streets until she had had the good fortune to be "converted" by a group of traveling evangelists known as the Little Brothers to Jesus.

She had played the role of a repentant Mary Magdalene very well, speaking to the few people who attended their meetings. It had been a rough life, but preferable to her brief sojourn on the streets. At least she had had a roof over her head, and if she were sick of meager food, the sight of dingy rooms, and the smell of poverty, she no longer needed to trade her body for a night's lodging with some lout from off a ship. And now she stared around the room where Clemency's footman had carried her after her faint and her murmured apologies concerning her illness.

She admired the fine furnishings, the wallpaper with its blue flowers that matched the draperies, and the deep-piled carpet. To be in a soft bed with fine linen sheets liberally scented with lavender was a luxury she had not appreciated enough in the days she had spent at Sayles. She did not want to leave it, would not leave it. Clemency had not looked very pleased to see her. It had been an error not to have confided her plans regarding her elopement. Clemency would never have betrayed her, she was positive of that. She would now have to concoct some sort of a tale putting the onus on Ralph. That would satisfy her cousin.

In the last eight months, traveling from town to town with the Little Brothers, literally living from hand to mouth, she had often thought of her dearest Cousin Clemency, who, but for an accident of birth, might have been dining off her crusts of bread and swallowing huge servings of humble pie! She might even have been prating of saving souls, when she was not at all sure any of the few poor fools who gathered to listen had a soul to be saved! She threw a burning glance at the Bible on the table beside her, wishing she could toss it out the window.

Unfortunately, though its contents bored her to extinction, she must needs keep it and refer to it as she continued playing the role she had assumed so many months ago. But at least she could do it here. She was convinced of that. If Clemency's mother had been present, undoubtedly she would have been sent packing. Lady Sayles was slow to forgive those who wronged her. However, Beatrix could easily handle Clemency, who, from the looks of her, had changed very little from the sweet, trusting girl she had been before her surprising marriage to Lord Colbourne, Lord Colbourne, of all people!

Not for the first time, Beatrix blessed the happenstance that had brought an old copy of the *Morning Post* into her ken. If she had believed in God or the Devil, she might have credited either power with this piece of good fortune. As it was, she only counted herself very lucky to have spent the night in a battered streetside hostel run by Methodists. The newspaper had been used as a "cloth" to cover the rough board where she and some other Little Brothers had been served soup. Her eye had fallen on the list of guests from the Regent's ball. Among those present had been the beautiful Lady Colbourne, née Clemency Barsford.

It had given her quite a jolt to learn that Clemency had wed Lord Caliban. And what had happened to his passion for the scrawny little Spaniard, whose passing had supposedly left him heartbroken? How had he and Clemency gotten together again? She remembered well the occasion of their first meeting. He had saved the chit's life. Her hands closed into fists as she recalled the terrible disappointment she had experienced on seeing her cousin brought safely home when she had happily been imagining her crushed and broken on the floor of the tower. However, that was water under the bridge, and . . . Her somber gaze brightened; she had a second chance, even if it did mean she would have to pretend to a repentance she was far from experiencing and to an affection that warred against her every feeling. She thought of another saying: "All things come to him who waits."

"*Beatrix* . . . your cousin?" Rodger stared perplexedly at Clemency.

She nodded. "I have put her in the Blue Room." She continued unhappily, "I sent Rose to look in on her again, and she tells me that Beatrix is still sleeping."

"She eloped, did she not?"

"Yes, with a Lieutenant Palmer. I have not been able to speak to her about him. Judging from her appearance, though, she has been through some very difficult times. Oh, Rodger, she does look so pitifully thin, and she was clad in such a ragged old gown, with naught but a thin shawl to protect her from the winds. And she's carrying a Bible."

"A Bible?" he echoed.

"She's joined one of those sects. She muttered something about the Little Brothers to Jesus. Have you ever heard of them? I have not."

"There are a great many of these groups about, especially among the poor. Still, from what I have heard about your cousin, which, I admit, is precious little, she did not strike me as a Bible student."

"Nor me," Clemency agreed, endeavoring to subdue the smile that tugged at the corner of her lips. Beatrix's regrettable condition and situation should not engender smiles. She added with some little reluctance, "I expect we ought to let her stay here." She regarded him dubiously, wishing he would withhold that permission and suggest an alternative—such as paying for a lodging in a boardinghouse or hotel.

He said, "If that is what you want, dearest, I am agreeable."

She did *not* want Beatrix to remain. If she should ever make a slip and call him by that dreadful nickname . . . But of course she never would . . . and she was so needful. She should not be thrust among strangers in a lodging house, not when she had relatives to take her in. Clemency could not, with a good conscience, send Beatrix away. They were closely related. Yet, though she realized she was being mean and uncharitable, she wished strongly that her cousin had not come. Given her past actions, her elopement without a word to anyone, she could not feel the same toward her. However, now was no time to dwell on that. For the sake of their old friendship, she had to let her stay, at least for a while. Maybe later, when she was more herself, they could find her a place in the country or wherever she chose to dwell. She smiled at Rodger and said, "You are very kind, my dearest." Moving closer to him, she put her arms around him and forgot Beatrix for the moment as she rejoiced in his warm embrace.

"An evangelical cousin?" Lady Maria turned amused brown eyes on Clemency as they sat in her post chaise being driven to one of her "finds," a hat shop where the miliner was not only amazingly inventive but also incredibly inexpensive. One could have three bonnets for the price of one! Lady Maria continued, " 'Tis almost like having an angel in the house—or do you not find it thus?"

"She has been with us only two days," Clemency said.

"Ah, so you've not been able to determine whether or not she is angelic?"

"She has kept to her room, poor thing." Clemency sighed. "She has suffered a great deal." She bit down another sigh. "I imagine her faith has given her strength."

"I hope she does not try and convert your servants."

"Oh, Maria," Clemency laughed. "I think that highly unlikely."

"I do hope so. I had an abigail who hummed hymns while she was arranging my hair and preached in the kitchen when the cook was preparing dinner. After the third soufflé dropped, I dismissed her. I do not expect you could do the same thing with a cousin, though."

"I could not," Clemency said. "She has suffered dreadfully."

"So you just mentioned. Might one ask what form her dreadful suffering took?"

"She eloped with an officer and—"

"You may stop there. I will tell *you* the rest. He had proposed marriage, but did not follow through."

"Oh, but he did—only he was killed and the marriage lines lost in America. His family has refused to recognize her as his lawful wife. They would not even see her when she went to them, and all her money was spent on a passage home. She was starving when she came to an evangelical mission and they took her in. She has been working with them ever since. She was terribly distressed when she fainted the other day—she had wanted to go back and help distribute food to the poor."

"Gracious," Lady Maria remarked. "Her tragic experiences have turned her into a zealot, I fear. My dear, you'd best pack her off, or I warn you, she will undermine your entire household and drive your husband to White's or Watier's or whatever hell he can find to escape her."

Clemency laughed, then sobered. "My husband feels deeply sorry for her."

"Is she young?"

"My age, or rather just a few months older."

"Is she pretty?"

"She used to be."

"And now no longer?"

"She is very thin—emaciated, really. And her skin is yellow."

"She needn't remain that way. I expect you are having your cook prepare all sorts of tempting delicacies for her?"

"I have told them to give her healthful food," Clemency said.

"My advice is keep her on a starvation diet. A lady in distress, particularly if she has any pretensions to good looks, can wreak havoc in a household—particularly where the gentleman is so attractive."

"I do not believe my cousin would agree with you."

"Is she blind?" Lady Maria demanded.

"I have often asked myself that question," Clemency said ruminatively.

"Be assured that you are fortunate." Lady Maria spoke crisply. "And let us hope that your indigent cousin continues to find his lordship unappealing, and vice versa."

Clemency said stiffly, "I have no fears regarding my husband, Maria."

"Indeed? Then either he is a paragon or you are less intelligent than I have always believed you to be. I pray that I am right—but I beg you to remember what I have just told you about 'distressed ladies.' "

"Rodger is a paragon," Clemency said softly. "You can have no idea—"

"Judging from my own experiences, I cannot . . . and here we are. Mind you, do not pay any attention to the first price she quotes. She will always come down."

Clemency returned home with two charming bonnets for herself and two for Beatrix. On arriving home, she went immediately to her cousin's room, only to be informed that she was in the library with his lordship. There was no reason, she told herself, that there should be a pounding in her throat as she hurried toward the chamber in question. It was all due to Lady Maria's silly chatter, of course. She had never been so annoyed with her friend as when she dared to suggest that Rodger might be attracted to Beatrix! Every day he seemed more attached to herself. Furthermore, he had told her that he hardly recognized Beatrix. He had seen her around the village once or twice and had thought her quite pretty. "I vow, my love," he had remarked when they returned to their own room, "your poor cousin looks as if she's aged twenty years."

As for Beatrix, she could have no interest in Rodger, not after what she had said about him all those years ago. Clemency's teeth clicked together. She grew angry every time she recalled that cruel gibe, spoken loud enough to be overheard and repeated!

She opened the library door to laughter, low and sweet from Beatrix, louder on the part of Rodger. She was, however, warmed by her husband's welcoming smile. Beatrix also had a smile for her. Clad in her battered black gown, she was curled in a large leather armchair. "My dearest Clemency," she cried. "Imagine, your lord refuses to believe what I tell him about America!"

"Really?" Clemency questioned. "Why not?"

"Because it seems to me that your cousin has been spinning tales the like of which I have read only in the works of the late Baron Munchausen."

"Late? Is he?" Clemency was momentarily diverted. "I thought the baron was a fictional character."

Rodger shook his head. "His death was reported quite recently. He died in Paris last month." His smiling gaze fell on Beatrix. "But I believe he left a sister."

"La, my lord, I have only told you the truth," Beatrix chided.

"Surely you have exaggerated the size and grandeur of Niagara Falls," he challenged.

Her wide blue eyes grew even wider. "I swear I have not. 'Tis against my faith to prevaricate. I can only say that you have no idea of their magnificence until you see them— veritable mountains of water. God has created America with a lavish hand! Everything there is immense—the rivers, the lakes, the woods. The trees seem to stretch as far as the sky. And sometimes you will find their branches intertwining across the roads, as if they were clasping arms in friendship. It does seem sad that the sounds of battle should be heard in what otherwise resembles a great natural cathedral."

"To my mind, the American conflict does seem a foolish war," Rodger agreed.

"Oh, indeed it is," Beatrix cried. "All wars are foolish!"

"Again, I can only agree," he said wryly.

"But how else could we contend against Napoleon?" Clemency asked.

"We could not," he returned. "There's the pity. Wars are foolish but inevitable, a collective expression of the anger arising from a series of preventable disputes. 'Tis a pity our vision is so restricted that we are unable to see the outcome of . . . But why discuss the impossible? And besides, I do not think my theory applies to Napoleon."

"Napoleon is the scourge of the Devil," Beatrix said. "Oh, the poor young men who have suffered because of him . . . 'tis so useless."

"Useless indeed." Rodger's brow darkened. With a slight bow, he rose. "I think I must rest. If you will excuse me."

"Of course, my lord." Beatrix spoke before Clemency could respond. "I hope I have not wearied you with my inconsequential chatter."

"No," he said quickly. "Only my own thoughts have conspired to weary me." He bowed and limped out.

Clemency would have followed him but was deterred by her cousin's plaintive voice. "I should not have mentioned the war. I was forgetting how much he suffered in Spain."

Words trembled on Clemency's tongue and she found she

could not keep from saying, "Had you, Beatrix? That seems strange to me."

"Strange?" Beatrix opened her eyes wide. "It has been a long time—"

"Too long for you to remember that you once mocked his sufferings?"

"M-mocked them? *I* could not have done such a thing!"

"You did. You called him Lord Caliban. You were overheard *and* quoted by various people in the village. He was told. It hurt him deeply."

"Oh, nooo," Beatrix almost wailed. "Oh, no, I could not have said anything so cruel . . ." She paused. "Yet . . . it does sound familiar. Yes, I think I might have. . . . I was a different person before I found God and was bathed in his light. Oh, Clemency, I hope you realize that I have changed."

"It seems to me that you have," Clemency admitted.

"Oh, I have, I have," Beatrix said breathily. "I do hope that he does not know 'twas I who was so heedless . . . so stupid."

"No, I've not told him," Clemency said.

Beatrix threw her a grateful look. "That was very kind of you, Clemency."

"I was not being kind," Clemency retorted with a surge of her old bitterness. "I did not want to cause him greater pain by discussing it overmuch. Nor did I want him to know that I had any connection with the slander."

"Oh, dear." Beatrix actually wrung her hands. "I cannot blame you. I can hardly believe those words came from me. Lord Colbourne is a very handsome man. I cannot see that his scar or his other infirmities detract from his looks at all. I was at my window yesterday and saw him ride away. He has a splendid seat on a horse."

"Yes, indeed he does," Clemency agreed with a proud smile.

"You are very fortunate, Clemency. He seems uncommonly fond of you."

"I am . . . uncommonly fond of him," Clemency said softly.

Beatrix looked down and appeared to be interested in a little Dresden china clown on the desk. She pushed it gently back and forth; then, raising her eyes, she said hesitantly, "Do you ever think of poor Damian?"

"Damian?" Clemency stiffened. "No, I . . . no, I am afraid I do not."

Beatrix said remorsefully, "I see that I have shocked you."

"You haven't." Clemency spoke defensively. "It has been a long time."

"Yet, if he had lived . . ."

"He did not."

"No, poor lad. He was killed the same day my husband went. They must have entered heaven together."

Clemency's eyes stung. She blinked away unexpected tears. "I am sorry."

"And I." Beatrix sighed. "I've not found anyone to take Ralph's place. Actually, no one could. Sometimes I pray that I will not live a very long time. I would like to join my beloved in heaven. Oh, dear . . ." She lifted tear-filled eyes to Clemency. "This conversation has turned very melancholy. I find that I, too, must rest, dearest Clemency."

After Beatrix had gone, Clemency sank down in the chair her cousin had recently vacated. She felt really shocked. She wondered what Beatrix, so very much in love with her late husband, would have thought had she told her the truth, told her that it had been months since she had had a thought to spare for the boy who had loved her and whom she believed she had loved. More tears filled her eyes and trickled down her cheeks. It was terrible to have forgotten him so quickly!

Thinking people contended that a belief in ghosts was irrational, and she had always agreed with them. However, she could not help feeling as if Damian's ghost stood near her, regarding her out of reproachful eyes. Mentally she apologized to it and hurried out of the library, needing her husband's reassuring presence.

As she came in sight of the door to his rooms, Clemency paused mid-step. He had been in a troubled mood and perhaps he would prefer to be alone. Mentally she damned her cousin for disturbing him, disturbing her, too, with her mention of Damian.

She recalled Maria's warning. It had given her something of a shock to find Beatrix in the library with Rodger. Yet, that was foolish. Beatrix was not laying snares for her husband, poor girl. Obviously she was still pining for the late Lieutenant Palmer—so cruel of his family to treat her so shabbily. If only in memory of their poor son, they should have welcomed her. Unfortunately, they had not recognized their responsibilities. Did it then remain for Rodger to give Clemency's cousin a permanent home? Though she did not credit Maria's advice, she still had reservations. She did not want a female companion. More specifically, she did not want a third person in the household. Yet to turn Beatrix away at such a time was too cruel, and whatever she had been in the past, she had changed, and not only physically. Mentally she seemed an entirely different person from the girl whose teasing confidences had both titillated and shocked her. A combination of trials, tribulations, and her newly acquired faith had taught her humility. Still, though Clemency believed in her cousin's conversion and approved the changes in her, she still wished that Beatrix had not sought them out. She also hoped that she would not make any more references to Damian!

Clemency knocked tentatively at Rodger's door.

"Come in," he called.

Entering his sitting room, she saw that the door to his bedroom was ajar. He was lying on his bed rather than the couch on which he was wont to rest.

"Are you feeling poorly, dear?" she asked solicitously as she came inside.

He shook his head. "No, I am only a little tired."

"I fear that Beatrix might have depressed you with her talk of war."

"No." A slight smile curled his lips. "She mentions it much less than people I meet at the club every time I go."

"You do not mind her presence here, then?"

"Not in the least. She'll be company for you, I'm thinking. There will be times when I will need to be away."

"I do not need company," she responded. "But I expect we must let her remain."

"I think we must, since she has nowhere else to go, poor girl. So many of the wives of men slain in the service of their country are in similar straits. Even when they are fortunate enough to receive a pension, it is not easy."

"I'd not thought of that," Clemency responded, wishing

that she had looked at Beatrix's situation from her husband's broader point of view. Naturally, he would be much in sympathy with war widows in general and not specifically with Beatrix. It was unworthy of her to wish that Rodger had objected more strenuously to the unheralded intrusion of her cousin.

"However," Rodger said, "we must see that she gets a new wardrobe—and urge her into half-mourning. With proper care and enough to eat, I imagine she will soon get her looks back, and then . . ."

"And then?" Clemency questioned edgily.

He gave her a conspiratorial wink. "I see no reason why we should not find her a bridegroom among one or another of the gentlemen we will invite for her inspection."

Clemency's eyes gleamed. "You are proposing a strategy?"

"Embarking upon a campaign, my dearest," he corrected. He added, "You are too far distant from me, my love."

"But shall not remain so," Clemency replied happily, and hurried to his side.

Their conversation concerning the disposal of Beatrix returned to Clemency's mind quite often in the following fortnight, mainly because her cousin proved stubborn when it came to the doffing of her sable garments. She was also most reluctant to take what she called "charity." It required considerable persuasion on Clemency's part and on the part of Rodger to coax Beatrix to participate in what she termed "the frivolities of choosing a wardrobe." Clasping her hands, Beatrix had said, "Consider the lilies of the field. They toil not, neither do they spin." She had been hurt rather than amused when Rodger had replied, "But you are not growing in a field, dear Beatrix."

Finally, however, she had acquiesced—but she needed more persuasion and the insistence of the mantua maker before she would allow Clemency to buy her a violet muslin morning dress and a white crepe gown for evening. She did accept, although very humbly, two black gowns, one in kerseymere and the other in a French washing silk. She admitted the necessity of several pairs of kid slippers and gloves as well as a peignoir, shifts, and camisoles, but was reluctant, again, to add a gray mantle and a black cloak to her wardrobe. Finally she acquiesced and also professed herself delighted by the bonnets Clemency had purchased for her, but refused more, insisting that she was very well content with what she had. Her expressions of gratitude, which were many, depressed Clemency. She preferred the old Beatrix, who had adored pretty clothes and who had been of a much gayer temperament. It seemed incredible that she could have changed so completely. However, she was quite annoyed a few days later when Lady Maria, hearing this opinion, remarked, " 'Tis not only incredible, my love, 'tis unlikely."

"You have met her but once. You cannot have formed an opinion so quickly," Clemency said defensively.

"I do dislike converts," Lady Maria complained. "I much prefer the unrepentant sinner."

"Her faith has sustained her."

"On the contrary, my dear love, you and your lord have sustained her. That violet gown you bought her is marvelously becoming. It makes her eyes appear almost purple."

"Her looks are improving, are they not?"

"Having seen her only the once, I would say that she is not uncomely, and when there is more flesh on her bones . . ." Lady Maria loosed a sigh and waggled a reproving finger at Clemency. "You should have taken *my* advice and starved her. Furthermore, in spite of her humility and all the objections she made to your purchases, I note that she did not refuse any of them."

"She tried. I would not hear of it."

"I am sure she must have anticipated that."

"When you get to know her better, you will agree with me, I am sure."

"Unfortunately"—Lady Maria pulled a long face—"I will not have that opportunity. Gerald has taken it into his mind that we must visit his aged mother in Yorkshire—this after I thought I had him weaned away from there."

"Oh, Maria, you are not leaving now—when everything is about to happen!" Clemency cried.

"I am in hopes that you are referring to the expected defeat of Napoleon," her friend remarked.

"What else could I mean?" Clemency gazed at her wide-eyed.

"I am not sure . . . but yes, we are leaving for York and I

am devastated, but there's no persuading him to wait. Besides, I have a suspicion that as 'twas with those giants of mythology who derived their strength from their native earth, a Yorkshireman must rest on his own soil every once in a while. I could wish that it were not now, but if it will put dearest Gerald in a better humor, I will not repine—though he insists I have spirits enough for the both of us." Lady Maria rolled her eyes.

"Oh, I will be sorry to see you go!" Clemency said regretfully.

"And I am very sorry to leave you, my love. Remember the sad experiences of Little Red Riding Hood and do not be taken in by clever disguises. A wolf in mobcap and spectacles is still a wolf."

Clemency regretted Lady Maria's departure and missed her sorely, especially since she had not found another friend as close among the ladies she met. However, she was not sorry to be rid of her dire warnings concerning her cousin. As she and Rodger agreed, Beatrix was quite unexceptional and certainly she made every effort to be as unobtrusive as possible. Still, it was impossible even for Beatrix to remain unaffected by the news reaching them from across the channel. In common with Rodger and herself, Beatrix eagerly scanned the London *Times* each morning. In common with them, she could talk of little else. And on the morning that they read about the allied forces storming the fortifications of Paris and penetrating the emperor's last defense, she came out of her shell to throw her arms around Clemency and around Rodger, also, though she blushed and apologized profusely for the latter burst of enthusiasm.

The news that Napoleon's giant war machine had been balked in its devastating sweeps across Europe gave rise to wild rejoicing throughout England. Whenever Clemency looked back on those hectic spring days, she saw them in terms of the balls, dinners, and routs to which she and her husband were constantly bidden.

There was a splendid soiree at Carlton House in honor of the Grand Duchess of Oldenburg, sister of Czar Alexander I, who arrived in London to the cheers of a populace who had waited on the streets for hours just to glimpse one who was closely related to a conqueror of the tyrant. There was also a dance at Almack's, and in accordance with their original plan, Rodger managed to procure a voucher for Beatrix. However, when told of this coup, she gently but firmly declined. "I am not really in the mood for celebrating," she had explained. "And besides, my faith does not allow dancing."

She had also declined an invitation to a reception given at the Duchess of Richmond's palace in honor of the restoration of the French king, Louis XVIII. Not even the assurance that his majesty would be present swayed her. She did consent to stand with Clemency and Rodger on the second-floor balcony on the afternoon of April 19 to watch that same king's triumphant ride through the city. He was escorted by a hundred men on horseback, by six royal coaches bearing, among others, a party from the royal household. Trumpeters proceeded them and in the gold-encrusted state coach rode his majesty and the Prince Regent, easily seen through the wide glass windows.

Prince and king were monstrously fat. Their faces were red and bedewed with sweat, something Rodger did not fail to notice and mention as the immense procession rolled past them.

"Oh, do not criticize them," Clemency begged, her eyes shining with excitement. "Think, that he has really abdicated!"

"I do." He had a loving look for her. "Though 'tis monstrous hard to believe."

"But it has happened!" Clemency clapped her hands. She threw a glance at Beatrix. "Is it not wonderful, my dear?"

"Wonderful, indeed," Beatrix said, but there was a melancholy expression in her large eyes as she added, "Again I must think of the many who gave their lives for this long-postponed victory."

In the white-hot excitment of the moment, Clemency barely heeded her until she glimpsed a brooding look in Rodger's eyes and guessed that he was reminded of comrades lost in Spain and Portugal. "I am sorry," she said hastily. "I was not thinking of the great price we paid for peace."

"Oh, I am sure Lord Colbourne understands," Beatrix murmured.

Clemency experienced considerable annoyance. A hot rejoinder trembled on her tongue, but Rodger, slipping an arm around her waist, said gently, "Of course, no one can fail to be excited by the defeat of Bonaparte. Can you imagine—the continent of Europe has been troubled by his presence for twenty-two years. You and your cousin were not born yet, but now we needn't fear that our children will grow up to be cannon fodder."

Clemency, looking at him, flushed, remembering his talk of an heir. He had never mentioned this matter to her since the day they had met in the woods and he had first voiced his proposal. Quite suddenly she wished that she might bear his child. She raised her eyes to him but found that he had an arm around Beatrix, too, and was looking down at her most solicitously.

"What is it, my dear?" he was saying.

Beatrix blinked tears from her eyes. "I had a child. He . . . died on shipboard. They . . . buried him at sea. Such a tiny mite. He lived no more than an hour and there was none to baptize him and . . . and see him safely into heaven Sometimes, in my dreams, I hear him crying . . . such a small, doleful sound . . . and I pray to God that he will be merciful and take my poor babe into his arms."

"Oh, Beatrix, you never told me!" Clemency cried.

"I could not speak of it. 'Twas an agony beyond compare. I wish I'd not mentioned it now."

"My poor girl." Rodger drew Beatrix against him. "You will bear other children."

"Other children?" she moaned. "But Ralph is dead."

"I cannot think you mean to mourn him indefinitely. You are young and beautiful. I am not being cruel when I tell you that there will come another to take his place. Life goes on, and I may say with certainty that one does recover from the pain of losing . . . loved ones."

"Oh . . ." Beatrix raised drenched blue eyes to his face. "I am sorry. I was so thoughtless. I had forgotten that you, too, have suffered. Your poor wife and your child as well. I do sympathize with you, with all my heart. I know how difficult it is to put these calamities behind us. I have tried. I have honestly tried, but as you see when one least expects it, one is plagued by memory."

Clemency's teeth were on edge, hating the turn the conversation had unexpectedly taken. Though she was sure her cousin was unaware of it, she was talking as if Rodger still actively suffered from that old sorrow. Then, looking into his face, she experienced a shock. He did appear very somber and his eyes seemed to be looking inward as if filled with a vision of his lost Inez.

Beatrix moved away from Rodger and turned her melancholy gaze on Clemency. "And you, too, have suffered, my love," she said feelingly. "One must not forget poor Damian."

"Damian, of course." Rodger nodded, his eyes straying to Clemency's face.

"They were so close as children," Beatrix continued.

"I knew no one else until you came," Clemency reminded her sharply. "Gracious, are we all to wallow in these old agonies? We, none of us, can bring the dead to life again, so what is the necessity of dwelling on them?"

"Oh, my dear." Beatrix was at her side in an instant. "I am sorry, thinking only of myself when I know how much it must hurt you to be reminded of him."

"It does—" Clemency began.

"Pray forgive me," Beatrix interrupted hastily. "And you." She turned back to Rodger. "Will you forgive me also, my lord?"

He stared down at her. There was a slight frown in his eyes. "There is nothing to forgive, my dear Beatrix. Come, the parade has passed by and it is very breezy out here. Shall we go in?"

"Oh, yes, it is windy," Beatrix agreed.

"Rodger, wait," Clemency said.

"Tell me inside, my love," he advised, moving back into the hall. But Beatrix was with them as she joined him, and she could not cling to him and assure him that Damian meant nothing to her, nothing at all. It sounded too heartless, especially in view of their grief. And why, why, why had Beatrix brought Damian's name into the conversation? Inadvertently Clemency recalled Lady Maria's warnings, but dismissed the thought quickly. It was only natural that her cousin should mention poor Damian. At the time Beatrix eloped with Lieutenant Palmer, her ears had been filled with ecstatic confidences concerning Damian. In those days, Clemency had never dreamed that anyone could replace him in her affections. He had been everything to her.

Had that really been true?

It seemed incredible now. Looking at Rodger, she did not see how she could ever have loved Damian. It had not been *real* love, only a young girl wanting to be in love. She felt immensely older, immensely wiser than her former self. It was a pity she had failed to impress her cousin with that fact. However, with the silly outpourings of callow passion she had visited on Beatrix, she could hardly blame her for believing that Clemency might still mourn Damian. But, she recalled, she had told her she never thought of him. Unfortunately, Beatrix, still suffering over the death of her own husband, had probably judged Clemency by herself. When she got Beatrix alone, she must impress upon her that she had mistaken affection for love and that she had never known what real love meant until she came to know Rodger.

"What is it you wished to tell me, Clemency?" Rodger asked.

She bit down a sigh. "Nothing of any importance, dearest."

"I see. Well, if you will excuse me, I think I will go to Watier's."

"Oh, dear." Clemency regarded him worriedly. "Should you ride out on these crowded streets at such a time? It could be quite dangerous."

"I will be able to manage, I think," he said coolly. "I am not wholly incapacitated, you know."

His rejoinder shocked her. "I did not mean . . . I was only thinking . . ."

"Sorry, I did not mean to bark at you, love." He kissed her lightly on the forehead and limped down the hall toward his chamber.

"If you will pardon me, my dear Clemency, you should not pamper him quite so much. He is very proud, you know."

Clemency whirled on her. All the impatience and annoyance she had been feeling in the last few minutes came out in her tart "I pray you'll not explain my husband to me, Beatrix."

"Ohhhh." Beatrix gave her a stricken look. "I am sorry. It is only that I wanted to . . ." She shook her head, and bursting into tears, started away.

"Beatrix . . ." Clemency hurried to her side. "I am sorry too. I did not mean to scold you."

"But I should not have said anything," Beatrix sobbed. "I am all at sixes and sevens, and today should be such a happy day. Just think—the wars are over and . . . and . . ." Beatrix shook her head, adding, "I must go to my room, I think." She gave Clemency an apologetic look. "I . . . fear I am not fit company for anyone."

Standing alone in the hall, Clemency felt like weeping. Inadvertently she had hurt Rodger, and it had been utterly wrong of her to flare up at poor Beatrix that way. Besides, she had said none of the things she had wanted to say to her cousin or to Rodger either. And though it was utterly reprehensible of her, she did wish Beatrix had not come—but of course Lady Maria was quite wrong about her. Lady Sayles would have been amazed at the change in her. She must also have been pleased. Clemency wished that her parents had elected to visit them this spring instead of going to Scotland to see Lydia. If they had been here, there would have been no question of Beatrix coming to stay with them.

Beatrix was glad that her chamber was at a goodly distance from those of Clemency and her lord. Yet, she was being overcautious, she decided as she regarded the heavy paneling of her door. No one passing down the hall could hear her smothered laughter. It was just that she was still unused to privacy. The walls of the lodging houses where she had stayed since leaving America had been replete with the sounds of howling children, weeping women, ranting men, and lovers discovering each other in language that yet assaulted her ears. Here in these luxurious surroundings, she could hardly believe she had lived such a life.

The thought of returning to it horrified her—but she would not need to go back. She had finally found an opportunity to fire the opening gun in a war no one knew she was waging! The bullet had found its mark—that bullet engraved with Damian Prior's name. She had caught Lord Colbourne's wince. Clemency had not noticed it.

Beatrix arose from her chair and paced back and forth across the room, thinking of those moments on the balcony.

Had she aroused his suspicions? Yes, she was sure she had. Everything had gone splendidly!

Several days ago she had determined that Lord Colbourne must be made to believe that Clemency, despite her apparent happiness with him, must still harbor an old passion for her lost lover. He would be hurt, then jealous, then angry, then indifferent.

She sat down at her dressing table and peered into the three-sided glass. Lord Colbourne—Rodger, Rodger, Rodger, as she called him in her thoughts—had told her she was beautiful. Had she really regained her looks, or was he only being kind? No, he was not being kind. Her face was fuller, but not too full, and her eyes did not seem so enormous. Her eyelashes were long and curling, her lips were full. Her figure was slender, but her bosom was a trifle heavier and her skin had lost its yellow cast. Yes, she *was* beautiful! And *he* had noticed!

How, she wondered, could she have been so blind all those years ago? Why had she not realized that he was one of the most handsome men she had ever seen, something out of a dream? In point of fact, he had figured in a good many dreams so exciting and explicit that to awaken from them was to be left full of agonized frustration. That she had been unaware of his attraction amazed and frightened her—she must have been addled. She shuddered. Years ago, one of her father's "housekeepers" had called her "addled," had said that she didn't think like other folk. "You be half-cracked," had been her dictum. Ridiculous witch! She did not know why the woman's words had stuck in her mind so long. Yet, at this moment, she was almost in agreement with her. Lord Colbourne was beautiful! She did not quite remember when she first realized she wanted him. It didn't really matter. But she *did* want him, and if she were clever, she would have him.

Clemency presented no barrier. She did not know how to handle him. She betrayed her anxiety over his condition too easily. Of course, he was still besotted with her. After all, they had not even been married a year. She would have to be patient. Yet, it was very difficult to see him looking at Clemency so adoringly, that silly little girl!

She was silly, but she was also beautiful. Her looks had

actually improved. Beatrix's eyes narrowed. Beautiful, rich, and wellborn, a rare prize, while she, her equal in looks and more than her equal in intelligence, was still suffering under the onus of her mother's questionable status. There was no sense dwelling on that. If she had not been endowed with the world's goods, she had an imagination that far surpassed that of her cousin.

She, for one, would never have invited another woman into her home. If she had been in Clemency's shoes, she would have given her money and bade her a hasty farewell. However, Clemency, the stupid and trusting, had opened the doors to her, and consequently it would not be forever that Beatrix had to watch Rodger as he gazed adoringly at Clemency. Unless she was very much mistaken, the beginning of the end of their love had been initiated this very afternoon!

It had been an inspired stroke to mention the brat, too. That misbegotten infant had been none of Ralph's begetting. She had borne it to the lout who had brought her back to England. She grimaced, remembering that she had believed it to be seasickness that had afflicted her toward the end of their voyage. She had been surprised because she had not suffered from it during her first crossing. Another surprise awaited her upon disembarking and deserting the lout in Liverpool—the queasiness had remained. It had vanished after several months, but Big Milly, one of the whores she met on the streets, told her she was breeding! She had also taken her to the filthy hospital where she had dropped the brat. She had been delighted to learn that it had been born dead. And now all the pain had paid off. Rodger had looked so stricken when she compared her loss to his own.

He must still grieve over the child and miss the Spaniard. His "beautiful" new bride had not succeeded in obliterating their memories, but she could—and would—make him forget, once she had him to herself. She knew well how to please a man. With a little more planning, a few words inserted here and there, she would wean him from Clemency.

Damian, so useless to her when alive, would prove most useful in death. Once Rodger was convinced that Clemency still mourned her late lover, she, Beatrix, would turn the full force of her arsenal upon him. Then it would no longer be a matter of taking charity from him. She could dispense it, could live in his castle on the hill as its doyenne and possess all the luxuries her soul craved.

Beatrix had a vision of Clemency, as she had looked the other night when going to a ball at Carlton House. She had worn the diamond tiara that had once belonged, she explained, to her husband's grandmother.

"You look like a princess," Rodger had said fondly.

When she, Beatrix, donned it, he would liken her to a queen.

9

Waltzing in the now familiar ballroom of Carlton House, Clemency glanced over the shoulder of her partner, Captain Sir Walter Farleigh, a grizzled veteran of the Spanish campaign and a friend of her husband. She was searching for Rodger but she did not see him. Passing the mirror, she glimpsed an image of herself and her red-coated partner. He was assiduously gazing at his feet, and his lips, she noted, were moving. He was counting, she guessed. The dance had only recently been introduced into polite circles. Though long a favorite of the Prince Regent, the waltz had been popularized by none other than Czar Alexander I, who had scandalized the haughty patronesses of Almack's by insisting it be included on the program of the evening he elected to be present.

She did not see Rodger, who had been watching her but a minute ago, nor did she find Beatrix, who had been sitting among the dowagers and other chaperons. Had she finally decided to dance? She drew a deep breath of annoyance. She herself had not wanted to join the dancers on the floor. She too would have preferred just to watch. Rodger, however, had insisted, almost angrily, too, that she waltz. He had been in an odd frame of mind lately. She feared he was becoming weary of the victory celebrations they had been attending. Yet it had been at his insistence that she had accepted so many of the invitations they had received during May and June. It was now July and they were still pouring in. However, when she had suggested that they return to the country, he had actually snapped at her, repeating his assurances that he was not an invalid. Of late, he seemed determined to prove that claim by abandoning his practice of resting in the afternoon. Instead, he went to Watier's or another club and, on occasion, he did not return until the wee hours of the morning. Beatrix's reminder that many of his old comrades were back in the city was, of course, correct.

They had entertained Sir William de Lancey, a handsome young man and, astonishingly, an American, who had fought under Wellington in Spain, acquitting himself so bravely that he had won a knighthood. She hoped that he might have cast the handkerchief, as it were, at Beatrix, but while he seemed to admire her, he also spoke rather shyly of a girl he had recently met in Scotland. Beatrix, she noted, had not looked in the least cast down. Nor had she put herself out to charm Sir John Waters, who, Rodger had explained, was a notable spy, who spoke all the dialects of the country like a native. Later, Beatrix had confessed that she could not bear those who followed that shady profession. It suggested a duplicity that she could not abide, even though assured that the information Sir John collected had proved invaluable to the British forces in Spain. There had been other young men at dinner, but her cousin, generally garbed in gray or black, only talked wistfully of her late husband, regretting that none of the officers introduced to her seemed to know him.

At length Clemency and Rodger had decided that they must give Beatrix more time to recover from what she was determined to believe was the love of her life. "And," Rodger had added at the end of one such discussion, "she is company for you, my love."

That, of course, was true. Inadvertently, they had drifted back into the old affectionate relationship they had enjoyed before Beatrix's elopement, with the one difference that Beatrix deferred to her much more than she had before. And of course there were no confidences to exchange, for Beatrix rarely spoke of her life in America or of the trials that had followed her return. However, there was no denying that she was pleasant and companionable. She also seemed very fond of Rodger, and he, in turn, was becoming quite attached to her. Clemency had the feeling that if Beatrix were to find someone to her liking and marry again, he would be genuinely sorry to see her go. As for herself, she was not sure. It was becoming difficult to remember just what it had been like before Beatrix returned. With a shock, she realized that Beatrix had already been with them close on four months.

Her thoughts came to an end with the cessation of the music. She was delighted that the waltz had finally ended. Her feet ached. She had been dancing nearly all the evening, but she had deliberately left one spoke in her fan empty of names. However, in her mind there was a name written large upon it—that of her husband. She still did not see him. However, she did spot Beatrix, seated once more among the dowagers. Parting from Captain Farleigh, she moved toward Beatrix, who, Clemency thought, was looking exceptionally well this evening. She was clad in the clinging white muslin that was among the new gowns she had been persuaded to accept now that the warm weather had descended in full force. Her hair, cut shorter, again in deference to the summer's heat, curled charmingly around her face, and if she had been of a mind to dance, she must certainly have been besieged by the young men who were casting longing glances in her direction.

As Clemency reached Beatrix's side, her cousin gave her a startled glance. "Oh, I have been looking for you, but in the wrong direction, it appears."

"Well, here I am." Clemency sank down on the chair next to Beatrix and half-slipped her feet from her sandals. "Oh, I am warm and weary."

"Are you? I am delighted to hear it," Beatrix said, and then flushed. "You will be wanting an explanation of that statement, I am sure."

Clemency laughed. "I would like one, I think."

Beatrix had been smiling, but now she sobered. "I know that you do not welcome any comments pertaining to your husband, my love. However, I do think it would be better for all of us were we to leave for the country."

"Oh?" Clemency regarded her anxiously. "Why do you say that?"

"Because—of course, I am not sure if you will agree—to me he seems very tired of late."

"I have thought so too," Clemency agreed. "But he does not take kindly to comments on the state of his health."

"I know that," Beatrix assured her. "However, he might agree if you were to say that you were feeling the heat."

"I am," Clemency groaned. "It's miserable, I think—so sticky. But of late, Rodger seems to doubt me. . . ." She sighed.

"Doubt *you*?" Beatrix repeated. "Surely you must be mistaken!"

"No." Clemency released another sigh. "He feels that every suggestion I make is directed at his well-being. As you yourself have already pointed out, he does hate being made to feel that I take his injuries into account."

"Then I beg you will put added stress on your own weariness, my dear," Beatrix said seriously. "He was uncommonly tired this evening."

"Where is he now? Have you seen him?" Clemency demanded, her anxiety increasing.

"I saw him go into the garden. I expect he is still there. I know you are bespoken for the next several dances, but do you think you might offer excuses?"

"I should be delighted to offer excuses," Clemency told her. "I will go seek him immediately."

She found Rodger in the garden, conspicuous because in that murmurous darkness, he sat alone on a stone bench, his elbow on his knee, his hand propping his chin, apparently deep in thought. He appeared completely oblivious of the couples who strolled down the paths or through the artfully arranged shrubbery and whispered in darkened arbors. Though she could not see his face, she felt he must be brooding. She did not acquit him of bitterness. Most of the younger men present at the Regent's victory celebrations had memories that tallied with his, and superimposed upon the dancers in the ballroom, she imagined they could see the melee of the battlefield with wounded soldiers pitching forward and falling beneath the flailing hooves of their mounts—and those same horses prone upon the broken ground, their bodies running blood as they screamed and perished.

It was unfair, she thought hotly, that Rodger—that all of them—should have had their lives so cruelly interrupted, their limbs shattered. She had a vivid image of that moment when she had looked down at Rodger from a tower window, and wondered why she was thinking of that now—and knew why. It had been the first and last time she had seen him in all the glory of his youthful strength. She shrugged that painful recollection away and came to his side.

"Rodger," she murmured.

He looked up quickly. "My love, I thought you must be dancing."

She shook her head. "I refused all dances for these moments. I think I will give my remaining partners my regrets." Sitting down beside him, she added, "I would like to leave."

"But you must not disappoint them," he protested. "And you would."

"It is either that or trip over their toes. I am so very tired, my dear. Cannot I persuade you to leave?"

His face was in shadow so she could not see his expression, but his tone was guarded. "You will need to persuade me that you want to leave. I have watched you, You are very graceful upon the floor—a natural dancer, in fact—and 'tis obvious that you love it."

"I did enjoy myself at the beginning of the evening," she admitted, "but it is hours later and I would like to get home. Indeed, I should like to go even further."

"Even further? To the ends of the earth?" There was a touch of mockery in his voice.

"To the country," she said seriously. "It is very warm in the city, do you not agree?"

"Would you forgo all the excitement that the Regent has planned for us?"

"Gladly! I have had—or rather I have endured—enough excitement. I am really very weary of it."

"Indeed? And here I was under the impression that you stood up to the rigors admirably. What has occasioned this sudden change of heart, my love?"

"It is not sudden, Rodger," she said patiently, regretfully recognizing the fact that he was suspicious of her motives. "I have been missing the country for quite some time now. Hyde Park is well enough, but it cannot equal the untrammeled paths at home. And it is a very long time since we have even given a thought to Devon. We have yet to ride out upon the moors and scan the rocks for hut-circles." That, she thought with some satisfaction, would convince him that she was not dwelling on his physical condition.

"Yes, we did say something of the sort, I remember. And

when I am better . . ." He paused and added reluctantly, "I cannot think that I am yet equal to the amount of walking and perhaps climbing that such a journey must needs entail, my love."

"Well," she said briskly, "once you are more rested you will be."

He regarded her quizzically. "What has brought about this sudden eagerness to leave for the country—and before the celebrations in the parks?"

Clemency stifled a sigh. Evidently he was still suspicious. "Do you want to remain for them?" she asked. "Then, of course, we shall."

"I had wanted you to see them. The fireworks will be magnificent. You'll not encounter their like again, I'm thinking. It is not every day that a Napoleon is defeated and dethroned!"

"If it is on my account, I would just as soon leave tonight, my dearest. 'Twill be monstrous crowded in the park. I prefer my park filled with trees and plants, not fireworks and other machinery."

"Very well," he suddenly capitulated, as if weary of argument. "We will go as soon as arrangements can be made."

"Oh, I am glad," she said on a breath. "I will tell Beatrix. She will be pleased too."

"Beatrix?" he repeated. "You'll never tell me that she is weary of town life also?"

"She has said so."

"And she sees so little of it." His tone was heavy with suspicion. He rose more swiftly than was his wont and stood staring down at her. "I do not like these schemes, my dear."

"Schemes?" she faltered.

His tone was icy. "I do not like to be coddled in cotton wool. Nor do I want you to be a burnt offering upon the altar of my indispositions!"

She backed away. "I cannot think what you mean, Rodger," she said defensively.

"I think you do," he accused. "And do you intend to keep denying yourself those pleasures that are yours by right, because you have joined yourself to Lord Caliban?"

"Rodger!" She stared at him aghast. "Who has called you that? Who has put it into your mind again?"

"No one had to put it there," he said bitterly. " 'Twas implanted already and continues to flourish as the green bay tree."

"No, no, no." She flung protective arms around him and then placed her hand over his mouth. "I beg you'll not think of that horrid slander. Oh . . ." Her voice broke, and moving away from him, she buried her face in her hands and began to cry in earnest.

"Clemency, love," he said huskily. "Forgive me for taxing you with my frustrations." He put an arm around her. "There is nothing more degrading than self-pity. Come, my beautiful." He kissed the top of her head. "We will go forth from Carlton House and from London, as soon as you wish."

"Clemency . . ." Beatrix came hurrying toward them. She looked at Rodger. "I wondered where she had gone. Young Molyneux is searching for her, as she promised him the cotillion. Is anything the matter?"

"Tell him," Clemency managed to say, "that I have been taken ill and must go home."

"Oh, my dear, I am sorry. I will go at once. And should you like me to summon the coach, Rodger?"

"No, I will perform that duty myself," he said dryly. "I am not entirely helpless, you know."

"I did not mean—"

"Oh, Lord," he sighed. "I did not mean to bite your head off, my dear. Do summon the coach, Beatrix. 'Tis well we are going, for as you see, I am not fit company for anyone tonight."

Beatrix said quickly, "I am sure that is an opinion held by none save him who uttered it, Rodger." Without giving him an opportunity to respond, she glided back across the garden.

Confronting a discomfited Lord Molyneux, she presented Clemency's excuses. She had been hard put to maintain the gravity that the news had warranted. She was extremely pleased with herself this evening. She had planted some seeds and they were sprouting already! Earlier, watching Rodger as he watched Clemency obediently accepting the many partners who crowded around her, mainly because of his insistence that she do so, she had said, "Clemency is supremely graceful and she's always adored dancing. I expect she's told you that she's particularly fond of the waltz?"

"No, she did not mention that." Some of the pleasure and pride that had illuminated his face vanished.

"Oh, yes. She used to complain bitterly because it was not more popular. She told me that she could waltz all night and never tire."

"She is certainly very graceful," he had commented.

"She looks so lovely—with her eyes shining that way." Beatrix had found it very easy to compliment her cousin, especially since she could read Rodger's mind so easily.

He was longing to partner his wife, of course. Unfortunately, it would be a long time before that particular wish could be granted. With her emphasis upon Clemency's apocryphal love of dancing, she had subtly suggested that her cousin could not enjoy being tied to a cripple. She had sown more seeds when she talked to Clemency. Knowing her as well as she did, Beatrix was positive she had agreed to dance only at Rodger's insistence. Undoubtedly she hated being away from him even for a minute. It wanted only a word in her ear and she would have done exactly as Beatrix intended she must.

Rodger, of course, had not welcomed the suggestion that they quit the ball. Clemency knew that. She would have furnished the excuses Beatrix mentioned and thought up other reasons for leaving London. She was a wretched liar. It had worked out exactly as Beatrix had planned. If she had been there, she could not have been more positive of the progress of events. Rodger would have been suspicious of Clemency's sudden desire to go home. Listening to his wife's inept assurances, he would guess she was acting on his behalf, alone. He would be extremely sensitive to any reminder of his injuries tonight, believing that he was depriving her of her pleasures in the waltz. However tactful Clemency tried to be, she must have rubbed a goodly amount of salt into his wounds. He would recover from that hurt, for of course, though he would never admit it, Beatrix was positive he did want to go back to the country.

He could not be enjoying all this fanfare attendant upon victory, not when he was unable to join his fellow officers on parade or even dance with his wife. Indeed, he must be truly wretched. Clemency, taking her suggestions to heart, would have augmented that wretchedness. Beatrix smiled. And the upshot of all this planning? They would not be quite as much in sympathy as they had been when she first arrived.

Once back in Somerset, Clemency would go out of her way to convince Rodger that she was not overconcerned about his health. That, of course, would make him doubly aware of her efforts. He would wax more uncomfortable. That, of course, was not enough to divide them. Beatrix raised her eyes to the brilliantly lighted ceiling that stretched between her and the heavens toward which she was really directing her triumphant gaze. Somewhere in that starry firmament were the three Fates, all of whom had blessed her. And again, it had been through a newspaper! The London *Times*, to be exact.

Two mornings ago, she had idly glanced at the editorial page, which Clemency had been scanning a few minutes earlier. It must have been those same Fates that had prevented her from seeing what Beatrix, running her eyes over the shipping news, learned—that the packet *Bellerophon* from America had arrived that morning, the eighth of July. Among its passengers was a Captain Sir Damian Prior! She had read the item twice just to be sure she was not dreaming.

Damian Prior was alive, and he would be home when the three of them returned! Her first impulse had been to tell Clemency. Fortunately, she recalled that her second thoughts were invariably better than her first! And those generous Fates had also arranged that Lord and Lady Sayles were visiting in Scotland with their eldest daughter, Lydia. Consequently, Damian's mother having fortuitously succumbed in February, there was no one to write and tell Clemency that her onetime lover had "risen from the dead," as it were. The only way she could have learned about it was through the newspaper, which had been subsequently torn in very small pieces and deposited in two wastebaskets.

No doubt Rodger, hearing about Damian's return, would wonder why Clemency had been in such haste to leave for the country. Beatrix was positive that she would be able to add some fancy embroidery of her own to these suspicions. She frowned. She had one nagging fear. She hoped Damian would be sound of mind and limb. God knows what had occasioned his disappearance! He might have been plucked off the battlefield and taken to some makeshift hospital, or he could have been a prisoner of war. No. If he'd been a prisoner, he must still be incarcerated, since that conflict was not ended. If he were a cripple, that would only complicate matters. If he were not, the contrast would give Rodger food for thought—and Beatrix would see that he dined well and often on that particular dish! Since she was no longer anywhere near her cousin and her lord, it was safe for Beatrix to smile broadly as she sought out the servant who would summon the coach.

Seated beside Beatrix in the huge traveling coach that was bearing them back to Porlock and thence to the castle, Clemency warmed to the familiar sight of green hills and the mighty old oaks and elms of the district. They had supped at the George and Pilgrim in Glastonbury and had wandered through the sad ruins of the abbey. Rodger had teasingly told her to keep her eyes on the ground because they might find an arrowhead that had dropped from King Arthur's longbow, since he was reputed to have frequented the abbey, as well as being buried there.

Clemency directed a side glance at Beatrix, who was looking out of the window. She wished that her cousin had not laughed at his remark, reminding him that Arthur was a figure out of romance. Beatrix had struck a discordant note that day, or perhaps it was just that she was *there* at a time when Clemency had longed to be alone with her husband. Indeed, it had surprised her that Beatrix had wanted to accompany them on their stroll. Usually she did not care to look at antiquities. But, explaining that she was weary of sitting for so many hours, she told them she wanted to stretch her legs. She had never left their side for an instant. True, she said very little, but she was present and must needs be included in their conversation.

Occasionally she had asked questions about what she was seeing, and these required answers, some of them quite complicated. In explaining the significance of the Holy Grail and the reasons for the destruction of the abbey in the time of Henry VIII, Rodger had kept the two of them from seeing as much as they might have done had they been alone.

It was selfish of her, Clemency knew, but on this afternoon she wished that Beatrix were still in America, or, she amended quickly, if not actually in a place where she had suffered the loss of her husband and where the war still continued, some spot where she would be comfortable *and* absent. With a shock, she realized that she had had precious little time with Rodger since the advent of Beatrix.

If only her cousin had been minded toward encouraging some of the young men who had been attracted to her. There was no use dwelling on that. Beatrix had not exaggerated when she told them that her heart had been buried with Lieutenant Palmer. Rather than regretting that stand, Clemency told herself sternly, she ought to try to put herself in poor Beatrix's place. In a very brief period of time she had lost both husband and child. She had been cast adrift by Palmer's family, had fended for herself for nearly a year, and had almost starved to death in the process, as witness her ravaged appearance when she first arrived. If anything were ever to happen to Rodger . . .

Clemency shivered. A goose had walked over her grave. That was how her nurse had described those odd chills that came from nowhere. This feeling, however, had come from somewhere, from her own ever-present fears for her husband. She glanced out of the window, trying vainly to catch a glimpse of him, but as usual, he had outdistanced the coach. She hoped that he would not be overtired by the time they reached home. Explaining that he felt more comfortable on horseback than cooped up in the hot coach, he had ridden most of the way from London. Coming up from the castle to London, he had shared the coach with her, but at that time, Beatrix had not been present.

Clemency turned a sigh into a deep breath. She did not want her cousin to ask why she was troubled. Beatrix was much more concerned about her than she had been in the old days. In fact, she really ought to be ashamed of the thoughts that had been coursing through her mind. In fact, she *was* ashamed of not being ashamed of them. Beatrix had been so very helpful on their journey. She had inspected their rooms at the two inns where they had stopped for the night, and finding them inadequate and noisy, had persuaded the innkeeper to give them other quarters more to their liking. She had also required the chambermaids to dust these same rooms and she had made sure that Rodger's valet and Clemency's abigail also had comfortable quarters.

Surprisingly enough, Rose was not as grateful for Beatrix's help as she might have been, saying, with a sniff, that she was appropriating *her* duties. Rose was not overfond of her cousin. Possibly that also rested on Beatrix's refusal to let Clemency hire a maid for her. She stubbornly insisted that she preferred to care for her own needs. Servants were terrible snobs, and also Rose probably recalled Beatrix's battered appearance when she had initially arrived at the house in London.

Clemency's eyes brightened. They had turned off the main highway onto the road that wound up the hill to the castle. Rodger would finally be able to rest. Midway up the hill, just before they arrived at the gatekeeper's cottage, Clemency could see her own home in the distance, and on the other side of the woods stretched Damian's estate. She was glad that they were not nearer. She would have found its shuttered windows depressing. Her mother, writing to tell her of Lady Prior's demise, had said that she had left the Grange in charge of a caretaker against her son's return. No one had ever convinced her that Damian was dead. What would eventually happen to the property? she wondered. Damian had been the last of his line. There was not even a distant cousin to inherit. It was a pity his parents did not have more children. Unfortunately, Lady Prior had been sickly. She had nearly died at Damian's birth and her physician had advised his father that his wife must not bear more children—if she did, he would not be accountable for her life.

Her own mother had marveled at that. She had given birth very easily, and so had Justine. Probably, she would too. Clemency flushed. She longed to give Rodger children. Judging from Beatrix's experience, as well as that of Lady Maria, she ought to have been increasing by now—but she was not.

"The pennant," Beatrix said suddenly. "It's flying."

Clemency glanced out of the window and saw the bright green-and-gold banner fluttering from its pole on the tower roof, an indication that his lordship was in residence. She nodded. "Yes, he sent the servants ahead, if you remember."

"Oh, yes, of course," Beatrix said. "I was not thinking." She smiled at Clemency. "I am looking forward to seeing your stately abode."

" 'Twill be yours as well," Clemency said. "I have given

instructions that you are to be lodged in the Rose Suite, which is similar to mine but on the far side of the hall. The windows are some of the few that give a view of the sea."

"Oh, lovely! I vow you do leave me without words, Clemency," Beatrix murmured.

"I cannot believe that, dear cousin," Clemency teased. "You have always had a ready tongue."

"I am sure my meaning's not escaped you. You have always had a ready understanding," Beatrix responded. "Ahhh," she added as the big coach drew to a stop. "I do think we have arrived."

At length they were out of the coach and stretching their cramped and jolted limbs, rejoicing in the firmness of the earth beneath their feet and in scenery that no longer seemed to be rising up and down.

The solid bulk of the castle was infinitely reassuring to Clemency as she craned her neck to stare at the pennant. In addition to being her home, it was a haven away from the hectic gaiety of London. Rodger would not feel it incumbent upon him to be off to one or another club to discuss the strategies of a war that could not fail to unleash a host of bitter memories. She could also make adjustments in their living arrangements and start inviting some of the families who lived in the immediate vicinity—friends of her parents. She had a moment of wishing that they might have taken that long-promised journey to Devon, but it was not far away and there would be time enough for that.

The sound of hooves on the winding roadway brought her out of her cogitations. Someone was riding up the hill, but who could be trespassing? It would have to be a bold soul, for the whole village knew they were back—the pennant attested to that. She glanced in Rodger's direction and found him talking to Jenkins and the coachman about the disposition of the luggage. However, as the sound of those hooves grew louder, he turned toward the roadway. In another second the rider had come into view, and in that same instant flung himself from his saddle. Grasping the reins of his panting horse, he came forward toward Clemency.

She had recognized the method of dismounting even before his familiar features registered themselves upon her bemused brain.

"Damian," she said faintly, and felt as if the earth had suddenly heaved beneath her feet. "Damian," she repeated. She felt dizzy but she did not faint. She was not prone to such spells, and in a second she had regained her equilibrium. "You are back," she said blankly.

"As you see, Clemency," he corroborated.

Rodger came to stand beside her. "Why, Damian," he said in a tone that mixed surprise and cordiality. "We had not heard this splendid news. I am so happy to see you, and looking none the worse for wear."

Hearing her husband's level tones, Clemency recovered in some degree, and now that the initial shock had passed, she gave Damian a searching glance and agreed with Rodger that he did, indeed, look well and very little changed. There were a few lines around his eyes and mouth, but that was only natural. She thought stupidly that the bayonet wound that had supposedly dispatched him could not have injured any vital part.

He said, "I beg that you will pardon me, my lord, for this precipitous entrance, but I had heard that my old friend and playmate was returned, and I thought I must greet her. Pray forgive me for not standing upon ceremonies."

"But of course we'd not expect that you would," Rodger assured him. "I am delighted to see you."

Beatrix came forward. "Damian, my dear," she said softly, "how good to see you again. And how wonderful to know that those who reported your death were in error."

"Thank you." He had a grave and pitying look for her. "I wish that I might felicitate you on the discovery of a similar error, but as it is, you do have my very deepest sympathies. Ralph was a fine soldier and my very good friend. I, too, shall miss him."

"I do thank you," she said, looking down. " 'Twas a sad loss."

"Will you not come in, Damian?" Rodger invited. "I am . . . and I know my wife is . . . most eager to hear what befell you in that battle where you were reported to have sustained a mortal wound."

Damian had been staring at Clemency, but now he fixed his eyes on Rodger. "Surely you and your wife will want to be settled first. I think I must return at another time."

"As you choose," Rodger said, "but first let us set a date for that other time. Could you come as early as tomorrow night?"

Damian's gaze returned once more to Clemency's face, and again he shifted it back to her husband. "Tomorrow night, yes." He added, "If that is agreeable with you, Clemency?"

"With me?" She stared blankly at him. "Yes, of course it is agreeable. I am most eager to know all that happened to you, Damian."

"I promise you, I will give you a lengthy account. You must name the hour, my lord."

"Shall we be fashionable and say seven?"

"Seven it is," Damian responded. He added, "I hope you will not think me remiss, my lord. I fear I have not yet offered you and your bride my sincere congratulations and my felicitations."

"I thank you, Damian." Rodger smiled.

"Yes, let me thank you also," Clemency said on a breath. She added, "And I have not told you how very sorry I am over the death of your mother."

His blue eyes were suddenly cold, his expression bleak. "I thank you, Clemency. Yet I am glad 'twas not grief that killed her. I am told she never gave up hope that I would return."

"No," she agreed. "She never did."

"Until tomorrow, then." He moved back, and a groom came forward to hold his horse while he mounted. Moments later a cloud of dust marked his swift passage down the hill.

Standing still as a statue and momentarily oblivious of her companions, Clemency watched Damian ride away. Her thoughts were chaotic. Believing as she had in his death, his sudden appearance had taken her breath away. The reproach in his eyes had filled her with guilt, but she ought not to feel guilty. The reports of his death had come from eyewitnesses, eyewitnesses upon the field of battle, where confusion was rampant and where a fallen man, even a man impaled by a bayonet, might not be dead. And Damian was not dead. He had come back to her—only she had not waited. Knowing him as well as she did, she had easily recognized the pain and resentment he was experiencing at seeing her wed to another.

He had poured out that hurt in one bleak comment: "*She never gave up hope that I would return.*"

"Clemency . . ." Beatrix came to her side. She said solicitously, "Had you better not come inside?"

Clemency regarded her blankly. "Yes, I expect I should." She nodded.

"I do not blame you for being shocked, my dear." Beatrix had a commiserating look for her.

"Yes, it was a shock," Clemency agreed. She added, "He looks much the same."

"He does seem older," Beatrix commented.

"I saw very little change."

"Had you better not lie down, my dear?" Beatrix asked solicitously.

"Lie down? No." she looked around her. "Where is Rodger?"

"He has gone inside."

"Oh, I hope he means to rest." Clemency started toward the door. "I had better see that he does."

"Clemency," Beatrix said quickly, "before you do, I would like to know where the Rose Suite is located."

"Oh, yes, of course," Clemency said. "I will show it to you." It occurred to her that it would be better to have a servant bring Beatrix to her rooms, but that would not be very friendly. It might hurt Beatrix's feelings. "Come." She put an arm around her cousin's waist.

The Rose Suite consisted of a commodious sitting room and an even larger bedroom. The walls were hung with a faded rose brocade which, nonetheless, was very beautiful. White marble fireplaces were in both chambers, and the bed, a huge four-poster, was hung with a rose brocade that matched the walls. The windows, once merely narrow slits, had been enlarged during the last century and looked out on a patterned garden. In the distance was a shining strip of sea.

Beatrix, her feet sinking into the deep pile of a pale rose Aubusson carpet, had moved through her new quarters exclaiming with a delight not entirely feigned. She had kept Clemency with her as long as she might, but finally her cousin had excused herself, saying she must find Rodger.

Beatrix regarded the door through which Clemency had just hurried with a smile considerably broader than the one she had worn a second ago. *Everything* was working out splendidly—including the unexpected appearance of Damian. Nothing could have pleased her more. No, that was not entirely true.

She had longed to introduce the item in the shipping news in a way that would cause Rodger to believe that Clemency's eagerness to leave London was based on her knowledge of Damian's return from the dead, as it were. Unfortunately, she had been unable to think of a way to introduce it. Still, Clemency's stricken—and, she suspected, guilt-ridden—reaction to the unexpected appearance of her erstwhile fiancé could easily be misinterpreted by her husband. Coupled with that was Damian's evident misery over her defection. Then Clemency, bless her, had allowed Rodger to witness her confusion as she stood there as immobile as Lot's wife turned to salt, watching Damian ride away.

Rodger had started toward his wife, but Beatrix had intervened, murmuring, "Poor Clemency's had a terrible shock. Best let me deal with her."

He had winced. For one revealing moment he had looked as stricken as though she had dealt him a physical blow. Then he had nodded and turned away. He had been limping almost as badly as when he had first come from Spain, she recalled with no little pleasure. Obviously his long hours in the saddle had told on him. He would not be able to refrain from contrasting Damian's wonderfully robust physical condition with his own. It was really fortunate that his leg was mending so slowly.

Of course, none of this would have occurred to stupid Clemency. Had Beatrix been in her place, she'd not have wasted a thought on Damian. She would have rushed after her husband, demonstrating with speech and action that Damian's return had surprised her—but nothing more! Nor would she have bothered to show her cousin through her suite. She would have left her to the good graces of some servant.

Clemency did not deserve a husband such as Rodger. She did not appreciate him. Beatrix flushed as she pictured herself in Clemency's place. He would never have any doubts as to her feelings for him. And—her eyes gleamed—there would come a time when he would know how she felt about him and when he would be pleading for her practiced caresses.

She gazed around the beautiful room. She did not doubt that the suites occupied by Rodger and Clemency were even more magnificent. She had a memory of that old disappointment when Clemency had not fallen to her death in the ruined tower. Now she was glad this mishap had not occurred. It would not have been very comfortable to be the sole remaining child at Sayles. However, with the help of that cooperative trio of Fates and her own ingenuity, she could and would be the third wife of Lord Colbourne, and that would be very comfortable indeed.

10

Coming out of Beatrix's rooms, Clemency walked slowly down the hall. She was thinking about Damian again. The shock of his sudden return still lingered, but now she was viewing it from another perspective—Rodger's rather than her own.

She came to a sudden stop as she regretfully remembered her reactions. But was it not natural that she should be startled and shocked? And was it not only natural that it had taken her some little time to regain her poise? Then, just as she was feeling more in command of the situation, his bitter observation had made her most unhappy, the more so since she could not help but feel that it was deserved. Unlike his mother, she had never doubted the accuracy of the reports about his death, or rather she had but very briefly, and her grief over his passing had been totally submerged in her growing love for her husband. Damian must believe her very fickle, and what would Rodger believe?

He might have remembered that his proposal had come fast upon her mother's decision to send her to London. She had wept, telling him that she could not forget Damian. He had mentioned his own sorrow over Inez. Then they had become immersed in each other. And then Damian had come back! It was possible, more than possible, that he had misinterpreted her confusion and her guilt. There was a distinct possibility that he might believe that she still cared for Damian. In her shock over his sudden appearance, she had acted very foolishly indeed. Was that why he had gone into the house so quickly? In ordinary circumstances one would have thought he'd have waited for her, but these were not ordinary circumstances. Damian had returned.

It was because of Damian's supposed death that she had married Rodger—but he knew about her change of heart, didn't he? But seeing Damian so little changed . . .

"Oh, God," she muttered, realizing that she should have gone to Rodger sooner. Why had she let her cousin detain her? She should have heeded her initial instinct and let a servant show her to her rooms. But she had not, and Beatrix had kept her talking. She must go to her husband immediately and reassure him that upon seeing Damian she had experienced no greater emotion than surprise!

As she neared his chamber door, it occurred to Clemency that of late she had been doing a great deal of reassuring Rodger.

The man, who had been a font of wisdom and understanding when first she knew him and in the early days of their marriage, had changed, and why? That fact puzzled her, mainly because it seemed so unlike him. She recalled that night at Carlton House when he, having urged her to dance, something she had done only to please him, had found him not pleased. He had looked on her so coldly and had seemed to disbelieve her when she told him she wanted to leave not only the dance but also London itself. That obvious doubt and suspicion had seemed totally foreign to his nature. Of course, he was depressed by his physical condition that curtailed so many of his activities. Still, he had not spared himself any, not in London nor on their journey home, as witness his determination to remain in the saddle for most of the hundred miles that stretched between London and Porlock. He needed rest and peace now. It was the greatest mischance in the world that Damian had returned at this moment!

If only her mother had been at home. Lady Sayles would have lost no time in writing to her, and then . . . Then what? She'd have been prepared to see him and she could have alerted Rodger and he would not have feared . . . But he could not think . . . More regrets attacked her. She looked down at her body, slim as a reed in the green muslin she had donned that morning. If only she were bearing his child, he could have no doubts. He ought not to be doubtful now, she thought with a trace of indignation. She had reached his door.

She knocked tentatively, and in a second Jenkins admitted her.

The valet's sleeves were turned back, indicative of the fact that he was massaging Rodger's leg. She looked toward the inner room. "Is he in much pain?" she asked anxiously.

The valet's gaze, slightly reproachful, lingered on her face. " 'Tis my opinion that 'e's done too much ridin', your ladyship."

"I know," she said regretfully. "But, as I am sure you are aware, there was no stopping him." She moved forward. "I will finish what you have started, Jenkins."

"But—" the valet began.

"This is not a request," she interrupted crisply. "You may go."

"Yes, your ladyship." The valet went out swiftly.

Coming into Rodger's bedroom, she found him lying with his eyes closed and his injured leg outside the covers, as she had seen it once before. She remembered the occasion well, for it was then that they had first been together. She settled down on the edge of the bed and ran her fingers gently over the scarred and pitted flesh, wincing as she felt the tenseness of the muscles.

He opened his eyes. "Clemency," he murmured with a slight frown. "There's no reason for you to be here. Jenkins—"

"Shhhhh, there is a reason. You need my magic touch. Now I beg you'll be quiet and let me apply it."

Much to her relief, he ceased to protest. She was even more relieved when, at long length, she felt the muscles relax. "There, my dearest," she said soothingly. "That's better, is it not?"

"Indeed it is." He smiled at her now. "There *is* magic in your touch, my dearest."

"Not magic—love," she corrected. She added, "Do you mind if I lie down beside you, my darling?"

He shook his head. "I would mind it if you did not."

Matter-of-factly she slipped out of gown and shift, and lying close to him, murmured, "It has been a tiring journey. You must rest now."

"I will take your sage advice, beautiful." He drew her into his arms, saying between passionate kisses, "But not yet."

* * *

Early in the morning, two days after their arrival at the castle, Beatrix, awakening early, gazed at the rose-tinted walls of her bedroom. The sun had just risen and its beams illuminated the colors in a way that made them appear almost iridescent. She noted the effect without pleasure. She had been long getting to sleep and that was mainly due to disappointment.

Damain had been at dinner the previous night and she had entertained high hopes for some embarrassment and strain, but the evening had been extremely convivial. She had noticed no awkwardness in Clemency's manner and Rodger had been at his most charming. Damian was no longer the brash boy she remembered. He had matured, and if he were suffering over the fact that his onetime fiancée was wed to another, he had given no indication of those inner feelings. He had looked very well in his fashionable evening attire. Beatrix, who had expected to see him in a dress uniform, found that he had sold out.

"I have a lingering stiffness in my shoulder, and the head wound I sustained still produces dizzy spells."

It had been the head wound that had caused his superior officers to believe him dead. It had deprived him of memory for some eight months. He had come to his senses in the middle of a fearsome tavern brawl. Some ruffian had struck him over the head with a grog bottle. Knocked unconscious, he had awakened to find himself being jounced about in the back of a farm cart. At first he had believed himself a prisoner of war being taken to a military base. Then, to his astonishment, he had found himself wearing rough homespun breeches and a dirty workshirt.

His hands had been rough and blistered, and when his confusion had dissipated, he realized that he had been working as a stableboy for a farmer who lived outside Buffalo. He subsequently found out that he had been discovered bleeding copiously from a wound in the shoulder and another in the head, where a ball had creased his skull, giving him the wound that had deprived him of memory. The farmer, who had taken him in, told him he had been stripped nearly naked by the scavengers who ranged over the battlefield after hostilities ended. Evidently he had been left for dead but had awakened and staggered toward the farmhouse, collapsing in the garden. One of the hands had dragged him in.

Guessing from his clipped speech that he was an enemy soldier, the farmer had, nonetheless, bound up his wounds, and taking advantage of the fact that his memory had gone, had employed Damian in his stables.

"He needed an extra man," Damian had explained in answer to Clemency's shocked question.

"One of his horses was giving him trouble and I was able to gentle it. His son, it seemed, had joined the militia and was off fighting the redcoats. Once I recovered my memory, he was all for turning me in. He even posted guard over me in the stables. Fortunately, I had made a friend of a half-witted fellow who worked for him and he helped me to get away. I managed to locate my regiment, rejoined it, and my commanding officer sent me home."

He had made what had obviously been a most grueling experience seem both humorous and entertaining, but Clemency, Beatrix had been pleased to see, was extremely distressed. She had hung on his every word, uttering horrified exclamations. However, her reactions had not appeared to trouble Rodger. He had seemed just as intrigued and amazed as his wife. Indeed, he had been in a very good mood, and the sense of strain that Beatrix had done her best to foster in him as well as in Clemency during the last months, was gone.

There was a good reason for that. It lay in the fact that she had seen neither her cousin nor her husband from the time they arrived in the castle until they came smilingly down the stairs the next morning with profuse but not very convincing apologies about having been extremely weary after their journey and going early and supperless to bed.

Beatrix rose and went to the window, staring into the gardens. They were bright with a profusion of roses, and as she looked, she heard the raucous squall of a peacock. The bird, tail spread, strutted into view, a magnificent sight. Through the trees she saw the glimmer of white marble. It was a small folly, fashioned after a Grecian temple. One of the pillars had seemingly fallen and the stonemason had inserted an artful crack in it. The gardener had coaxed ivy to grow over it and to clamber up the standing pillars as well. Clemency had told her that Rodger's grandfather had commissioned the folly and also the little stone grotto that lay near a flight of stairs leading into yet another stretch of garden. Inside the grotto was a deep pool stocked with carp similar to those that thronged the moat.

On her first evening at the castle, Beatrix had strolled through the gardens, remembering a time when she and Clemency had been wont to speculate what lay behind the high walls of Colbourne Castle.

Now she knew. On that same night, Beatrix also explored the castle itself, entering the various chambers, marveling at their fine furnishings and exquisite works of art. Luxury was in evidence everywhere—from the smallest malachite box to the magnificent tapestries that covered so many walls. She had also discovered the long gallery, and there hanging on a wall had seen the portrait of Rodger as he had been before he went off to war. His features had been classically beautiful. Yet, he was even more beautiful now, she thought, wondering, as she often did, why she had not been able to see it in those days when she had jokingly dubbed him Lord Caliban. She frowned. Next to the painting was the portrait of Inez, darkly lovely, in a red gown, a Spanish shawl hanging negligently from one shoulder. If she were Clemency, she would have insisted that the beautiful likeness be removed and stored in some attic. She frowned. Next to that painting was the recently completed portrait of Clemency done by Sir James Carmody, paling in comparison, she thought with the lovely and exotic Inez. Of course, the latter portrait was flattering, or else the woman had lost her looks very quickly once she reached England's inhospitable shores.

Beatrix had accompanied Clemency to three of the sittings, and Sir James had murmured something about her being a good subject, too.

"You ought to have your portrait painted, Beatrix," Clemency had agreed.

She had scoffed at the notion. She had no husband to pay for that privilege, and upon Clemency's insisting that she would be glad to assume that responsibility, she had still refused, saying that there was no space where it could hang.

"There will be one day," Clemency had said comfortingly.

"There will be," Beatrix now muttered. "And I will have your portrait taken down and burned to ashes, dearest cousin."

She had gone out of the portrait gallery and come back to the drawing room, huge and also splendid, with a fifteenth-century enameled triptych on the sculptured marble mantelpiece. And there were the state rooms as well. Among them was the startlingly beautiful bedchamber where Queen Elizabeth had slept during one of her progresses. It had been very hard to view such luxury all around her and to remember, too, the splendors of the London mansion.

She had left London reluctantly. She had wanted to attend the celebrations in the parks and in the palaces, too. However, she had believed the renunciation of these pleasures worth it because of Damian's return.

Clemency, she knew, did not give a fig about the excitement in London. She was not impressed with her surroundings. She was so much in love with Rodger that she would have been happy in a hut—or so she said. Beatrix sneered. It was easy enough for Clemency to make such extravagant statements. Thinking of her easy life, of winning one handsome man and then another even more handsome, and extremely wealthy besides, Beatrix seethed with envy and frustration. The contrast between the two men had been marked last night—Rodger had been a thousand times more attractive than Damian.

Damian had not half Rodger's charm or beauty. Still he was handsome—some might call him an Adonis. Her eyes gleamed with wry amusement. Venus, Goddess of Love, had wed the crippled Vulcan and been unfaithful to him with Adonis. The analogy intrigued her. Rodger was still upset about his infirmities—even though they were mending. If there were only some way of making him believe his Venus was drawn to healthy Adonis . . . but unfortunately, Clemency showed no signs of cooperating. Her happiness had been written all over her face last night. It was impossible to guess what Damian had been thinking.

Beatrix turned away from the window and surveyed her beautiful and luxurious surroundings with lackluster eyes. She wanted more—everything—and it seemed to be unobtainable! She had to get out of here and think or, rather, plan.

Coming out of the castle, Beatrix walked down the hill and across the bridge. She had been aimlessly wandering, but seeing the woods that lay in line with the castle and then with Damian's estate, force of habit brought her into them and onto a path that lay between tall elms. The sun was higher, and now she remembered the pool. On an impulse she walked in what she hoped was that direction. She had never entered the woods at this particular point, but a short time later she glimpsed its waters through the trees. A few more steps brought her to its banks. Sinking down, she stared into waters that brought a beguiling reflection of her face. In her mind's eye she could see Clemency's face, too. They had often sat there talking "secrets," secrets which mainly concerned Clemency's love for Damian. Beatrix had listened and smiled and hated her. Yet, how cleverly she had masked her hatred, while her cousin, guileless and unsuspecting, chattered on, believing she was talking to her true and best friend!

That old bond had certainly served her well, but—she glared at the pool—their return to the country no longer held the same promise. It had started so auspiciously, too—with Damian suddenly appearing, startling Clemency and hurting Rodger. Then, their difficulties had all been resolved through that mysterious legerdemain called "love." The structure of doubt and distrust that she had built brick by brick had toppled to the ground.

A sound startled her—the windy snuffle of a horse. She rose swiftly, bending down to pick up a stick, remembering belatedly that old warning about vagrants and poachers—but it was neither a vagrant nor a poacher that came through the trees looking gloomy and with a downward curve to his well-shaped mouth.

"Damian," she murmured.

"Beatrix!" He regarded her in amazement. Then, with a trace of harshness to his tone, he added, "What are you doing here?"

"Trespassing," she said lightly. "Actually, I came here to wait."

"Wait?" he questioned. "For whom? Have you found a new lover? I hope so."

She shook her head. "That part of my life is over. Ralph is dead."

With a slight frown Damian said, "I cannot understand why you did not go to his family."

Beatrix looked down and haltingly produced the fiction she had invented for Clemency. With an artistic quaver she concluded, "I do not know what I would have done, were it not for Clemency's great kindness in taking me in."

He appeared shocked and surprised. "I know Ralph's people. In fact, I spent a great part of one leave with them. They were very pleasant to me. It seems unlike them to be so cruel to Ralph's bride."

"I was very bedraggled by the time I made my way to their home. I had lost my baby and my looks as well. I had nothing to prove that I had been married to him—and they found it easier not to believe me. They gave me a pound note and sent me away." As she spoke, her mind was racing. It would be disastrous if Damian did not believe her, particularly since a scheme had suddenly flashed into her mind. It was so daring and yet so simple, given the two people she must impress, that she had difficulty controlling her excitement.

Damian said, "I could write to them."

"No!" Beatrix drew herself up. "I want nothing from them. I wish never to see them again." Her lip quivered. "They almost spoiled my memory of the happiness I shared with Ralph. I am well enough here—"

"In Caliban's castle?" Damian said bitterly. " 'Twas a turn of events I never anticipated."

She winced inwardly at his use of the name, but she did not reprove him. The bitterness that marred his countenance had its foundations in what she had suspected. He had put on a good front last night, but it had been patently false, and he had given her the impetus she needed. She could now proceed with her plan. She said softly, "Clemency is very unhappy, you know."

"Unhappy!" He looked at her incredulously. "She did not seem so last night. Indeed, I have never known her to look so blooming!"

"The poor child has learned well the art of dissembling. 'Twas necessary for her own safety."

"Her safety?" Damian echoed, his brows drawing together in a frown. "What can you mean, Beatrix?"

"Rodger is fearfully jealous, you see."

"Actually, I did not see," Damian said. "He did not seem at all jealous. I am sure he was aware of our engagement, and yet he invited me to dine with them and seemed in the best of humor."

"You do not know them as I do." Beatrix was warming to her inventions. "I have lived in their household upwards of four months. You have no idea how often I have had to shield and comfort Clemency from her husband's wrath."

"To shield and comfort *Clemency?*" Damian repeated skeptically. "In the old days—" he began.

She held up her hand. "I know exactly what you are going to say. In the old days, I made sport of her. I was heedless and envious. I admit that freely."

" 'Tis not necessary to admit that 'freely' to me. I know you were," Damian said frankly. He added, "You are suggesting that you have changed."

Beatrix clasped her hands and lowered her eyes. "Yes, I have changed, Damian. You have no idea how very good Clemency has been to me. I came to her with naught but rags on my back. And like the Good Samaritan who reclaimed the beggar, she took me in. She has been kindness itself—which makes it doubly difficult for me to stand by and witness her misery."

"Her misery?"

"Rodger knows of your former love. He has taxed her with it very often. You see, it was her family forced her to marry him. She tried to resist them, but the pressure was too unrelenting. She is very gentle, you know."

"But not weak, if that's what you are suggesting," he said.

"No," Beatrix said ruminatively. "I would not call her weak, but 'tis difficult for her to stand up against constant persuasion. And, poor child, she thought you were dead. Rodger, from what she has let drop—she never actually criticizes him—was extremely persistent and her parents thought it an excellent match. They are old and wanted to see her settled. But I need not explain them to you. You've known them all your life."

"No, you need not explain them to me," he agreed with a trace of bitterness. "I am fully aware that Lady Sayles, for one, thought Clemency could do much better than wed a mere baronet."

It was with considerable difficulty that Beatrix kept her hands clasped. She was in a mood to clap them. She was in a mood to jump up and down. Damian wanted to believe her.

That was exactly what she had hoped would happen. "That is true," she told him regretfully. "They were never in favor of your marriage. They thought it was a mere pact between children and that both of you would outgrow it." It was really lovely, she thought gleefully, how well the truth was blending in with her lies. She added, "Clemency told me that she was minded to run away, but she had no place to go. Her sister Justine, with whom she might have stayed, was equally in favor of the union. Her brother and her other sister, as you know, are never in communication with her."

"Yes, I know," he said gloomily. "They could be living on the moon, as far as poor Clemency is concerned." He was silent a moment and then added, "But if she is as unhappy as you seem to believe, she does mean to hide it very well."

"She did not hide it on the afternoon you appeared. She took to her bed shortly after you left and she did not even come down to supper. But I pray you'll not mention that when you see her. It would distress her to know that I have confided these matters to you. She doesn't want you to know that she's unhappy. She wanted only to arrange a meeting with you. She entrusted me with that."

"She told you to arrange a meeting?" he echoed.

"You asked me why I was here this morning."

"You told me you came her to wait for someone," he reminded her.

She shook her head. "No, I said that I came here to wait, and then we spoke of other things. I did not have the chance to tell you that I was waiting until the sun would be a little higher in the sky. I do not have a watch and that is my way of ascertaining the hour. I was on my way to see you, but I thought it too early to come knocking on your door. Consequently, our meeting has been most fortuitous. Clemency wants to see you, Damian, but alone. Perchance you could meet her—at this pool?"

He was silent a long moment. Then he said bitterly, "And pray, what use would that be, with her wed to Lord Caliban?"

"Oh, you are bitter," she said commiseratingly. "Can you imagine how Clemency feels, now that she knows you are back? At least see her and give her some word of comfort."

"God!" He ran his hands through his hair. "And what comfort will I derive from this errand of mercy, when my own heart . . ." He broke off. "You cannot imagine what it was like to awaken after what seemed a night's sleep and find that the better part of a year had passed. My first thought was of Clemency. As soon as I might, I wrote to her, but evidently she never received my letter."

"The ship might have gone down," Beatrix said, thinking that was very likely and inwardly rejoicing that that dangerous letter had never arrived.

"Possibly it did. These are uncertain times. Uncertain, confusing, miserable. God, I do not want to see her. I wish to hell the regiment would have me again. I need to be out and away from here. Damn you, Beatrix, I was trying to achieve some peace of mind, and you have opened all the wounds again."

"Oh, Damian, I am sorry," she cried. "Believe me, I have had my share of anguish too. But do see Clemency, if not for your sake, for hers. She feels so terribly guilty."

"Guilty?" he repeated. "Why should she feel guilty?"

"Because she thinks she should have been stronger and waited. Believe me. I know her. Her heart is breaking. Tell her that you understand that . . . Oh, I cannot put the words in your mouth, but you do understand what I mean, do you not?"

He nodded. His eyes seemed more gray than blue, an indication of how deeply he had been touched by her tale of Clemency's despair. He said, "Very well, Beatrix, I will see her. I will do my best to see that she does not continue to suffer. Tell her that I will meet her whenever and wherever she chooses."

"Oh, I do thank you, Damian. You are kind."

"And you are kinder. I never dreamed that you would come to care for Clemency so much."

"I am older now and I know what it means to suffer loss." Beatrix fixed melting blue eyes on his face.

"I am sorry for that, my poor girl. I wish something could be done."

"I do not, not any longer," she said with a little catch in her voice. "God has told me to forgive them, and I have done so with my whole heart. As Christ said from his cross, 'Forgive them, for they know not what they do.' "

"Uh, yes." He looked embarrassed, as people often did

when she mentioned God or Christ. She bit down a derisive little smile. "I must go," she murmured. "I am in hopes that I will have an answer for you by tomorrow morning at this time. Can I hope that you will meet me here?"

"I will," he promised.

"I do thank you, Damain—for Clemency. She will be so elated." She moved out of the glade. It was not until she was halfway up the hill that she sought the shade of a tree, and standing against the trunk, laughed until she was weak.

"You cannot be serious!" Clemency stared at Beatrix out of wide horrified eyes. "*Damian?*"

"As I stand here." Beatrix's eyes slid away from Clemency's distressed countenance to look at the beautiful room. It was far larger than the one she occupied. Of course, that was only natural since it was part of the master suite. Generations of Colbournes had been born here. She could not think of that now—or how much she longed to move into these lovely, lovely rooms, herself. She must concentrate upon the matter at hand.

"He seemed in a particularly good mood last night," Clemency said. "I was quite heartened by his attitude, and so was Rodger."

"He is not." Beatrix gave her a reproachful glance. "How could you expect that he would be? It was all pretense with him, and I agree that he carried it off beautifully. But his heart was breaking, Clemency. You are the first thing he remembered when he regained his memory. Can you not envision his agony upon learning how many months had gone by? He knew that you must believe him dead."

"How could I believe otherwise?" Clemency said defensively. Memories were pouring back into her mind, memories that had almost been obliterated by her present happiness. She had been despairing, she recalled—and when her mother insisted she must go to London, she had experienced an even greater agony. It was very difficult to recall the misery of those days in view of her present passion for her husband. It seemed to her that she had loved him all of her life, but that was not true. There had been Damian at a time when she had not really known what it was to love. It had been a childish infatuation—but Damian would not be able to understand that. She said, almost resentfully, "Damian should understand—"

"He understands only that you wed Rodger not six months after his supposed death," Beatrix cut in.

"But that was because . . ." Clemency began, and paused. "At the time, I thought I never would recover from Damian's death, and Mama was insisting I go to London. Rodger understood. He had lost his wife. That was our original reason for coming together—so that neither of us would be forced to marry where we did not choose. We were friends. We thought we would be compatible if not deliriously happy. It was only afterward that I realized how much I loved him."

"I doubt that Rodger thinks often of Inez," Beatrix murmured.

Clemency said gently, "I do not believe that he will ever forget her, but we are happy."

"You must explain to Damian how it happened," Beatrix urged. " 'Tis only fair."

"I wish you might provide that explanation," Clemency sighed.

"I would—but 'tis not me he wishes to see. I doubt that he would believe me. He might think you lured by Rodger's wealth."

"He could not!" Clemency cried.

"Could he not?"

"Does he?"

"I do not know what he thinks. I only know that he is miserably unhappy."

"I cannot believe that he will be any the less unhappy if I see him," Clemency said. "I cannot tell him that anything of my old love for him remains."

"At least see him," Beatrix urged. "You are sensible. It will be helpful just to talk some sense into him. Besides, it is necessary."

"Necessary?"

"You would not want him to put a period to his existence."

"He wouldn't!"

Beatrix looked down. "I am not at all sure of that," she said in a low voice. "He was, as I told you, quite desperate when I encountered him at the pool."

"Very well, I will go to him," Clemency said unhappily.

"When?"

"I will talk to Rodger and perhaps we can both—"

"No," Beatrix protested. "You could not do that. You have told me the circumstances of your marriage. Very likely Rodger will prevent you from seeing him. He might even call Damian out."

"He wouldn't!" Clemency cried.

"He might easily believe you are making excuses to see Damian again. What other reason could you give? That Damian is dying of love for you? How would your husband react to that? And what would poor Damian think, seeing you arrive with Rodger at your side? Best meet him in private and have done—then there will be no repercussions or complications. You did not see your face when Damain arrived, but I did, and so, unfortunately, did Rodger. It was easy to see he suspected the worst."

"Oh, God," Clemency muttered, remembering Rodger's leaving while she was still watching Damian ride away. She recalled her own qualms concerning his suspicions. She had managed to alleviate them, but there was no telling what he would think if she insisted on seeing Damian again. She would have to explain far too much. She turned troubled eyes on her cousin's equally troubled face. "I imagine you are right. Very well, I will see Damian alone. Tell him I will meet him by the pool."

"When?"

Clemency pondered. " 'Tis Rodger's habit, as you know, to rest after our midday meal. I imagine that would be the best time."

"Yes, I do believe you are right. He will sleep, and by the time he awakens, you will be home. Do you wish to make it tomorrow at three?"

"At three," Clemency agreed.

"I will tell him," Beatrix said. "I will go to his house immediately."

Watching Beatrix as she quitted the room, Clemency felt very uncomfortable. She would have preferred to tell Rodger the whole of the situation, but as Beatrix had said, it would be awkward. Besides, she could not guess how Rodger would react, being informed that Damian was still in love with her. If she explained that she was going to see him, he would naturally want to come with her, and that *would* distress Damian. She owed something to her old love, but Damian would not understand that. Her face grew warm as she remembered other meetings beside the pool, meetings sparked by his gentle caresses and by his far-from-gentle kisses. She had returned those kisses, had clung to him, had told him over and over again how much she loved him, and now she would have to explain . . . But what could she say? The task of bringing understanding to him was one she wished heartily that she might avoid. Perhaps she would be wiser on the morrow. She truly hoped so!

Much the same sentiments that had plagued her the previous afternoon were going through Clemency's mind as she rode through the woods bound for the pool.

She had not told Rodger that she intended to ride after their meal. She rolled her eyes. It had been a very difficult hour and a half for her. She had been on tenterhooks during that repast, fearing that Rodger would ask her to remain with him during his rest. She had been desperately searching for excuses when his voice had broken in on her chaotic thoughts.

"You seem uncommon edgy, my love," he had commented. "Is there anything the matter?"

"Matter?" she had answered, and forced a smile. "No, I was not aware that I seemed edgy. I am not, not in the least."

Her very assurance had been edgy and she had not looked at him. Fortunately, Beatrix had come to her rescue. "I expect 'tis the weather. You'd not think that with these thick stone walls we would feel the summer's heat to such a degree."

"It is warm." He had nodded.

"Uncommonly warm," Clemency had agreed gratefully. "I think that after we have eaten, I will take a walk in the rose garden." She had continued, daringly, "Will you join me, Rodger?"

His answer had both relieved and concerned her. "I think not, my love. I have been feeling a bit run-down of late and in the summer I am often prone to bouts of malaria."

"Then you must rest, of course," she had said. Thinking of that exchange, she felt the chill that always came when she was reminded of her husband's uncertain health. It was so unfair that he should continue to suffer from maladies contracted nearly four years ago. It was the fault of the war—everything that had happened to him could be blamed on that. Yet, if it had not been for the war, she would not have been wed to him and happier than than she had ever been in her whole life. She tensed. She had come in sight of the grove where lay the pool and where Damian waited. And now it was up to her to reassure him and comfort him—because their love had been another casualty of the war.

She slid off Apollo's back, and taking him by the reins, moved toward the trees, wishing now that she had never chosen this particular spot for their rendezvous. It held far too many memories. Reluctantly she thought of a younger, excited Clemency, tying her mount to one of the low-hanging tree branches and hurrying to meet an eager Damian.

She attached the reins to the adjacent branch of a tree and went into the clearing by the pool. He was standing there staring into its green depths. He did not turn as she approached.

"Damian," she murmured, and was further assaulted by her memories as he turned.

His eyes were bleak and brooding. He said harshly, "I have been asking myself why I was fool enough to come."

His comment confused her. "I thought you wanted to see me."

"I did . . . I do. I have dreamed about this meeting for months. Even when my mind was a blank, washed clean of all I had known in my former life, I think I dreamed of you, Clemency. *Clemency*. Do you know what that means? I shall tell you. It means a 'disposition to be merciful.' 'Twould have been more merciful if you had not come. No, it was merciful of you to come . . ."

"Damian," she said unhappily, "please . . ."

He moved toward her. "I am told you are miserable. But you were comforted uncommonly quick, were you not? And I was forgotten in less than a year, not even half a year, I'm told."

"You were not forgotten," she cried. "Only—"

"Only Lord Colbourne with castle in hand came to woo and was not turned away. You could not resist his many attractions. Was that it?"

"No, that was not it. I married him—"

"Oh, Christ, married . . . those words . . . you *married*," he groaned.

"Damian, dear, I beg you will listen to me," she cried.

"I do not want to listen. I want to look at you," he said passionately. "I did not dream that you could become more beautiful, but you are. Are you really unhappy? I can hardly credit it. The other night you sat at that table like a queen. You did not look unhappy. You smiled, you laughed. Were you entertained by my tale?"

"You seemed . . . I thought . . ." She faltered. "Oh, Damian, how can I explain?"

"Do not explain," he begged. "Do not say anything." He covered the space between them in two strides, and seizing her in his arms, kissed her suffocatingly. She tried to struggle, but she was no match for his strength. Panic surged through her. Panic and anger. It was a long moment before he released her.

"Oh . . ." She put a hand to her mouth. Her lips felt bruised. She said angrily, "How could you?"

He turned a deep red. "I thought that was what you wanted," he said roughly.

"Wanted?" She regarded him incredulously. "No! Why would you imagine—"

"Why?" he interrupted. "Why did you arrange this assignation, then?" He glared at her.

"Assignation! It was nothing of the kind," she cried hotly. "I came because I was told you were unhappy. I came because I wanted to explain matters. What other reason would I have for coming?"

"What indeed?" he demanded harshly. "Only Beatrix told me that you were miserably unhappy. She hinted that you might still care for me."

"She couldn't have!" Clemency cried. "Unless . . ."

"Unless what?"

"Unless she wanted to spare your feelings. . . . She might have meant it as a kindness."

"Is Beatrix really so kind?" he mused.

"Oh, yes, she is a different person. She has suffered a great deal and borne it so bravely. She hates to see others unhappy, but she should not have led you to believe that I still cared for you. Rather I do care for you, Damian, I shall always care for you—but in a different way. I am sorry if I am hurting you . . ."

"You do love him, then?" he said hopelessly.

"With all my heart, Damian. It is true that when I first wed him, I was most distressed over you. Oh, my dear, I did not understand my heart at all. You may hate me for saying this, but I have learned the difference between affection and love. There is a wholeness to love that . . . that . . ."

"I know that, Clemency," he said miserably. "I thought you did, too. You led me to believe—"

"Because I believed it too," she interrupted. "That is why I originally accepted Rodger's proposal."

"Because you thought you loved me?" he asked ironically.

"Listen to me, Damian." She looked at him earnestly. "Please."

He moved away from her and settled down on the bank near the water. "I am listening," he said resignedly.

Beyond the grove of trees, Beatrix crouched near Clemency's chestnut. It had been difficult to control her impatience, and for a brief moment she had feared that the only scheme which had occurred to her would prove as unfruitful to her as all the others she had evolved in regards to this meeting she had arranged.

When she had originally talked Clemency into meeting Damian, she had had it in mind to find some way of alerting Rodger to their plans, but outside of directing him to the woods, she found herself stymied. In betraying Clemency, she would not only be betraying her part in the plan, she would be sent packing. Rodger would never thank her for her good offices on his part. Consequently, she had racked her brains in vain. Then Clemency herself had provided the solution. She had decided to ride rather than walk! She had confessed to not feeling up to snuff and she had looked a trifle peaked, too, Beatrix thought—but her state of health was of little matter. She had ridden here and, as always, had tethered her horse to that hanging branch she had used for years. Beatrix had hoped for that, since the tree in question was a good distance from the pool. Clemency, deep in her role of comforter, would not hear the dry summer grasses crackling under her footsteps. Or if she did, she would not identify the sound as a footfall. That she had not had been proved a few minutes ago when Beatrix had made her move.

The chestnut was looking down at her. She patted its nose and whispered to it. She had always had a way with animals, she thought with some little satisfaction. She quickly unknotted the reins, and giving the horse a smart slap on its rear, sprang back, and as it snorted and leapt forward, she dodged back, fleeing into the forest, plunging deep among a growth of ferns she had noted earlier. That sound was muffled by the hooves of the chestnut as it sped away. In another second she was rewarded by the sight of Clemency hurrying out of the grove with Damian behind her. They looked startled and alarmed. In another moment they were out of her sight, searching, no doubt, for the horse.

"I thought I had tied him sufficiently tightly."

"Evidently you did not."

"Did you hear him snort? I wonder what startled him?"

Damian's reply was muffled.

Beatrix, a hand over her mouth to stifle her laughter, left her hiding place and went back the way she had come, following a path that would bring her to the castle well ahead of Clemency.

Thanks to the cooperation of those three Fates, the first part of her plan had gone exactly as she had expected it would. The horse would return riderless to the stables. Clemency would take a much longer time to trudge back to the castle, even if Damian carried her before him part of the way. she would have considerable difficulty inventing an explanation as to why her walk in the rose garden had turned into a ride through the woods. It was a shame, at least for her, that Clemency was basically truthful.

If such a mischance had happened to her, Beatrix, she would have torn her dress, placed a few scratches on her arms, and rolled in the dust. A limp would also be in order, and no one would question the fact that she had been tossed from her saddle. She did not credit Clemency with similar ingenuity.

And what would be the result? Rodger, alerted to the fact that her riderless horse had returned to the stables, would be naturally upset. Clemency, distraught and frightened, would have considerable difficulty explaining what had happened. Meanwhile, she, having reached the castle long before her cousin arrived, would carefully cover for her in a way that might easily be disbelieved. It was not quite as satisfactory as the scene she had originally envisioned—in which Rodger, led to the pool, would find his wife with her onetime lover. Unfortunately, she had been unable to implement that particular plan. However, this one was equally satisfactory. She could be reasonably sure of that!

11

Beatrix's entrance and egress from the castle had been through a crevice in the garden wall, one almost concealed by vines. She had found it on her second morning at the castle. Several bricks had fallen and no one had bothered to replace them. Early this morning she had visited that spot again and found to her delight that the crevice was just large enough to accommodate her. Subsequently she had crawled through and made a little heap of stones to mark the place.

She had found it easily enough on her way back and she had crouched by the walls, her ears straining to hear the clink of the gardener's shears or the chop of the hoe. Some of the men were wont to hum as they worked, but all was silent now. Slipping through the aperture, she carefully rearranged the vines. In a few moments she reached the grotto pool and washed the dirt from her hands and face. She was shaking the dust from her garments when she heard Charlie, the head groom, yelling, "Saddle 'is lordship's 'orse."

Beatrix's eyes lighted. She was positive that Clemency's mount had returned, and she had feared that Rodger would have already gone off to search for his wife. She was pleased that he had not. She was not quite sure what she would say to him, but, she reasoned as she hurried up a path that would bring her to the front of the castle, she would think of something. She was nearing the huge oaken door that opened on the main hall when Rodger, booted and spurred, emerged from it, looking alarmed. She also thought that she read confusion in his glance.

Reaching him, Beatrix looked at him in artfully simulated

surprise. "You are riding?" she questioned. "I thought you had intended to rest this afternoon."

His face was marked with strain. "Clemency's horse has returned—riderless," he rasped.

"Oh, no, what could have happened to her?" Beatrix cried. "I told her . . ." She bit her lip and broke off.

"You knew she was going riding?" he questioned.

"I . . . thought she . . . she might." Beatrix faltered. "Oh, dear, she must have been thrown. 'Tis very treacherous through the . . . the . . . around here. Badgers—I mean, their holes . . . Oh, gracious, I must sound sadly confused."

His frowning gaze rested on her face. "Do you know where she went?"

"I think . . . but I am not sure . . . And besides . . ."

"You are not making yourself very clear, Beatrix," he commented. "Do you or do you not know where my wife went?"

The sound of hooves was in her ears again. Out of the corner of her eye she saw a groom leading Rodger's gray stallion Balthazar toward them. She clasped her hands. "I am sorry, Rodger, but I have sworn that I would not betray Clem . . . I mean . . . Oh, Rodger, pray forgive me." Her easy tears welled up and slid down her cheeks.

"My dear Beatrix, please tell me what's amiss. What is this talk of betrayal?"

"N-nothing . . . I beg you will forget it. Clemency took me in, I owe her my loyalty, but while we t-talk, she might be in . . . in dire trouble. Please go look for her." She burst into tears and dashed back into the garden. From a spot near a large oak tree, she watched Rodger mount the gray. Her eyes glinted with amusement. Another idea had occurred to her, and she would soon plant it in soil that was now fertilized and ready to receive what would grow in it.

Standing at the foot of the hill, Clemency stared up at the castle. It seemed very far away, and the road was so steep. From this distance it glittered like glass under the rays of the unrelenting sun. She had hard thoughts for her chestnut, who was probably in the stable by now, his head thrust into a bag of oats. How could he have slipped his tether? She had tied him securely—at least she thought she had. And poor Rodger must be so worried. He would imagine that she had been thrown. And now she would have to tell him the truth, a rather awkward truth, since she had mentioned nothing about her meeting with Damian before.

"Put the blame on me," Damian had instructed. "Say that I begged you to come. 'Tis no more than the truth."

But the meeting had been mainly of Beatrix's arranging. Clemency frowned and flushed, remembering her initial panic when she found the horse had bolted. Her first thoughts had been of Rodger. "He will be terrified that I have been hurt or even killed." She had glared at Damian accusingly. "I never would have come had not Beatrix told me that you were desperate enough to contemplate suicide."

"Whaaat?" He had regarded her out of wide, disbelieving eyes. "I never said such a thing!"

"It did not sound like you," she had agreed.

"My dear Clemency, much as I love you—and I do love you—such a thought never crossed my mind. It is true that I am unhappy over your marriage, but not, my dearest girl, enough to put a pistol to my head or a dagger to any other vital part." He had actually laughed, and she, much to her surprise, had also laughed. Their mutual merriment had had the effect of making them both feel much better, and suddenly Damian was no longer her discarded lover, but the friend he had always been. She was reasonably sure that he felt the same way, for he had visibly relaxed.

However, Beatrix's report had puzzled her. "I do not understand it," she had said. "Why would Beatrix believe—"

"Best ask her," he had interrupted. "And my advice to you is to tell Rodger of her machinations."

"Machinations?" she had repeated. "You are suggesting that she willfully misconstrued your feelings and mine?"

"It would not surprise me." His smile had fled and he had looked uncommonly grim.

"Oh, no, Damian—what reason would she have for that? Besides she is much changed. She has become very devout. She has begged me to open the chapel so that she might go in there to pray. She is forever reading her Bible—and I think she knows most of it by heart."

"The Devil can quote Scripture," he had quipped.

"No, she is wholly sincere. After Lieutenant Palmer's

family refused to harbor her, she was in dire straits and she was rescued from starvation by an evangelical society, which she joined."

"Saint Beatrix?" He raised his eyebrows.

"It's true," Clemency had insisted.

"Well, I did catch an evangelical turn of phrase to her speech," he had commented dryly. "But it did surprise me that Palmer's family would not take her in. However, that's not your concern or mine. Look, my love, do you need to tell your husband that you met me? You could always say that you'd gone riding and—"

"Oh, no," she had protested. "I do not like lying to him. And there's no reason to lie. I will tell him exactly what happened."

"Best let Beatrix be your witness and explain her part in our meeting."

"I do not need a witness," she had flashed. "He will believe me. Why should he not?"

"Why indeed?" He had brought her hand to his lips. "No one fortunate enough to be wed to you would distrust you for long. They would know, as do I myself, that you are the very soul of integrity."

Beatrix, Clemency decided, must have based her conclusions concerning Damian's desperation on his attitude rather than anything he had said. He *was* unhappy—there was no doubting that. And certainly she had led her cousin to believe that she was equally unhappy—instead of confused and bewildered as she had been that first day that Damian had suddenly appeared. Basing her opinions on Clemency's old passion for Damian, Beatrix must have discounted her protests to the contrary and decided that she was concealing her true feelings. Or was that true?

A flicker of suspicion stirred in her consciousness. Had Beatrix, as Damian hinted, purposely tried to make trouble between herself and Rodger? But what would be her reason? She could think of none. And nor could Beatrix have anticipated the complications that had arisen because her chestnut Apollo had gotten away. If that had not happened, no one would have known why she had left the castle grounds and she would have been back long before Rodger awakened.

For a moment she *was* tempted to take Damian's advice

and not mention their meeting. However, that was dangerous. Lies engendered more lies, and as her mother had always said, one did need a good memory to be a liar. Clemency shook her head and smiled ruefully. Apollo would not get any sugar from her tomorrow morning. It was really too annoying, but it was amusing, too.

Rodger was very fond of the poet Walter Scott and could recite whole cantos of his *Lay of the Last Minstrel*. She could imagine him quoting to her, "Oh, what a tangled web we weave/ When first we practice to deceive." Undoubtedly he would tease her unmercifully. With a groan she started up the steep winding road to the castle.

Beatrix had waited and waited, and finally, standing at the far end of the road, she saw Rodger returning. He was riding slowly. His horse was covered with foam and he was hung over in his saddle. He looked the very picture of weariness. She watched as the gatekeeper admitted him, and now she saw that Rodger seemed relieved. He had been informed that Clemency had returned.

As he started up the driveway, she came out from where she had been standing. He reined in immediately and stared down at her in some surprise. "I am told that my wife has returned safely," he said.

"That is true." Beatrix nodded. She swallowed convulsively. "I have been waiting for you. I must speak to you."

"Clemency has not taken any hurt, has she?" he demanded anxiously.

"No, but I thought you must want some explanation of my reticence. After you rode off, I was most disturbed."

"Disturbed?" Rodger echoed. He dismounted and stood facing her. "What is amiss?"

"I was not honest with you. I have prayed about it and God has told me that I owe you the truth."

"The truth?" he questioned.

Beatrix nodded. "You see, I knew where you could find Clemency, but I had been *sworn* to secrecy." She heaved a great sigh. "Still, it does go against my nature and my faith to bear false witness. Also have I read God's instruction against the flattering tongue and against the man who goeth in to his neighbor's wife."

"His neighbor's wife?" Rodger's eyes narrowed. "What are you trying to tell me, Beatrix?"

"I am . . . Oh, dear, this does go against the grain with me! Clemency has been so kind to me, but," she burst out, "I am telling you that you never should have returned to the castle, not at this time. Oh, God, what ill wind blew you and Clemency here at a time when Damian arose from the dead? I know she was faced with too great a temptation. I knew it the day we returned and she stood there staring after him, fighting with her better nature. I pray you will forgive her for being weak. We women do not have the strength of men. I was weak today when I did not tell you at once that I knew where she went. 'Twas to meet Damian, of course. She swore me to secrecy, as I said. She told me you would never, never understand and she had to see him. Mind you, I do not think there was more to the encounter than a wish to see him again . . . but still I should have told you what she intended. Unfortunately, I was confused. I thought my loyalty lay with the one who had succored me and lifted me from the mire. However, I never agreed to lie for her. That goes against my conscience and I went to the chapel and prayed about it. The Lord has spoken to me in the stillness. He has told me that I must reveal my part in this deception."

"I see," he said heavily, his gaze turned bleak.

"Do you, and do you forgive me?" She lifted anguished eyes to his face.

"Yes, I forgive you. I know that you are a woman of great principle."

"I am, but I was not always. 'Twas hard won. I was once a sinner—until I accepted Jesus Christ and his Father. But now I feel only pity for those who are not as strong as I have become. And, again, I must impress upon you that Clemency did want to comfort Damian. He was greatly cast down. She told me that she could see that last night. She knows him so well—as I told you, they were very close before he went away—almost too close. It used to worry my aunt. And so naturally Clemency thought that poor Damian was owed an explanation as to why she did not hold to her promise and wait for him."

"I wish she might have explained all this to me as well." He frowned.

"She feared you would not understand. Neither of us did. That is why I did not hasten to tell you that I knew she was with Damian—by the pool. I shall quite understand if you wish me to leave."

"To leave? No, of course not. You are not to blame for this sorry little intrigue."

She stared into his frowning face and quickly lowered her eyes. "Oh, dear, I do wish you would not call it so."

"Can you think of a better description?" He smiled mirthlessly.

"I would, if I were in your place, be inclined to give dearest Clemency the benefit of the doubt. And I think you must, too. Still . . . if you'd deign to take my advice, I would not make Damian too welcome here." Her hand flew to her mouth. "Oh, dear, what am I saying? I am Clemency's friend and her close relation. She saved my life—but in the quietness of the chapel, God came to me and warned me that I have an even closer relationship to him . . . an allegiance that cannot be broken. Oh, dear." She wrung her hands. "I am afraid that Clemency will look upon me most hardly. She'll think I have no loyalty."

"She will know nothing of what you have told me," he said curtly.

"Does that mean you will not tell her?"

"I will not betray your confidence," he said dully. "And I suppose I must thank you, Beatrix."

"Oh, dear, I see that I have hurt you. Would it have been better to leave you in ignorance?" As he shook his head, she whispered, "Clemency is very fond . . . I mean, she does love you, Rodger. I know she does."

"I must be getting in," he said.

"Oh, Rodger, I pray you will not look so . . . so . . . Oh, dear, I shall pray for you. I shall pray for you both."

A short time later, Beatrix knocked softly at Clemency's door. On being admitted, she found her cousin lying on her chaise longue. She was looking extremely weary. "My dear," Beatrix said in accents of regret, "I think you have exerted yourself too much today."

"It was uncommonly warm," Clemency sighed. "A pox

on that horse! I almost think he developed fingers in his hooves."

Beatrix laughed. "That is a quaint conceit, I must say. Be that as it may, Rodger is back."

"Oh, is he!" Clemency sat up.

"I met him as he was riding to the stables."

"Did you? I hope he's not too tired." Clemency regarded her anxiously. " 'Twas such a shame to have interrupted his rest—and 'tis so hot outside."

"It is. . . ." Beatrix hesitated and then added, "I know I should not have taken it upon myself, but I told him you were back and I explained you'd gone to meet Damian. I told him why, too."

Clemency's eyes widened. "Did you? Why did you not leave that to me?"

"I had intended to . . . but he looked so worried, not finding you . . ."

"I see." Clemency frowned. "I wish . . . Oh, well, never mind. What did he say?"

"Not very much."

"Oh, Lord, I expect he is very angry with me."

"If he is, 'tis a passing thing." Beatrix looked down. "I know he'd not remain angry with you for long."

Clemency regarded her cousin with considerable annoyance. "I expect that you believed you were acting in my behalf, Beatrix, but I do wish you'd not interfered on this particular occasion. I am quite capable of providing my own explanations."

"Oh, dear." Beatrix gave her a stricken look. "I did not mean to interfere, truly I did not. But he looked so confused, I felt he must be told something. You know I have only your best interests at heart . . . always and forever."

"I suppose that when he hears the whole story, he'll understand." Clemency tried to quell an anger that was two parts anxiety. Probably she ought to soothe Beatrix, too. Her big eyes were full of tears. Undoubtedly it was wrong of her to wish that dear Beatrix was at the other end of the earth. She could not refrain, however, from saying, "I do wish I'd told him the truth in the beginning."

"You are blaming me, are you not?" Beatrix sighed dolefully.

Clemency swallowed the logical answer and said with some difficulty, "I expect I must blame myself for making everything so complicated. I ought to have explained immediately. Damian, by the way, is not suicidal."

"He seemed so yesterday," Beatrix said earnestly. "He was so desperate . . . but perhaps you think I am lying?"

"No," Clemency said slowly. "You have no reason to lie, my dear. I expect you mistook his air of gloom. 'Tis fashionable to be gloomy. Lord Byron has made it so." Clemency's laugh was not entirely successful. She threw a look at the connecting door. "I expect I must have it out with Rodger. 'Twill serve nothing to prolong the evil day."

"Why do you not wait?" Beatrix asked. "He is very tired."

"I think I had better take my own advice in this matter, Beatrix," Clemency said almost sternly. "I am sure he'll want an explanation from my own lips. I do not want to leave him perplexed, as I am sure he must be." She rose and went to her mirror. "Oh, dear, I do look a fright. My nose is red and my hair's a bird's nest. I'd best ring for Rose. No, I think I can manage my horrid hair . . . and perhaps a dash of powder for my nose."

"I will comb your hair," Beatrix offered.

"There's no need."

"Nonsense, my love, of course there is. You've never been able to arrange your curls properly, and you should always look your best for dear Rodger." Beatrix moved to the dressing table and took up the comb. "Sit down," she ordered, indicating the chair.

"Oh, very well." Though she was still annoyed, Clemency managed a smile. "You do have a way with hair. Whatever will I do when you leave?"

The comb dropped from Beatrix's hand. "You want me to . . . to leave?"

Again Clemency had some difficulty in masking what she was beginning to fear was a forlorn hope. She said gently, "Of course not, my dear. I was only thinking of that evil day when some gentleman offers for you and you accept. I cannot think that will be very far off—with you looking so lovely."

Beatrix said, "I do thank you for those kind words,

Clemency, but you may be assured I will be with you a very long time."

Clemency's teeth came together with a click. However, she managed a smile as she said, "You may change your mind, you know."

" 'Tis not likely," Beatrix said firmly. "I loved my dearest Ralph above all other men. I worshiped him as I might a . . . heathen idol. I put him above God himself. And God has punished me for my great sin. He took my husband and my child. I know that in this life I'll not be able to wed again."

"I cannot believe God would be so cruel," Clemency assured her earnestly.

"The way of the transgressor is hard." Beatrix picked up the comb..

Remembering that she faced a mirror, Clemency hurriedly produced another smile. "I will pray, too, that you be forgiven, my dear," she said earnestly.

Clemency had expected to find Rodger in the library, but she was told by Maria, one of the parlor maids, that immediately upon his return his lordship had gone to his room. That surprised her. One would have thought he must come to her in search of the explanation he must surely want. Yet, thinking on it, she guessed that his long, fruitless ride in the hot sun must have wearied him to the degree that he could only think of resting. She emitted a sigh of relief. From what Beatrix had told her, she had expected some manner of reproach, but evidently he was not as angry as her cousin hinted he might be. She returned to her room. She was half-inclined to open the connecting doors, but probably it was best to let him sleep. She could do with some sleep herself. The long walk in the sun had tired her greatly. They would meet at supper.

He did not come to supper.

Staring at her husband's empty place, Clemency had an anxious look for Beatrix. " 'Tis such a pity. He could have been spared these needless exertions. I think I'd best go to him now."

"If he is resting—" Beatrix began.

"No matter, I must see if he is feeling poorly. His leg, you know." Clemency rose from the table and hurried upstairs. She knocked tentatively at Rodger's door.

Jenkins opened it. Much to her surprise and indignation, he planted himself firmly on the threshold as if actually barring her way. " 'Is lordship's not feelin' 'is best, milady. 'E's issued strict orders that I mustn't admit nobody."

Clemency visited a freezing look upon the valet. "I am not nobody, Jenkins. Please be good enough to stand aside and let me enter."

For one pregnant moment it seemed as if the man had no intention of obeying her, but then he nodded and moved aside. "Yes, your ladyship," he muttered.

Sweeping past him, Clemency turned back to say coldly, "You may go."

"Yes, milady." He bowed and went out.

Clemency frowned. Jenkins deserved a harsh set-down. His attitude, a strange combination of servility and stubbornness, left much to be desired, even though he did seem totally dedicated to Rodger. Indeed, he seemed to have constituted himself her husband's unofficial guardian, but surely he did not need to bar the door against his wife! Something must be said to Rodger concerning the man's officiousness—but these comments must be reserved for a later time. She went on into the bedchamber.

Rodger was lying on his back. He looked very pale and his eyes were shut. However, as Clemency came to stand at the foot of the bed, they opened. His gaze was so hard and frigid, it shocked her.

"Did not Jenkins inform you that I was resting?" he inquired.

"He did," she said. "But I was concerned about you, my darling." She longed to settle down on the edge of the bed and kiss him—but he looked so forbidding that she did not dare. He must be even angrier than Beatrix had hinted. Unconsciously she grasped the footpost. "I hope you did not take too much harm from your ride."

"No, I did not take too much harm from it," he said.

"Oh, Rodger," she burst out. "I am indeed sorry that you were forced to go out searching for me. I knew you must be alarmed when Apollo returned without me. If only I could have reached you in time, but—"

"But you were not walking in the rose garden, were you?"

She tensed. His eyes had narrowed and his tone had been extremely caustic. "You must know I was not. Beatrix told me that she explained where I was and why."

"Yes, she explained," he agreed.

"She did tell you about Apollo breaking free from his tether while Damian and I were talking, did she not?"

"She told me that, too."

"I am sure you are wondering why I did not tell you I would be meeting Damian."

"It did surprise me," he admitted.

She regarded him nervously. She could not quite fathom his mood. Was he hurt or angry? Probably he was both. She wished she could supply him with a more cogent reason for what he must consider her arrant deception. If she were to provide it, however, she must needs involve Beatrix, and some of his anger would fall on her. That would not be fair—Beatrix had only been trying to help her.

"Damian, you see, sent me word that . . . that he was miserable. He suggested that he might do something desperate if I did not meet him. But I thought you might not like me seeing him again, and I thought, too, that you might not approve his asking me to come. I expect I was being overcautious—"

"Have I seemed such an ogre to you?" he interrupted.

"No, but I was confused and also I was most concerned about Damian. I knew I would not remain long with him, but also I felt I could not refuse his request. So I went. I did not stay with him long, either. I was just about to leave when Apollo galloped away."

"That was most unfortunate," he said coolly.

"Yes, it was 'Twas a very long walk back, and all uphill."

"Damian ought to have taken you."

"He offered, but . . . well . . ."

"It would have been awkward," he said.

"Well, it would have been, since . . . Oh, dear Rodger. I cannot blame you for being extremely annoyed with me. But that is all there was to it."

"I see. I thank you for coming to explain the situation, my dear."

She regarded him uncertainly. His manner was still so cold. "I do hope you believe me," she said nervously.

"Is there any reason why I should not?"

"No, none."

"Then of course I believe you. As for Damian . . ."

She tensed. "You are not thinking of calling him out or anything, are you?"

"My dueling days are at an end, I fear. I was about to say that you may see him whenever you choose."

She released a caught breath. "I do thank you for being so very understanding, Rodger. I knew you must be, once I told you what happened."

"I am, but I am also extremely weary, my dear. I was close to falling asleep when you came in, so I would appreciate it if we ended this conversation. I need to sleep, and so, I think, must you, after all your exertions this day. Will you please send Jenkins to me on your way out?"

Clemency felt a throb at the bottom of her throat. There was something intensely odd about his manner. He seemed most unlike himself, and she did not understand his coolness of tone. That seemed to belie his insistence that he believed her explanation. Yet why would he not believe her? More important than that, why had he dismissed her so coldly? He must be much more weary than she had imagined. Otherwise he would have wanted her to remain with him. She said, "Of course, my love. I am very sorry that I kept you from your sleep." Obediently she left the room.

12

Clemency lay in bed. She felt empty inside and that was because immediately upon awakening she had been extremely sick. It was the third morning she had felt so queasy. It was really horrid. She had thought when it first happened that she had eaten something that disagreed with her. However, she should have recovered by now. She reached for the cup of tea Rose left for her and sipped it. That did seem to make her feel better. She wondered if her inexplicable nausea had anything to do with her current state of mind.

Mr. Mitchell, the family physician, had once told her mother that strong emotions often produced adverse bodily reactions. She was certainly prey to a very strong emotion—an anger that, at times, bordered on fury. It was coupled with a large sense of resentment. She had always loathed injustice in any form, and Rodger was being totally unjust! She never would have suspected that he could be so obtuse or so implacable.

In the fortnight that had passed since her meeting with Damian, he had been totally unreasonable. In spite of his assurance that he had believed her explanation, obviously he had been lying. He did not believe it. In the beginning, she had been terribly hurt and anxious to justify herself—even though no justification was necessary, not that she could see. She had told him the truth!

"Damn him," Clemency muttered with a glare at the door between their rooms. It no longer stood open, had not been opened for a fortnight. It remained as closed as his mind!

There was no challenging him on his obvious disbelief. Neither by word nor look did he ever refer to it. He was polite, pleasant, and distant, as distant as any stranger. The camaraderie that they had enjoyed might never have existed. And in the last week she had scarcely seen him. He had explained in that new, overly polite manner he employed whenever they were together that he was occupied with the affairs of the estate.

" 'Twas sadly neglected when we were in London enjoying ourselves, my dear," he had said.

Had they enjoyed themselves in London? she wondered bitterly.

Yes, they had. He had been a different person then. He had been warm and loving and kind—in short, the man she had always known. What had happened to him? It seemed, almost, as if he had been stolen by wicked fairies and a changeling put in his place. Yesterday was a case in point.

He had remained at home, closeted in the library with Mr. Murchinson, his man of business. She had Beatrix to thank for that information, Beatrix to thank for having demeaned herself by trying to effect some manner of reconciliation, where none was desired, obviously! Beatrix had suggested that she try to talk to him after Mr. Murchinson left.

"He does not want to talk to me," she had snapped.

"My dear, he does. I am sure he is sorry for the strange way he has been acting."

"Are you suggesting that you know my husband better than I do?"

Beatrix had looked very hurt. "It's only that I do not believe either of you is thinking very clearly these days, my love. Naturally, I would never try to explain Rodger's odd behavior, but jealousy does cloud the understanding."

"He has no reason to be jealous. He has never been jealous before "

"You never gave him cause."

"I did not give him cause this time."

"Yes, but the fact that you did not tell him the truth immediately does make a difference. I hold myself accountable for that, and I am most desperately sorry. My advice was completely wrong. If it would help, I would be glad to explain my part in it."

"No, you thought you were acting for the best. I do not want to bring his wrath down on your head as well."

"My dear, you are an angel!"

"No, I am not," she had disputed hotly. "No angel would want to black both of Rodger's eyes."

"My dear!" Beatrix had been shocked. "A soft answer turneth away wrath."

"I have given him far too many soft answers."

Clemency ground her teeth, hating herself for the lingering hope that had made her agree to Beatrix's gentle persuasions. No doubt her cousin had believed she was acting for the best, even though she had admitted that she found Rodger's attitude entirely incomprehensible.

"Eventually he must realize his mistake," she had insisted. " 'Tis a pity Damian is away, else I am sure he would come to your defense."

"How do you know he is away from home?" Clemency had asked.

"I went to see him in hopes that I could get him to corroborate your story, but his servant told me he had gone on a journey."

"I am glad he is gone," Clemency had cried. "I wish never to see him again."

"I am sure you do not mean that, my dear."

"I do! No, I expect I do not, but I wouldn't want him to corroborate anything. I am sure you thought you were acting in my best interests, Beatrix, but I cannot help but feel you were being a little naive in these circumstances. Rodger would never listen to Damian. Obviously he believes that Damian is the cuckoo that invaded his nest!"

"My dear . . ." Beatrix had gazed at her wide-eyed. "What a dreadful thing to say!"

"I believe in calling a spade a spade."

"My darling, certainly I cannot blame you for being hurt and confused, especially since you have been wronged. But I cannot bear to see the two people I love best in this world so estranged, and for no good reason. It is all a sad misunderstanding. Go to him. You might find him in an entirely different frame of mind."

"Very well, I will try," she had agreed reluctantly.

She had come into the library a few moments after Mr. Murchinson departed. She had steeled herself for the interview and also promised herself that she would be as dignified as possible. However, upon entering, she had found Rodger sitting at his desk with his head buried in his hands and his shoulders hunched.

"Rodger!" She had run to him. "What's amiss, dearest? Are you ill?"

He had looked up quickly, and for once his gaze had not been guarded. Instead, it had been full of agony. However, before she could say anything more, it was as though a mask had dropped down over his face, robbing it of all expression, rendering his eyes blank. He had said coldly, "My dear Clemency, I know that you are under the impression that you have married an invalid, but let me assure you that I am in the best of health."

His chill tones had frozen her to the bone and had made her wish strongly that she had never heeded Beatrix's well-meant advice. With equal coldness she had replied, "I am pleased to hear that, Rodger."

"I thank you, my dear. Was there something you wished to say to me?"

"No," she had answered in even colder tones. "I find I have quite forgotten what I meant to tell you. Pray excuse the interruption." Holding herself stiffly, she had gone out of the room. She had resisted a strong impulse to slam the door. That would *not* have been dignified.

It was all such a tempest in a teapot! she thought crossly. No, it was more than that. In fact, though he had never mentioned it, she wondered if that sword-thrust that had created his scar might not have gone deeper and addled his brain. Perhaps he was prone to spells of madness. She had heard of such afflictions. They often attacked members of ancient families. She threw a wry glance at the wall next to her bed. Hanging there was a tapestry worked by the second Baroness of Colbourne in the year 1302, shortly after the castle had been built. This castle had replaced a cruder effort erected by the Colbourne who had left Normandy with William the Conqueror. She did not know how far back the line stretched in France. Then, there was another possibility. Jenkins had told Rose, who had passed the information to her, that he was concerned over his master's long absences from the castle.

" 'E be goin' about too much, that's wot Jenkins says,"

Rose had explained, reflecting the valet's worry in her own eyes. " 'E's not restin' enough. An' Jenkins is afraid 'e might get sick again wi' the fever wot 'e caught in Spain."

Malaria.

Clemency knew very little about the disease, but she had heard that fever could also disturb the mind—yet he did not have any other symptoms.

She drew a long breath and expelled it in a sigh. Just the other day she had received a letter from her mother telling her that they were on their way back to Sayles. They might even have arrived by now. That meant that they would want to entertain Rodger and her. What if he refused to go? What would they think? She felt a sudden longing for her mother and for her home. She wished that she might go back and stay there—but of course her parents would never countenance that. And—

There was a tap at her door. She threw a glance at the communicating door and tensed. A moment later, she relaxed. Whoever wanted her was in the sitting room. "Who is it?" she called.

"Beatrix, my love." Her cousin opened the door a crack. "Have you decided to have all your breakfasts in your chamber?"

Clemency grimaced. "I do not want breakfast."

"My dear." Beatrix came to stand at the foot of the bed. "I know that you have still not achieved a reconciliation—but I still insist that Rodger will come to his senses. When he does, he will not want a wraith for a wife."

"And I say he would not care if I were worn down to a skeleton!" Clemency retorted bitterly.

"You must not starve yourself, my love." Beatrix frowned.

"I am not starving myself. I do not feel like eating. I would not be able to keep any food down. I am dreadfully queasy."

Beatrix regarded her with alarm. "Are you? How long has this been going on?"

"For the last three days."

"Have you tried purging?"

"No, I do not think I need it."

"Well, actually," Beatrix said thoughtfully, "I am in agreement. I think it is because you are suffering over Rodger's inexplicable withdrawal. I must say I do not understand it myself." She came to sit on the edge of the bed. "Oh, Clemency, I cannot bear to see you so unhappy. Pray, let me intercede for you. I mean with Rodger."

"No," Clemency said sharply. "If he will not listen to me, why should he listen to you? I do not want anyone to intercede for me. I am not at fault. He is."

"Oh, dear . . . oh, dear, I cannot understand any of this. Ralph and I had our misunderstandings, but they never lasted more than a few hours. What can be the matter with the man?"

"He is mad, I think."

"Oh, no, my dear. He is only hurt. You should try to reason with him."

"I cannot believe that I am hearing aright." Clemency sat up straight, her fists clenched. " 'Tis impossible to reason with him. You know that. Why do you keep at me with these ridiculous suggestions?"

"Because I know that he is miserably unhappy."

"Good!"

"I cannot speak to you when you are in such a mood. I will pray for you, my dearest. I shall pray for you both—that you achieve your old understanding." Beatrix shook her head and glided out of the room. Once she was in the hall, she quickened her steps and raced down the stairs. Rodger would still be in the breakfast room, debating as to whether or not he should come up to see his wife. Rose, damned interfering little wretch that she was, had told him Clemency was not well! That he had been concerned was only too evident. However, he had seemed relieved when she volunteered to see Clemency. His remarks, though, had been rather ominous.

"I am beginning to think that I have been very hard on poor Clemency," he had said thoughtfully. "After all, we must take into account that she has known young Prior most of her life."

Beatrix had said nothing, hoping that her silence would prove more effective than words, but now she had *words,* words that must impress him and forever destroy any chance of a reconciliation! If all went as she foresaw, it would be more than possible that she would be occupying Clemency's place before the year was out!

She slowed down to a sedate walk as she neared the small octagonal chamber where they breakfasted. As she had hoped, he was still at the table drinking coffee. He looked up as she came in and she could not like the anxiety she saw written large upon his countenance. However, she thought with considerable satisfaction, he would never look anxious again—at least not over Clemency's welfare.

Since they must not be interrupted, she slammed the door and stood against it, looking at him wide-eyed. "Oh, Rodger," she cried piteously.

He looked up startled and alarmed. "Is it Clemency?" he demanded, rising swiftly.

"No." She shook her head. "I cannot bear it. Oh, I cannot."

"My dear Beatrix, what is amiss?" He demanded.

"Oh, Rodger, Rodger . . ." Beatrix collapsed into a chair. "That girl, that wretched, conniving . . . and that we should be so closely related. Oh, I am so ashamed— even though 'tis not my shame. She told me the whole of it just now. She is utterly without scruples! And she seemed to take it for granted that *I* would stand by her and aid her in her deception. And the terrible part of it is that I might have, once. But no longer. I have repented of all that I have done. I have been absolved of my sins. I am saved." She raised her clasped hands and her eyes toward the ceiling. Then she let her hands fall to her side and she bent her head. "I have accepted Christ, our Savior. I am washed in the Blood of the Lamb. But that is something *she* would not understand, who pays only lip service to her God. For old times' sake I have tried to help her, I have kept her confidences. I have never told you that it was she who called you 'Lord Caliban.' "

"Clemency?" He stared at her incredulously. "I cannot believe it."

" 'Tis the truth—may God strike me down in my tracks if I lie. And 'twas in church. She saw you come limping in and she was astounded. She said she would never have known you for the same man. She . . . I know it will wound you deeply when I say this, but I cannot keep silent any longer. She said, 'Sir Knight, I dub thee Lord Caliban,' and she laughed. Damian, who was with us, also laughed. I wanted to sink through the floor."

He sat down again and stared at her. " 'Twas in church that I heard it, a young woman's voice. I heard the laughter, too."

"It was she, but I did not want to tell you. I owed her some loyalty and I found I could not bring myself to repeat that horrid name. But now all loyalty is at an end. You must know her as she is, stripped of all pretensions—as she soon will be, for her sin is compounded and increased. In biblical days, would she be taken to the town square and stoned . . . for her adultery."

"What do you say?" he whispered.

"She is a whited sepulcher, she does look beautiful on the outside, but inside is she full of corruption and sin . . . which she will bring into the world."

"I do not understand. You are not making sense, Beatrix."

"I am sorry. I am having difficulty revealing this ghastly truth to you. Rodger, she is with child! And told me so and prayed that I intercede for her and beg you to forgive her for her dalliance with Damian. 'You would not want me to bear a bastard,' was what she said. 'I need my husband's name, so I pray you, Beatrix, speak for me, because he will not listen to me.' " Beatrix began to sob. She rose from her chair and fell to her knees. "Forgive me that I must be the bearer of these dreadful tidings. But mayhap God will forgive me for baring her secrets . . . but I could not see you, who are so good, so terribly betrayed and shamed."

He said slowly, "She is sure that the child is Damian's?"

Beatrix nodded and got alowly to her feet. "She has told me that she has not been with you for the last fortnight. Is that true?"

He looked at her with a mixture of shock and anger. "She told you that?"

"She told me everything, everything, including the fact that she is sure that the child is of Damian's begetting. You see, the sickness, the morning sickness, usually appears directly after an encounter."

"She has been to see him again?" he demanded.

"She has gone often. You have made that very easy for her, my poor Rodger, being absent so much. You should have watched her more closely."

He clenched his hands. "Damn her, damn her, her child

will not have a father, 'tis true—for I will spit Damian Prior on the end of my sword or send a bullet through his head.''

"Alas, if that were only possible, Rodger—for though I do not hold with violence, I can only feel that he deserves your wrath. But unfortunately, he is gone. That is why Clemency is so desperate."

"Oh, God, God . . ." he said brokenly.

"Yes, you must call upon God to see you through this agony, this callous betrayal. He will help you to bear your sorrow. He is merciful. I wish I might remain also, but . . ."

He regarded her bleakly. "Why do you think you must go?"

"You cannot want me to stay." She began to sob. "Not after what I have told you. I would fain have held the news from you, but my conscience would not let me, my conscience and the duty that I owe to the Almighty."

"You need not go, Beatrix," he sighed. "I would not have you lose your home because of this."

"This is not my home," she said woefully. "I have no home."

"On the contrary, my dear. This is your home as long as you choose to remain here." He rose. "If you will excuse me, I must go."

"To her?"

"No, I cannot look on her at this moment," he said wearily. "There are papers to peruse . . . estate matters." He was limping very noticeably as he left the room.

Beatrix waited until she no longer heard that uneven step in the hall. Then she went up the stairs to her own chamber. She closed the door—but, again, it was only when she was lying facedown on her bed with her face buried in a pillow that she gave way to her triumphant and gleeful laughter.

Clemency had just learned that she was increasing. "Are you sure?" she asked Rose, who had just given her opinion on that delicate subject.

"Oh, yes, milady, me sister Kate 'as 'ad three an' each time she was sick as a dog in the mornin's. Sometimes it lasts longer. Sometimes it takes all day. But mostly it comes in the mornin'."

"I see." Clemency vaguely remembered her sister Justine

saying something of the sort. "Will I be sick every morning until the birth?"

"Oh, no, milady, it gets better after a while, an' then you'll feel just fine." The abigail smiled fondly at her and added, " 'Is lordship ought to be pleased, milady."

His lordship. Clemency frowned. "I expect I must tell him," she mused.

"Oh, yes, milady." Rose stared at her in surprise.

Clemency bit her lip. She had not intended to speak out loud. "I do not expect that he is home," she said hopefully.

"I think 'e is, milady. 'E be in the library. Oh, milady, 'tis wonderful news."

"Um," Clemency murmured. "I hope he will think so." She flushed. It was unlike her to take Rose into her confidence, and it seemed to her that the girl was looking at her very strangely. It was not difficult to ascertain what she must be thinking. Rose had expected her to be excited and thrilled by the news. An ironic smile twitched her lips as she recalled how much she had longed to give Rodger a child. Her heart had ached for the little son who had been born dead, and for his father's agony. Her heart was not aching now. In fact, she was not sure how she felt about bearing the child of this man who had changed so inexplicably and who looked at her so coldly and seemed to avoid her as much as possible, but, she reasoned regretfully, he would have to know about it sooner or later. She said resignedly, "I expect I must get dressed, Rose."

"What do you wish to wear, milady?"

"It does not matter." Clemency shrugged.

"The green muslin, milady?"

"Very well."

Informed by the butler that his lordship was still in the library, Clemency walked slowly through the hall. Arriving at the library doors, she hesitated. If she knocked, Rodger might tell her to go away. Again, her anger at his inexplicable attitude rose. He did not deserve to be told anything, but her sickness would continue, and undoubtedly she must see a physician and learn what to do during her lying-in period—though undoubtedly her mother could advise her. She had half a mind not to tell him anything; but that, she decided, was cowardly. He ought to know, and perhaps the news would gladden him. She frowned, dismissing that particular speculation. She was not some dog hoping for a pat on the head from a master who had been administering nothing but punishments. Rodger had been punishing her ever since he had discovered her in a lie. Had no one ever lied to him before? Now was not the time to think about that. She opened the door and came inside swiftly.

He was sitting at the desk, his head resting on his folded arms. She moved forward and stopped, resisting a wish to ask him if he were ill. He did not relish such questions, and at this particular moment she was not really interested in his health or the lack of it.

"Rodger," she said.

He sat bolt upright, staring at her. His eyes were blazing. "Well?" he rasped.

Clemency took a step backward, wondering at the anger that seemed to be directed at her. What could be the matter with him now? she wondered. "I have something to tell you," she said carefully.

"Yes?"

Confusion warred with fear. He was looking at her with such hatred. Hatred? Had she misinterpreted his expression? No. She quelled an impulse to leave the room. He would believe her afraid of him. She had good reason to be, she thought. However, she was not going to turn tail and flee. She was *not* afraid of him or anyone else. She said steadily, "I am going to have a child."

"Are you?" he said stonily.

Clemency's fear increased. Obviously the man was not sane. She said as calmly as she could, "Yes, I thought you would want to know."

"*Did* you? Might one ask why you held this information from me for so long?"

"What?" she demanded incredulously.

"Has your hearing gone awry? I asked: why . . . you . . . did . . . not . . . tell . . . me . . . about . . . these . . . fine . . . hopes . . . sooner?"

His manner of phrasing his question as well as its content confounded her. Her fear increased. "They are not hopes. I am expecting the child, and the reason, my lord, that I did not tell you before was that I did not know about it until this morning."

"Didn't you?" His voice now held a silky tone she had never before heard from him.

"I begin to think your understanding is sadly clouded, my lord."

"I beg to disagree with you, Clemency. It has never been clearer than at this moment. I presume you wanted to tell me because you were hoping to acquaint the real father with this information."

She felt as if someone had drenched her with cold water. She began to tremble. "The . . . real father?"

"But he is not here, is he? He has gone. That is most unfortunate, my dear. Did he leave before or after you informed him of his happy expectations? Mayhap he did not want to shoulder such a responsibility?"

Clemency backed away. "Who does not want to shoulder . . . What are you saying?"

"I am saying that your dearest Damian has failed you. That is the truth, is it not? And you are willing to use my name to cover your shame."

"Name" and "shame" rhymed. Clemency wondered why she should think of that when what was left of her world had just tumbled down about her ears. She was really frightened now. She said, "I think you must be mad. I could wish that Damian were the father of my child. I could wish that anybody save you had fathered the infant—for 'tis said that insanity runs in the family!"

He rose. "Out of sight, wanton!"

His scar flamed scarlet against his white face. He looked, she thought, like the very incarnation of Wrath. She said scathingly, "If I were you, Rodger, I would consult a physician— for sure you must be in danger of Bedlam." She walked swiftly from the room, and dashing up the stairs, rang for Rose, pacing up and down impatiently as she waited, and trying, albeit not very successfully, to collect her thoughts. She had to be calm, even though her worst fears had been realized. This man, whom she had once revered and loved, was afflicted with madness—and very likely, it was hereditary!

"Why were you so long?" she cried when Rose finally appeared. "No matter, we must go home."

The abigail looked at her in astonishment. "Home, milady?"

"My home. Sayles. I wish to leave as soon as possible, and I charge you: do not tell anyone of my intention. Just pack any garments that were mine before I wed his lordship. And do not take any of the jewelry."

"But, milady, why—?"

Clemency stamped her foot. "Do as I ask, Rose. And I beg you'll not question me. And, oh, yes, do you know where my cousin might be?"

"I believe she is in her room, milady."

"Fetch her, please. I am sure she will want to accompany us."

"Yes, milady." The girl scurried out of the room.

A few minutes later, Beatrix came hastily into Clemency's chamber. "It cannot be true!" she cried. "You are not leaving Rodger?"

Clemency turned a cold, composed face toward her. "Yes, it is true. I am leaving within the hour."

"But why?"

"Because I want my child to be born in a safe place."

"Your child? You are not expecting!"

"Yes, I am. Rose has told me that I have all the symptoms."

"My dear, but this is joyous news! Surely it will bring your husband to his senses. Have you told him yet? You must tell him—no matter what your differences may be, you know."

"I have told him and it has only served to drive him further into madness. He . . . he has dared to accuse me of infidelity . . . of . . . of bearing Damian's bastard."

"Clemency!" Beatrix's hands flew to her ears.

"I am sorry if I have shocked you, Beatrix, but it is true."

"But that does sound m-mad." Beatrix sank down on the bed. "Oh, I have never been so shocked!"

"Nor I . . . and I will bear the child of this . . . this madman!"

"Oh, my love." Beatrix rose and put her arms around Clemency. "What can I say?"

"There is nothing to say." Clemency wrenched off her betrothal and wedding rings, putting them down on her dressing table. "My life with Rodger is at an end. Rather I should say *our* lives, for surely you must come with me."

"Oh, my dearest, if only I could," Beatrix sighed. "I do not know what I will do now."

Clemency gave her a startled glance. "Why can you not come with me?"

"Your mother, child. She would never let me set foot inside Sayles, I am sure of it."

"Oh, that is water under the bridge . . ."

"I hate to suggest that I know your mother better than you, Clemency. Suffice to say that I would not want to put your kind invitation to the test. No, my love, I will go back to London."

"You cannot do that. There's no place for you to stay."

"There is the mission," Beatrix sighed.

"Oh, Beatrix, no. You must not even dream of it. I do not have money . . . but here . . ." Clemency moved to her jewel box. She looked in the bottom and brought out an emerald ring. "This was given me by my uncle. It's nothing of Rodger's. I am leaving all he gave me behind. Take this and sell it. 'Twill fetch a good price and allow you to live comfortably. Let me hear from you and I will send you such monies as you need."

"I cannot!" Beatrix cried.

"You must, and 'tis my advice that you leave as soon as possible. You are not safe here."

"Oh, my dearest, what can I say . . . except may God smile upon you. Who would have expected matters to come to this? I thought your marriage was made in heaven!"

Clemency swallowed a sudden lump in her throat. "I, too, once had that impression. Unfortunately, we were both mistaken."

"Again, I am left without words. My . . . my heart is very full. I never anticipated . . . but why belabor the point. All I can say is that my thoughts will be with you always and I shall pray for you, my dearest Clemency."

"Thank you, Beatrix. I wish you well, wherever you may go." Clemency kissed her.

"And you, my love," Beatrix said fervently as she returned the embrace.

13

Beatrix stood at the window in her room—still her room after six months, lacking only a few days. Her hot gaze was in the distant stretch of sea which, from this vantage point, looked calm. It was not calm. It swelled and seethed. Last week a ship had gone down in its chill waters and most on board had perished. She compared it to herself, serene and calm on the surface, seething beneath, longing to do for Clemency what the ocean had done for HMS *Valiant*. Until Clemency was gone, she would achieve no more than she had already with Rodger. She had his respect. He thought her a good and godly woman, mainly because she had mouthed platitudes concerning her faith until she was sick of uttering them. There were times when she actively hated the man she loved— mainly because he really did not see her and certainly he did not love her.

Despite the fact that she had faithfully nursed him through a bout of quinsy in August, when he had called constantly on Clemency and despite the fact that she had cosseted him and read to him as he recuperated, he had been up and away the minute his health was restored. He had not returned until the first week in November. And when he was back he had overdone both his walking and his riding—spending hours each day overseeing his property and discussing improvements to the tenants' cottages, a waste of money, she thought bitterly. They would not have the sense to appreciate it and, as for Rodger, he had not only strained his leg, which up until then had been improving steadily, he had been bedded with another attack of quinsy. He was still feverish—she had spent most of the night tending him and, again, Clemency's name was on his tongue, though he never mentioned her when he was well.

She woud not have any peace until the girl was dead and he a widower. She smiled. If all went well, he would be in that condition before another day passed. The note she had sent to Sayles would do the trick. She did not doubt that Clemency would meet her at the pool. She had prudently kept in touch with her cousin, sending her notes about Rodger via Charlie, whose word could be trusted. He had never betrayed the fact that he was her messenger, nor had he made any secret of his admiration for her. Most of Rodger's servants did not like her—but Charlie did. His bold dark glance pierced her garments each time she came into the stable yard, and while his manner was always respectful, his eyes issued invitations she heartily wished she might accept. It would be lovely to lie with him in the stable loft, down in the straw. She willed these desires away. Charlie must return soon with Clemency's answer. She was sure that it would be in the affirmative. She was glad it was a fair day with no snow on the ground and the pool not frozen over yet.

Clemency could swim, of course, but not when she was close on six months gone with child and the water so frigid. This time there would be no Lord Colbourne to rescue her. She would disappear, and if the pool ever offered up its dead, she would be called a suicide and her body buried in unconsecrated ground. Rodger would grieve, and in his grief, he would turn to her.

Clemency sat in the sunny parlor at Sayles, stitching on a small white gown. She had only recently begun to make clothes for the baby, whose kicks were becoming much more vigorous.

Justine, who had come on a brief visit at the end of November, had said, " 'Twill be a boy, love. They are always more rambunctious."

Remembering those words, she also remembered Justine's anxious face. "I do wish you were happier, my love. This should be such a joyful occasion for you both. I cannot imagine what can be ailing the man!"

"He is mad," she had responded.

"It does seem so," Justine had agreed. "But Mama insists that that taint has never been associated with the Colbourne family."

"So she has told me, too, but what other reason could you provide for his actions unless you agree with him that I have been unfaithful?"

"Of course, I do not agree with him, dear. Knowing you, the idea is unthinkable. But do you have any enemies, love? Someone who could have poured these ugly suspicions into his ears?"

"No one," Clemency had insisted. Now she stared out of the window at the autumnal landscape. The foliage was dying in splendor this year, helped by a warm spell in October. The trees were golden, red, even pink—and the ground, covered with more vivid leaves, bore a resemblance to some great medieval tapestry. As she watched, more leaves fell, a golden shower, and Clemency averted her eyes, for she had glimpsed the great bulk of Colbourne Castle. Inexplicably, Lady Maria was in her mind. She wondered why she should suddenly think of her at this moment. No, actually and actively, she missed her bright presence—but that was not why she had thought about her. She was remembering her warning about bringing Beatrix into her house. She could imagine what that forthright lady would say were she aware that Beatrix remained at the castle, while she was back in her parents' home. Maria would be sure that she had been proved right. Lady Sayles would have agreed with her.

" 'Tis shocking that she should stay there with Rodger," her mother had said tartly. "And I beg you'll not prate to me of how she's changed. Leopards do not change their spots and sinners do not become saints."

"Many sinners have become saints, Mama," Clemency had pointed out. "St. Francis, among them."

"I would not liken your precious cousin to St. Francis," Lady Sayles had said dryly. Unconsciously she had echoed Damian. "The Devil can quote Scripture."

A slight grimace curled Clemency's lips. Beatrix often finished the notes she sent with some little quotation from the Bible. She had tried to read some of these to her mother, but Lady Sayles had scornfully refused to listen. Beatrix had been all too correct in her contention that she would not have been welcome at Sayles.

"I cannot imagine why you let that creature come to stay with you," her mother had scolded. "Your memory is very short. Imagine leaving us without a word of thanks. Bad blood will tell!"

Clemency's glance strayed to the table near her chair. There was a note, and she must conceal it before her mother came in and recognized her cousin's sprawling and distinctive handwriting. There was always the off-chance that Lady Sayles might ask her what Beatrix had to say about Rodger. She had no intention of divulging the contents of this particular communication. It would have caused no end of trouble.

Beatrix wanted to meet her at the pool. It was the very first time she had suggested that they see each other in person, which meant she must have something of singular importance to confide, something she dared not put in writing. That had been implied if not spelled out in her note.

Clemency had scribbled a reply to Beatrix and sent it back with Charlie. Fortunately, she could still ride, and when her parents took their noonday nap, she would meet Beatrix at the designated spot. Ironically, the plan was very much like the one her cousin had proposed at the time she had gone to meet Damian, which appointment had ruined her marriage and—though she was loath to admit it—her life. Yet, as she always assured herself when she entertained those futile regrets, she was fortunate she had discovered what manner of man she had married. She wished she were meeting Beatrix sooner. She could not see her until two in the afternoon—three hours from now. She released a short impatient sigh. She was worried. She feared her cousin would be telling her something about Rodger's mental state, and she anticipated the worst. One of the reasons Beatrix had stayed on at the castle was that Rodger seemed to find comfort in her presence.

"I feel it is my bounden duty to remain with him," she had written in an earlier note. "For I was hungered and ye gave me meat. I was thirsty and ye gave me to drink. I was a stranger and ye took me in. Naked and ye clothed me. I was sick and ye visited me.

"It was you who did all these things for me, Clemency,

but it was Rodger who permitted it, and since I cannot pay you back as I would choose, I will try to do my little best for him." She had added, "My dear, I *have* come to fear for his sanity and I pray God each day that he will be merciful and in his great wisdom will restore Rodger's mind as it was before."

Clemency felt a movement and put her hand on her stomach. Would her child inherit his father's malady? She could not believe that there was not some madness in the family. Probably they had kept it well-concealed, had bribed servants and locked away those who were violent. And would Rodger become violent and need to be locked away and chained like an animal? She shook her head and whispered, "May God forbid it." One day she would succeed in totally hardening her heart against this man who had hurt her so deeply, she thought, and then she remembered the early days of their marriage.

They had been so happy! He had been so kind, so loving, so wise, so tender. And now, according to Beatrix, it was as if that marriage had never existed. "He never mentions your name, my dearest. It is as though he had never met you. I have ceased to argue with him, ceased to assure him of your love for him, ceased to defend you in any way—for it only brings on the most violent outbursts. On one occasion he seized me by the throat and tried to strangle me, but I called on God to rescue me and, amazingly, Rodger immediately calmed down and was most contrite afterward. But I pray you will pardon me if I do not take your part anymore. I do not dare."

Clemency blinked, and was intensely annoyed. Her eyes were wet. She brushed a hand across them. It was her condition, of course—that is what made her all weak and watery. Yet it had been cruel of Beatrix to tell her about Rodger's reaction to any mention of her name. If her cousin had been estranged from her husband, she would not have made her suffer needlessly. . . . Lady Maria was in her mind again—Clemency recalled her doubts of Beatrix. It seemed to her that Beatrix wanted her to suffer . . . but that was ridiculous. She only wanted her to understand Rodger's condition and to impress upon her that the man she married no longer existed. Beatrix was right. He did not exist. To all intents and purposes, he had died.

Once more she thought of changelings and wished, almost, that Beatrix had not sent her the note, because there were two and three days together when she did not think about Rodger, did not wonder, did not speculate and mourn the man he had been. However, she did hope that the infant she was bearing would be a daughter instead of the son Justine had predicted. It was small and petty of her not to bear the heir he had mentioned when he had so shyly proposed to her. But daughter or son, she remembered bitterly, he would never acknowledge that the child she carried was of his begetting!

What did Beatrix want to tell her? Was it to do with his state of mind or was it something else? But what else could it be, and what did it matter? She was minded not to go. She would not go!

She would go. She knew she would not be able to keep from going. Though she hated to acknowledge it, there was a tiny thread of hope in her mind . . . Perhaps . . .? She shrugged and shook her head. Most likely Beatrix, as always, would corroborate her worst fears.

"Clemency." Lady Sayles came quickly into the parlor. She blinked. "My, it is uncommonly bright in here. You have a visitor, dear child." She moved to the window and drew the draperies. "The sunlight's monstrously trying," she added distractedly.

"A visitor, Mama?" It was odd how her heart had suddenly begun to beat faster. She was intensely annoyed at a second fugitive hope that arose and vanished like morning dew in the sunlight. She knew full well that it could not be Rodger, and besides, she never wanted to see him again and he never wanted to see her again—he who had not mentioned her name once in nearly six months! "Who would that be, Mama?"

"Damian, my love. He is most anxious to see you. I told him you would probably not want to receive him and he has insisted that I give you the opportunity to refuse or not refuse." Lady Sayles fixed her faded blue eyes on her daughter's face and added earnestly, "My dear, I think you should see him. I think you must see him."

"Damian?" A sharp rejection trembled on Clemency's lips. However, her mother's strange attitude forestalled its utterance. Lady Sayles seemed far more excited than the occasion warranted. And after all, it was not Damian who was responsible for breaking up her marriage and destroying her happiness, it was her husband and, inadvertently, Beatrix, who had arranged that fateful meeting in the first place.

Beatrix, of course, had had the best intentions in the world and it was totally irrational to blame her for what had happened—or was it? Occasionally—more than occasionally—the thought had crossed her mind that Beatrix was not as ingenuous as she seemed. But why . . .? She could not speculate upon that now. Her mother was awaiting her answer. "Why do you think I should see Damian, Mama?"

" 'Twould be better for him to tell you that himself," Lady Sayles said mysteriously. There was a touch of accusation in her voice as she added, "You'd not believe me, but perhaps you will believe Damian."

"I do not understand, Mama. What have I refused to believe?"

"A truth that has always seemed obvious to me, my dear." Lady Sayles's face darkened for the moment. She added maddeningly, "But enough, I beg that you will see him."

Her mother's manner was proving more irritating and more confusing to Clemency by the minute. Lady Sayles had never approved of Damian, and primed on her explanations concerning the part he had unwittingly played in her present predicament, she had roundly castigated him, saying that she had never thought him a suitable companion. Consequently, Clemency's curiosity would allow no other response than the one she gave, albeit raising her eyebrows as she said, "Very well, Mama, I will see him. Could you show him in here?"

"Of course, my dear." Lady Sayles practically scuttled from the parlor.

A moment later, Damian came in and, much to Clemency's surprise, he was unaccompanied by her mother. She was further surprised by his appearance. He was much more fashionably garbed than usual. He had also put on a little weight and at first glance he seemed like his old friendly self, only happier. However, his face changed as he saw her and his gaze turned grave. She stifled a sigh, realizing that though he must have been primed by her mother, he had not expected to see her looking so pale and thin. In the last months, even the bright hue of her hair had faded and there were dark circles under her eyes.

"My dear Clemency." He came forward and kissed her hand. "I have a great deal to tell you, and some of it, I hope, will drive the gloom from your countenance."

She attempted a smile. "Do I appear so gloomy, then? I assure you that—"

He held up his hand. "I do not want you to give me any assurance until you have heard what I have to say about many things."

"Oh!" she said in exasperation. "I fear that you mean to be as mysterious as Mama."

"I do not intend to be mysterious at all," he contradicted with a fleeting smile. "First off, my dear, before I tell you anything else, I am married."

"Married!" Clemency exclaimed. "Are you? When?"

"A month ago in Edinburgh. Forgive me that I did not write and inform you at once, but there was a time when I was so besotted that I could think of nothing but my own happiness."

"I do understand," Clemency said a little sadly. "One can be very happy. Your bride is Scottish?"

"Not entirely, though she has Scottish relations on her mother's side. The MacIvors."

"Oh, I am so very pleased for you, Damian," Clemency told him warmly. "Who is she? Have you known her long?"

A flurry of emotions chased themselves across his countenance. He looked pleased, then angry, then triumphant. "I have known and not known her long. I met her first when she was sixteen and in the schoolroom. At the time, I hardly noticed her . . . then I had occasion to return, and when I saw her again 'twas liking at second sight and loving third, and all in a matter of weeks. Her maiden name's Palmer." He fixed his eyes on Clemency's face and said with a peculiar clarity, "She is the younger sister of Lieutenant Ralph Palmer. Her given name's Patricia Ellen. Her family and now her husband call her Pat-Ellen. She is very beautiful. Dark like her brother and with gray eyes. She's tall—almost as tall as you. You'll meet her soon."

"I shall look forward to it," Clemency said. She added in

some surprise, "You went to see the Palmers, then? And Lieutenant Palmer has a sister? Beatrix never mentioned . . ."

Damian's smile vanished so abruptly that it seemed as if it had been literally wiped from his face. His eyes grew amazingly chill. "Beatrix, my dear, did not know that Ralph had a sister. She knew nothing about his family, having never met them."

"But she did," Clemency cried. "She—"

He held up his hand. "I know what you are going to say and I must remind you of something you have probably forgotten in the wake of all that has happened following our encounter last summer. Your mother has explained about your leaving Rodger and also about his inexplicable attitude. At any rate, I have told you that I was surprised that the Palmers had turned Beatrix away. I stayed with them and knew them to be warm, loving people. I could not imagine them being so cruel to Ralph's bride, especially if she were breeding.

"Consequently, on an impulse, I decided to ride up north to York. I felt a need to be away from . . . everything. Also I decided it would be better for all concerned if I made myself scarce. And"—a mocking little smile played about his mouth—"ironically enough, I wanted to help Beatrix with Palmer's family if, indeed, her story were true. Imagine my consternation upon learning that they had not rejected our sainted little Beatrix, because, my love"—he paused and his eyes narrowed— "they did not have the opportunity. She never came near them and they'd never heard of her."

"They'd never *heard* of her?" Clemency whispered. "But—"

He held up a hand again. "They'd never heard of her because it's not often a man describes his mistress to his parents or to his siblings."

"His . . . his mistress?" Clemency breathed. " 'Tis not possible. She said . . ."

Damian's blue eyes were hard. "She was never anything else, Clemency, dear. Ralph gave me the impression he was wed to Beatrix . . . but now I believe it was to save her so-called reputation. I do know that he had been head-over-heels in love with her and 'tis my belief that she played one of her tricks on him and he decided not to wed her. Probably it happened on shipboard. I do not know. I do know that he was betrothed to Lady Janet Murray, a girl his parents knew and loved. He'd written to her the day before he died. He also wrote to his parents explaining that he was coming home on leave and would wed Janet at that time. Pat-Ellen would have been her bridesmaid. As it was, Janet fortunately found another and is happily married now."

"Oh, I am glad," Clemency said warmly. "But . . . but Beatrix, she was only his . . ."

"Mistress and naught else. Another reason he let us believe in the marriage was Beatrix's background—her gentle birth. Certainly she was several cuts above your average camp follower."

"Beatrix insisted—" Clemency began.

"Beatrix is a liar," Damian stated baldly. "A most accomplished liar but, in a sense, I owe it to her that I met my darling once again." His face softened. "She is the dearest girl, though she did lead me a merry chase at first. I was not her only suitor, though being her late brother's friend did give me an edge. There was another most persistent . . ." He broke off, flushing. "I will not try your patience with all that. I have much more to tell you."

Clemency said, "I long to meet her, but Beatrix . . . perhaps she felt she must save face and that is why she invented such a tale. That would certainly be understandable."

His eyes grew even harder. "Trust you to find excuses for her. There are no excuses, Clemency, dearest. This is not the only fabrication she's been guilty of. There are others far more dangerous and damning. I have just come from the castle, and—"

"The castle," she interrupted. "You . . . you went to Colbourne Castle?"

He nodded. "I arrived here yesterday afternoon, and if I'd not been so occupied in showing Pat-Ellen around the Grange, I presume one or another of my servants might have given me some inkling of all that has taken place since I left, but be that as it may, I was definitely prepared when I went to the castle this morning to see you and tell you what I'd learned about sweet Beatrix. I was not sure what you would do with the information, but I felt you must have it. I remembered that Beatrix had told you I was suicidal, and me that you still loved me—I thought those were harmless exaggerations given out of concern for my feelings and yours . . . but on pondering them, I decided they were not and she must have had some ulterior motive—"

"What happened when you went to the castle this morning?" Clemency interrupted impatiently.

"I was just coming to that. I was met by the butler, who glowered at me and seemed minded to slam the door in my face. However, I said I wanted to see you and he told me that you were not there, which did surprise me. However, then I said I'd speak to his lordship and he explained that his lordship was not receiving visitors because he was bedded with a quinsy."

"He's ill again?" Clemency questioned. "I'd not heard of it."

"Let me continue," he ordered. "I would have left upon hearing that, had not Beatrix suddenly emerged from a passageway. She looked astounded to see me, and I asked about you. She told me loudly that I must go immediately before his lordship learned that I was there. But, of course, that only whetted my curiosity, and I did not go. I stood my ground and demanded to know where you were, and of a sudden Rodger came down the stairs. He was clad in a dressing gown and nightshirt and he was leaning heavily upon the balustrade and carrying a cane as well. He looked very badly, bone-thin, haggard, and wild-eyed. I scarce recognized him!"

"Oh, God . . . oh, God," Clemency moaned. "I know. He has gone mad, Damian, or very near it. He has accused me of . . . of . . ."

"I know, my dear," he said soothingly. "And I beg you'll not distress yourself by repeating those ridiculous charges. I know all about his misapprehensions now. Your mother's told me the whole of the tale. But of course I was in complete ignorance this morning, and naturally I was unprepared to hear him call me a seducer and accuse me of getting you with child!"

"I am sorry, Damian. I tried to convince him, but one cannot reason with the mad."

"And who was it told you he was mad? Beatrix, I expect."

"No, 'twas my opinion. The things he said, Damian, and all stemming from our meeting."

"He did not base his accusations on that, my love. I must tell you about Beatrix. While he was raging at me, she kept interrupting and telling him on the one hand that she had ordered me to leave and on the other that he was too ill to remain below in these drafts and must return to his bed. She also added that I'd come to see you like the bold-faced rascal I was. Out of their going back and forth, I got the impression that Rodger firmly believed me to be carrying on with you still!"

"Still?" she breathed.

"Still! And I told him he had to be wanting in the upper garret, because you loved him and had told me so the last time I was here, which had been months ago. And Beatrix said I was lying and that I would burn in the fires of hell—"

"What?" Clemency stared at him incredulously. "Beatrix said that?"

"She did. And then Rodger said something that explained entirely the direction from which the ill winds were blowing."

As he paused, Clemency said impatiently, "What could he have said?"

"He told me, my dear, that you never loved him—that it was all pretense because it had been you who'd called him Lord Caliban and jeered at his infirmities."

"What?" she cried, aghast. "I never . . . 'Twas—"

"Our sweet, gentle, kind, and truthful Beatrix," he said mockingly. "I know. I was there too, and heard her. I was about to tell him the true source of that quotation, but luck was with our Beatrix, for at that moment he suddenly turned white as a sheet and fainted."

"Oh, no." Clemency pressed her clasped hands against her bosom.

"I tried to kneel at his side, but Beatrix screamed that the servants must eject me forcibly because 'twas my fault their master had swooned. They had withdrawn while we three were going at it hammer and tongs, but at her screech, they came hurtling back, four big muscular footmen all looking monstrous determined and flexing their muscles like a Pet o' the Fancy about to climb into the ring. Consequently, I, believing discretion to be the better part of valor, departed." He had spoken lightly, but now, staring into Clemency's wide distressed eyes, he added, " 'Tis your sweet Cousin Beatrix, my love, who has sewn the dragon's seeds in your garden."

She stared at him for a long time, her gaze bleak and still doubtful. "It must have been Beatrix who told him I called him Lord Caliban."

"I cannot imagine he received the information from any other source. There were but three of us who knew who invented that nickname. You, myself, and Beatrix. Dragon seeds to disrupt a marriage, my sweet."

"Why?" she whispered.

"Jealousy, envy, and all-around bad character. She's always resented you, always tried to steal what you possessed, beginning . . ." He paused, shook his head, and then said doggedly, "Beginning with myself."

"You?" she said confusedly. "I do not understand."

He flushed. "I have kept this incident locked inside of me since I was fourteen, but 'twas Beatrix initiated me into . . . I exaggerate when I dub them the . . . er, joys of love. She was furious when I, shamed and miserable, refused to seek further instruction, though she did her best to drive me to it by tempting me with a thousand knowing glances, brushing up against me . . . I will not refine any more upon this incident."

"She and you?" Clemency gazed at him with wide, disbelieving eyes.

He nodded. "By the pool, shortly after her arrival at Sayles." He grimaced. "I do not hold any brief for myself—I was a willing and most curious pupil, at first. But I did not enjoy the instruction. She teased and mocked me for my shyness and said she'd known lads of twelve who were better at the game than I. She spoke disparagingly of you, too, in those days, made mock of you, something else I preferred not to tell you."

"I wish you had," she whispered.

"I wish I had too. But you seemed fond of her and thought her equally fond of you. Also I thought you might turn from me."

Clemency said slowly, "She was always so sweet to me. That is why it was so hard for me to understand her going off without so much as a word." She paused and added in a low voice, "You and then Rodger. She must covet him as well."

"There's no doubt that she does."

"Do you think she's been with him, too?"

"I cannot give you any answers." He frowned. "But I would guess not."

"But you do not know," she pursued.

He regarded her with pity. "How might I know unless I had been told?"

"How did he seem to you?"

"As I have explained. Ill. That, I think, must preclude any dalliance with the divine Beatrix."

"He did not seem . . . mad?"

"No, only furiously angry at me and at you. Poor man. Our accomplished little Beatrix must have been stoking his fires for many a day."

"It does make sense . . ." Clemency said slowly. "Yes, it does make sense. I have half-suspected that Beatrix . . ." She paused and then continued, "He changed so dreadfully. And now that I think of it, there were indications of that even in London. He seemed not to believe me when I told him I did not really like to dance. He was always urging me to it. I expect—"

"Yes," Damian interrupted. "The spider was spinning her web."

"Then, when I met you, he was so suspicious and doubting, when he'd been so warm and affectionate before. There was a disappointed look in his eyes and he had *told* me he believed my version of what happened."

"What did you tell him?"

"The truth. He seemed to accept it, but he was so cold, and he stayed away from me. At first I was a miserable. Later I grew angry. It seemed so unlike Rodger not to believe me. And . . . and when I told him about the child, he accused you of fathering it—during one or another of our meetings. And we'd only met the once. I could not understand his suspicions. I could not understand the change in him. What else could I believe save that he'd sustained some terrible injury in the war, something he'd never mentioned or, worse yet, something he'd inherited and which might be the legacy he'd pass on to our child." She shuddered.

"And all the while, that something was our dearest Beatrix."

"If that is true, how could he have believed her?" Clemency's eyes gleamed with fury. "How could he have countenanced such lies, who'd known me, lived with me . . ."

"And who was grievously wounded, partially crippled, painfully scarred . . ."

"But beautiful . . . his features still perfect, and as for his leg, the doctor said it will grow in strength and—"

"He saw only the scar, and he had once been in total control of his body—not dependent on a cane, not needing to rest and so on. Then I returned. God knows what she must have said to him, what subtle poison poured into his ears, and the whole clad in the trappings of her spurious faith."

"Oh, Damian." Clemency clutched his arm. "We must go. We must go to the castle—now."

He regarded her anxiously. "Are you well enough, my dear? There's likely to be a great deal of unpleasantness once we beard the lioness in her appropriated den."

She held his eyes with her own. "I will be able to face her. I assure you that I am strong."

"Your mother's told me—"

"That I have been at times . . . despondent. Yes, but—" —her eyes narrowed—"I would very much like to meet my cousin earlier than we'd intended, and at the castle rather than the pool."

"The pool?" He clutched her arm. "What can you mean?"

Clemency extracted Beatrix's note from her work box and handed it to him, explaining hurriedly about the communications she had been receiving.

He scanned the note and frowned. "I do not like this . . . to make you come so far, and in secret, of course. None would have missed you."

Clemency regarded him in astonishment. "You cannot believe that she meant to do me a mischief, can you?"

"Mischief is her stock in trade," Damian observed grimly. "You'd been planning on meeting her, I assume?"

"As I told you. Yes."

" 'Tis doubly fortunate that I came. I do think it safer to meet her at the castle."

"When shall we go? I'd like it if we might leave immediately, or . . ." She glanced down at her gown, an old merino which she never wore beyond the confines of her home. "Would you wait until I have changed into something more suitable for . . . paying calls?"

"A suit of armor would be the most suitable," he commented with a grin. He added, "After all it is a quest—"

"A quest, Sir Knight, indeed!" Clemency hurried out of the room.

A chill wind had sprung up, sending a host of gray-tinged clouds scurrying across the sky. From the bottom of the hill the castle looked singularly forbidding, more fortress than home, something that had never occurred to Clemency when she had lived there. The same thought must have been passing through Damian's mind, for he said with a lift of his eyebrow and a twist of his mouth, "In the old days, they would have raised the drawbridge after my departure."

"And rolled out the war machines," she agreed.

He brought his horse nearer to her mount and looked at her concernedly. "I wonder if 'twas wise for you to come."

She returned his gaze steadily. " 'Tis still my home," she asserted firmly. "There's been no formal separation."

"Then, onward and upward," he urged with the mischievous gleam in his eyes that she had seen so often.

"Shall we race as far as the gatekeeper's cottage?" she inquired.

"Not up that grade," he warned. "The road's already been muddied by the rains. Control your impatience, my dear."

"Oh, I expect you're right. I must be cautious. You'd probably have won anyway."

"Perhaps . . . but I see you winning something more important than a piddling race."

There were unshed tears in her eyes. "How can I ever thank you, Damian?"

"We're to the gatekeeper's cottage," he said a little gruffly.

The man came out immediately, a lowering look in his eyes which vanished as he recognized Clemency. "Your ladyship." He grinned. " 'Ave ye come back, then?"

"For the nonce, Perkins." She had a warm smile for him. "And how is your wife?"

"She be fine, your ladyship."

"And the little ones?"

"They be fine too. They'll be ever so glad to 'ear you've returned, your ladyship."

Clemency swallowed a lump in her throat. "I thank you, Perkins. Do give them my best wishes." She turned to Damian. "Come."

As they started up the road again, Damian, bringing his horse nearer, muttered, "And here I thought he was a rather surly brute."

"No, not at all. That's his gatekeeper's face. He's pleasant enough when you get to know him. His wife's a lovely woman and their children are adorable."

"I hope we'll receive an equally warm welcome from the other servants. Those four footmen looked primed for a scuffle." Damian rolled his eyes.

"Henry, Calvin, George, and Silas are most protective," she commented wryly. "I pray they'll not have forgotten me."

"Were I to lay bets on the fact that they have not, I would find myself considerably the richer, I'm thinking."

"You do cheer me, Damian," she said gratefully.

Reaching the summit of the hill, they dismounted and led their horses to the posts that stood near the top of the carriageway.

They had reached the massive door of the castle, and despite her brave words, Clemency's heart was pounding heavily. She clutched her cloak tight about her. It was dark green and new-made for her by the village seamstress, and she rejoiced in its hood as well as the thick folds that concealed her increasing figure—the bulk of her baby being more visible because she had lost so much weight of late.

Damian slipped his arm around her shoulders and held her against him for a moment. "Be of good cheer, my dearest," he murmured. Then he lifted the knocker and slammed it against its plate with a force that must have raised a flurry of echoes through the hall, Clemency thought.

It was a moment before the door was opened by the butler. He frowned as he saw Damian, but then as Clemency held aside her hood for a moment, his face lighted amazingly.

"Your ladyship!" he exclaimed, pulling back the door as far as it would go.

"Good morning, Travers," Clemency said softly. She felt another lump in her throat. He must have heard a great deal of gossip, but it was obvious that it made no more impression on him than on the gatekeeper. As she entered, followed by Damian, she saw Jenkins cross the hall. She would have greeted him, but he did not give her that opportunity. With a surprised glance at Damian, he turned and hurried up the stairs. Had he gone to warn Rodger? Evidently Beatrix was not without her faithful supporters. Jenkins, she recalled with a pang, had never been very friendly. Then she remembered that her hood shaded her face—he might not have recognized her. A moment later she was delighted that two of the footmen who had threatened to oust Damian must have guessed her identity, for they were all smiling at her most cordially. She moved toward them with the intention of asking after their families—but was halted mid-step as her cousin's voice rang out in surprise and anger.

"How dare you admit this man after I gave you express orders that he was not to be allowed here? And you, Damian, I wonder that you had the effrontery to return!"

Clemency looked up and tensed. Beatrix was standing on the first landing. As usual, she was clad in gray, but a huge circlet of diamonds blazed on her third finger, left hand—one that Clemency recognized. It had been her betrothal ring. If she had been inclined to doubt Damian's tale, this alone would have substantiated it. Had Rodger given it to Beatrix? Out of her new awareness, she doubted it, and remembered the ring she had forced on her cousin just before her departure. Beatrix had been reluctant to accept it, mainly because she had had her sights set on not one but all her jewels—and the giver as well! Clemency moved out of the darkness, and flinging back her hood, said coolly, "Damian came here at my invitation, Beatrix."

"Clemency!" Beatrix thrust her hand behind her back. "What are you doing here? What has Damian—?"

"I thought," Clemency interrupted, "that since there was so chill a wind blowing, 'twould be better to meet you here rather than at the pool. Besides, I have been informed that my husband is passing ill. I presume he is in his rooms. I think I must go up to see him."

Beatrix's eyes narrowed, "I do not understand you, Clemency. You know he'll not see you. I am sure that he made that very clear to Damian, and I cannot believe that you are in ignorance of what passed earlier this morning. Nothing has changed in the last hour. He will not see you and he has forbidden all mention of your name."

"You've told me a great deal, Beatrix," Clemency said evenly, "but still, I have given this matter considerable thought and I feel that, after all, a wife's place is at her husband's side—in his time of need."

Beatrix clutched the newel post. "He has me to care for him. 'Tis me he needs. I do wonder at your temerity, coming here with your paramour—"

"Beatrix." Damian interrupted what gave promise of being a virulent diatribe. "I am indeed glad that my wife did not accompany me upon this . . . er, courtesy call. She would have been pained indeed to hear this slander."

Beatrix took a step backward, staring down at him incredulously. "Your wife?"

"You did not give me an opportunity to tell you that I am no longer a sorrowing bachelor but, instead, a happy benedict and have been in this exceedingly pleasant condition for four bliss-filled weeks. But enough! Clemency and I have not come to pass the time of day with you. She has informed me that she wishes to see her husband." He turned to Clemency. "Should we not cease this fruitless discussion and go directly to his rooms, my dear?"

"Yes, I think we must. Immediately." Clemency started up the stairs.

"You may not . . . must not see him," Beatrix shrilled. "I have told you that he might do you an injury. He is not himself. And since he cannot bear to hear your name, what makes you believe that he would have you near him? I warn you, Clemency—"

"I am very much afraid, Beatrix, that your warnings have ceased to matter to me," Clemency retorted coolly.

"And if he attempts to injure her, I shall be there to protect her," Damian said smoothly. He moved up the stairs behind Clemency.

Beatrix stretched wide her arms. "You shall not come up! I forbid it. Calvin . . . George, you know what to do. Show them out. Throw them out if need be!"

The footmen stared at her blankly. "We cannot do that, ma'am. 'Tis 'er ladyship, don't ye see," George protested.

"Aye." Calvin nodded solemnly. " 'Tis 'er we takes our orders from."

"Be damned to you! Do you not know that I am mistress here?" Beatrix screamed. "Mistress of this house . . . mistress of his lordship, too!"

"I do not believe you!" Clemency cried.

"You may believe me—for 'tis true!" Beatrix retorted.

"It is not true!" The denial, weak but firm, came from overhead.

Clemency stared up into the darkness and let out a little cry as she saw her husband, flanked by a watchful Jenkins and leaning on the balustrade in the upper hall. He glared down at Beatrix and she, seeing him, seemed actually to dwindle in size. Her arms dropped to her sides. She opened her mouth and closed it.

"What did you mean by telling my wife that lie?" Rodger demanded icily.

Beatrix reeled, and for a moment it seemed as if she would fall, but she steadied herself by clutching the post again. Raising wild accusing eyes to his face, she cried, "Look at her, Rodger, she has dared to come back—with her lover tagging behind her. She is shameless, wanton . . . and 'he goeth after her as an ox to slaughter, or as a fool to the correction of the stocks . . . as a bird hasteth to the snare and knoweth not it is for his life!' "

Rodger said, "Why are you wearing that ring?"

"You gave it to me, Rodger. Do you not remember?"

"I gave you nothing," he contradicted coldly.

"You did, you did," she cried. " 'Twas when I nursed you through the fever. You do not remember . . . you do not remember that you said you loved me and wanted me?"

"I could not have been that delirious," he said contemptuously. "You are a liar and possibly a thief."

"I tell you, you do not remember!" she cried desperately.

"Beatrix," Damian said loudly, "I did not give you the

maiden name of my wife. 'Twas Palmer. She is the sister of the man you called husband. She has said she would very much like to meet you, and her parents too have expressed a similar desire, having never known of your existence until I mentioned you."

Her face was a mask of hatred. "You—may you rot in hell, Damian Prior."

"Oh, Beatrix!" Clemency exclaimed.

"And you," Beatrix screamed. "Why did you not break your damned neck in that tower that day? I prayed you might. I . . ." She suddenly rushed down the stairs and lunged at Clemency, who stepped aside hastily, clutching tightly to the banister. Overbalancing, Beatrix fell forward and rolled down some six steps to the bottom, and leaping to her feet, sped to the front door and dashed outside, slamming it behind her.

One of the footmen stepped forward and hurried toward the door. "No," Clemency exclaimed breathlessly. "Let her go."

"My dear," Damian protested. "This is not a time when clemency is needed."

"Oh, yes, she is," Rodger said in a tone filled with shame and anguish. Relaxing his hold on the balustrade but still taking support from Jenkins, he came down to the first landing. "Oh, Clemency," he said brokenly. "Are you really here? I have missed you so terribly."

She hurried up to him. "My poor Rodger." She put her arms around him and then cried out, for he had fainted again.

Rodger moved restlessly on his bed and opened his eyes. He sighed deeply as he stared at the wide expanse of mattress. "Was it another dream, then?" he muttered. "I thought . . ."

"What did you think, my lord?"

He turned swiftly and looked at the young woman who sat in an armchair pushed close to the side of the bed. "You *are* here."

She nodded gravely. "I am, my lord."

"I feared I might have dreamed you. I have dreamed of you so often and awakened only to . . ." His gaze strayed past her to the window. " 'Tis twilight already," he muttered. "I remember 'twas sunny not more than a minute since. I must yet be dreaming." His face fell. "It did seem so real."

" 'Tis the potion that confused you," she said. "You fainted and were in pain. We gave you something to make you sleep."

He stared at her, his gaze wandering over her face and body as if he were still trying to assure himself that she was really there. Then he said slowly, "Yes, you are right. The potion did confuse me. Beatrix . . ." He frowned. "Where . . .?"

"She's gone, and took with her Charlie from the stables, as well as Apollo and your gray. We did not discover the thefts immediately. We were too concerned with you."

"No matter, she is gone." He released a long sigh. "Believe me," he said earnestly, "she was never my mistress."

"I do believe you, my lord," she said gravely, and bent a troubled gaze on him. "I can wish that you'd been as trusting."

A spasm of pain contorted his features. "I have no excuse, my dearest—or say rather that I had no defenses against the potency of her tears and the seeming sincerity with which she voiced her accusations. She called upon God to be her witness. She seemed so terribly unwilling to betray you. She talked of her duty to you but swore she had a greater duty to me and to God, as well as to her own conscience, when she told me that you were consorting with Damian and that you'd confessed to her that you were carrying his child."

"Oh, God," Clemency groaned. " 'Twas she who told me that I should not mention my meeting with Damian to you. 'Twas she who arranged it in the first place—telling me that he'd threatened suicide because he found me wed to you. I would not put it past her to have loosened Apollo's reins that day. She knew well enough where we were."

"I think it more than likely." He shuddered. "Especially in view of what she said about the tower."

Clemency nodded. " 'Twas Beatrix who said we must go across the floor . . . and I was never one to refuse. I prided myself on my bravery."

"And might have died for it!" He stared at her in horror.

"And might have died, indeed, if you'd not come and saved my life," she murmured lovingly.

"And you've saved mine," he sighed. "These last months, I have wanted to die, you know. That I did not was only because I had in mind what Shakespeare has called 'the canon 'gainst self-slaughter.' "

"Rodger!" She looked at him in horror. "Oh, she has much to answer for. Still," she added with a regret she could not quite mask, "if Beatrix had concocted such inventions about you and sworn to them upon her precious Bible, I'd not have believed her."

He flushed. "I fear I saw only my crippled body, which I could not help contrasting with Damian's young strength. And Beatrix had told me you'd jeered at my injuries . . ."

"And called you Caliban," she said mournfully. "Yes, Damian told me that. Did you not know me at all? I cannot think you did, else you must have realized I would never have been capable of such wanton cruelty—and toward one who had saved my life!"

He said slowly, "I should have . . . but when I first mentioned that nickname to you, you looked so stricken, and it seemed to me in retrospect that you'd also seemed ashamed. Coupled with her accusations, it did appear—"

"As if I had been guilty," she interjected. She nodded. "I did feel guilty, since it was my own cousin who'd spoken those words. I taxed her with it at the time. I was furious with her. Then, when she came to us in London, I also felt guilty about letting you shelter her. I reminded her of what she'd said. She seemed deeply troubled. She asked me if I had ever told you that 'twas she who'd spoken thus. I told her I had not. I little dreamed how she would twist my confidence." She gave him an apologetic look. "I should not blame you, I think, for believing her. I believed her too."

He reached for her hand and held it tightly. "How could you not, who are all goodness and gentleness. She came to you with a Bible clutched in her hand . . ."

"And duplicity in her heart," she sighed. "I feel like such a fool."

" 'Tis not you who were the fool. Oh, God, Clemency, can you find it in your heart to forgive me?"

"There's nothing to forgive. We were both her dupes. But"—her eyes flashed—"I will never forgive her for hurting you so terribly. My poor love, can you not believe that your beauty goes deeper than a shattered leg and a scarred cheek? Those infirmities are taken into account by none who know you. If you were in truth a Caliban, it would make no difference, for no one would see your twisted features—only the goodness and the kindness shining through."

"Oh, Clemency"—he sat up—"how may I atone to you for all you've suffered?"

The smile her mother had decried so long ago returned to illuminate her face. She said lovingly, "Let me see . . . first you must buy me a new betrothal ring, for the other's gone, I fear, with Beatrix."

"I will buy you ten," he vowed, smiling too. "And what else? A diamond necklace?"

"I . . ." She paused, for she had felt a stirring. "I think that in four and a half months' time I will have a present for you."

"A present?" he repeated.

"I pray you've not forgotten that you're soon to be a father, my lord."

"Oh, Clemency . . ." Tears stood in his eyes. "Oh, my dear love, I do not know what to say."

She slipped from the chair to the bed. Putting her arms around him, she said softly, "You need not say anything, my very dearest. But I pray you are not too weak to kiss me."

Moments later, a breathless Clemency was able to assure her lord that her hopes had been gloriously fulfilled.

L'Envoi

On Monday, October 5, 1818, Covent Garden was filled almost to capacity. The lovely actress Miss O'Neill was playing Juliet opposite the celebrated Charles Kemble. And while some of those present felt that his Romeo was inclined to rant too much, he was still very popular. Tickets to the performance were dear and everyone had brought extra hankerchiefs—or so said one member of a lively foursome which occupied a box comfortably near to the stage. However, they were not so near that they could not see and be seen by the assembled members of the *ton*.

Many quizzing glasses were raised as fashionable bucks in the pit stared at the ravishing brunette and the beautiful redhead who sat in the front of the box in question. Their escorts, a tall, handsome young man with fair hair and blue eyes and a dark, strikingly attractive gentleman a few years his senior, received similar and languishing glances from the ladies. The latter also noted that the brunette's gown, a silver-gray satin that matched her eyes, was the very latest crack of fashion. They also admired the redhead's green silk gown, but it was her emerald necklace that made them sigh with envy.

The occupants of the box were totally unaware of being the center of this combined attention. "And now," the brunette said as she turned to her companion, "You must tell me, Clemency . . ." She paused and flushed.

"What must I tell you, dear Pat-Ellen?" Clemency prompted.

"Well, I want to know why I do not feel in the least ill even though Mr. Thayer, our physician, insists that I am increasing." She added nervously, "Do you believe that is normal?"

"Not only normal, but extremely fortunate," Clemency replied. "Though this time I feel much more the thing myself."

"This time." Pat-Ellen gazed at her round-eyed. "You'll never be telling me that . . ."

Clemency nodded. "Yes. I want my babies as close together as possible so they'll not be lonely as I was when I was growing up. As it is, 'twill be May before I have the baby, and by then little Rodger will be about two years old."

"Such a darling," Pat-Ellen enthused. "And beautiful—with his hair such an unusual shade, like old wine, Damian says."

"That would make it purple," Clemency laughed, "rather than the auburn I hope it is. But he does resemble his father, does he not?"

Pat-Ellen looked vague. "As much as any baby resembles anyone," she said finally.

Clemency laughed merrily. "You wait, my sweet, until you have borne your infant. From the moment it draws its first breath, you'll find resemblances to everyone in your family, and everyone in your family will be finding them, too. Rodger's great-aunt mentioned ancestors lost in the mists of antiquity!"

"I am sure of that." Pat-Ellen also laughed. "Oh, I am excited and I am glad you will be coming back to the castle in November. We are leaving tomorrow, as you know. I like it here in London but I much prefer the Grange. Shall you be going off to Devon to see more hut circles before you return?"

Clemency shook her head. "It's too cold, and also Rodger thinks it's too strenuous for me at this time. But if you want to know the real truth, his interest in the ancients has declined. Though I have no doubt it will revive once our son's old enough to accompany us on our forays into the past." Clemency cast a fond look over her shoulder at her husband, and then, opening her eyes wide, she turned to whisper to Pat-Ellen, "Look at Rodger and Damian—with their quizzing glasses turned on those boxes over there. I do believe they are ogling the *courtesans!*"

Pat-Ellen looked back. "Why, I believe they are—shameless creatures."

"Our husbands or the Fashionable Impures?"

"Both," Pat-Ellen said indignantly. "And look at that little blond over there. She's practically naked. I expect she's the one who's taken their fancy." She tapped her husband's knee with her folded fan. "You remember, Damian, my love, what happened to Peeping Tom when he looked upon the bare Godiva?"

He gave her a fond look. " 'Tis not her unveiled charms that beckon me, who can see someone far more fair and just as bare as the fabled Godiva in my home each night."

"I vow you do shock me, sir." Pat-Ellen blushed, but spoiled her reprimand with a giggle.

At that same moment, Rodger leaned forward and murmured in his wife's ear, "Perhaps you would like to satisfy your curiosity as to our target. 'Tis in the third box on the right, just one away from the stage."

"I do not see why you should want to look at such a creature," Pat-Ellen complained.

"I think Clemency might find the sight extremely edifying," Damian commented.

Seeing Rodger and Damian exchanging telling glances, Clemency took the proffered glass and turned it in the specified direction. Her first view was that of an elderly gentleman, very wrinkled of countenance, not aided by the quantities of rouge he had slathered on his cheeks or by the dark curly wig he had clamped on his head. He was clad in a puce satin evening suit which, again, was not flattering to one whose years might easily number seventy-five or more. But it was the woman with him that now drew her eye. Her gown was a flaming red cut so low that her full breasts were nearly exposed, or would have been had she not worn a diamond-and-ruby necklace that half-covered them. Diamond-and-ruby drops hung from her ears, and an immense diamond glittered on her finger. She was laughing and shamelessly flirting with the old man, who seemed to be enjoying her company greatly. It was another moment before Clemency recognized her.

"Beatrix," she mouthed in shock, glancing at Rodger and Damian.

"Quite," Damian agreed. "In the flesh, or very nearly."

"Oh, you!" Pat-Ellen pouted, seeing her husband's quizzing glass raised again. "I do wish you'd stop peering at that abandoned woman."

"Judging from what I can perceive, she is far from abandoned," he observed. "The wages of sin are fixed by the hour in some circles, so I've been told."

Clemency raised the quizzing glass a second time. She had caught sight of someone else in the box—a tall, handsome young man in the dark livery of a footman. He was standing against the door and his face was familiar. In a moment she had identified him as Charlie, the groom who had fled with Beatrix. In that same instant she saw her cousin stop fondling the old man and send a most loving look in the direction of the onetime groom, who blew back a kiss. Beatrix smiled and turned away. As she fell to fondling her elderly escort once more, Charlie fastened his eyes on a young girl in the next box. She, in turn, fluttered her fan, peeping over it with a most provocative glance. He blew several kisses in her direction.

Clemency was not minded toward biblical quotations, but one popped into her mind at that moment. Handing the quizzing glass back to her husband, she said, "I see the handwriting on the wall."

"What would you be meaning by that, my love?" he asked.

She would have amplified her remark by some mention of chickens coming home to roost, but it was too late. The curtains were parting and the play was beginning and she did not want to interrupt what promised to be a happily lachrymose evening with any speculations as to Beatrix's eventual disappointment. It occurred to her that none of those present would be in the least interested—and with Rodger's loving hand resting lightly on her bare shoulder, she turned her attention wholly to the stage.

JOIN THE *REGENCY ROMANCE* READERS' PANEL

Help us bring you more of the books you like by filling out this survey and mailing it in today.

1. Book Title: _____

   Book #: _____

2. Using the scale below, how would you rate this book on the following features? Please write in one rating from 0-10 for each feature in the spaces provided.

POOR	NOT SO GOOD		O.K.		GOOD		EXCELLENT
0 1	2 3	4	5 6	7	8	9	10

   RATING

   Overall opinion of book .... _____
   Plot/Story .... _____
   Setting/Location .... _____
   Writing Style .... _____
   Character Development .... _____
   Conclusion/Ending .... _____
   Scene on Front Cover .... _____

3. About how many romance books do you buy for yourself each month? _____

4. How would you classify yourself as a reader of Regency romances?
   I am a ( ) light ( ) medium ( ) heavy reader.

5. What is your education?
   ( ) High School (or less) ( ) 4 yrs. college
   ( ) 2 yrs. college ( ) Post Graduate

6. Age _____ 7. Sex: ( ) Male ( ) Female

Please Print Name_____

Address_____

City _____ State _____ Zip _____

Phone # (____) _____

Thank you. Please send to New American Library, Research Dept., 1633 Broadway, New York, NY 10019.

About the Author

Ellen Fitzgerald is a pseudonym for a well-known romance writer. A graduate of the University of Southern California with a B.A. in English and an M.A. in Drama, Ms. Fitzgerald has also attended Yale University and has had numerous plays produced throughout the country. In her spare time, she designs and sells jewelry. Ms. Fitzgerald lives in New York City.